Back in the Saddle
Sequel to Cowgirl Up

Ali Spooner

Back in the Saddle
Sequel to Cowgirl Up

Ali Spooner

Affinity
Rainbow Publications

2017

Back in the Saddle
© 2017 by Ali Spooner

Affinity E-Book Press NZ LTD
Canterbury, New Zealand

1st Edition

ISBN: 978-0-947528-50-8

All rights reserved.

This is a work of fiction. Names, character, places, and incidents are the product of the author's imagination or are used fictitiously and any resemblance to actual persons living or dead, businesses, companies, events, or locales is entirely coincidental

Editor: JoSelle Vanderhooft
Proof Editor: Alexis Smith
Cover Design: Irish Dragon Designs

Acknowledgments

I would like to thank my fans for following my stories, providing great feedback and encouragement. Writing wouldn't be so much fun without you. Thanks to Affinity, Irish Dragon for the cover art and the team of editors, readers, and publishers who continue to help me grow as a writer.

Dedication

To Rhonda. Tap, tap, tap. (Readers, if you've watched the movie *Bridegroom* you'll catch this.)

Table of Contents

Also by Ali Spooner

Chapter One

Cameron Bohannon knelt on the floor of her bedroom while she filled the final box with picture albums. Her rapidly graying hair fell into her eyes, and when she brushed it back with a hand, one of the books fell open to a picture of two young women walking hand in hand down a beach of sugar-white sand. Cam's heart ached as memories of that day filled her mind, and she choked back the well of tears pooling in her eyes.

"That was our first vacation together, Sheila," she said to the empty apartment. She struggled to imitate the smile she'd worn that day. "Definitely one of our best times together," she whispered while she trailed her fingers across the images in the photograph. "What I wouldn't give to be back there now."

Blaring music from the apartment above brought her back to reality. She gently closed the album and placed the lid on the box.

Cam picked up the last box, locked the door behind her, and slid the key into the mail slot. After loading the last of her belongings, she closed the tailgate on her truck. She leaned against the bed of the truck and took a final look at her apartment.

"Where will life take me now?" she asked. With a deep sigh, she opened the door and climbed in behind the wheel. She had sold most of her meager furnishings and donated the rest to charity. Cam was determined to make a complete fresh start.

For years, she'd seldom seen the small one-bedroom apartment she rented, and admitted she was one of the few people known to be able to kill a cactus. It wasn't that she had a brown thumb; she was just gone for such long stretches even a cactus couldn't survive the neglect. For the last ten years, she had served as a veterinarian for a national rodeo corporation, and now at fifty, she was determined to find a spot to settle down and plant her roots. She hoped to find a place to open a small practice and enjoy sleeping under the same roof for more than a few nights at a time. *It will be nice to have a home again.*

Cam reached for her sunglasses to curb the glare from the early morning sun and turned her truck south.

Earlier in the month, she'd received a call from Tom Cone, a fellow vet who planned to retire and move to South Florida with his wife. Cam had agreed to meet with him, and her first stop when she reached her destination would be his office. While she drove, her mind wandered back to the last fifteen years. Her long-term lover, Sheila, had died in a car crash while on her way home from work, sending Cam's life spiraling into chaos. Overwhelmed with grief, Cam had tried to drown her pain with alcohol. She'd convinced herself life without Sheila was worthless. Cam would have successfully wasted her life away if not for Harley Boone.

Back in the Saddle

Harley, a cowboy at a local ranch and a frequent participant in the rodeo circuit, easily recognized the signs of the alcoholic funk she'd fallen into and called her out on her behavior. With his constant encouragement, and a lot of tears, Cam had realized the mistake she was making. Hurting herself this way would not bring Sheila back, and she would most certainly not approve of Cam's behavior. Harley's friendship and guidance had helped her find her way again, and with his recommendation, she'd landed a job as the rodeo vet. The constant travel kept her mind busy, and over time, her heart began to heal.

Now, Harley was coming to her rescue again. He had recommended her to the retiring vet in hopes of her taking over the practice. Harley worked for the MC2, one of the large ranches in the area Dr. Cone served. After she met with Cone, she planned to track Harley down. She hadn't seen her friend in a couple of years and looked forward to reuniting with him. The thought left her wearing a grin.

†

Cam had two final stops to make before she left town. Getting flowers was the first. Cam pulled her truck into the lot of a small flower shop and entered to pick up a dozen yellow roses. They were Sheila's favorite. Whenever she had brought them home, she would ask Cam to sing "The Yellow Rose of Texas" to her. The memory brought a smile to her face but renewed the ache in her heart.

The clerk behind the counter greeted her with a warm smile. "I was wondering if you'd be in today. It's so beautiful outside."

"That it is." Cam made her selection and went to the counter to pay for her purchase.

3

"See you next time, Doc."

"Have a great day." Cam left the store. Her next stop was the cemetery to visit Sheila's gravesite. Whenever Cam was in town, she placed fresh flowers on Sheila's grave. Her boots had worn a path to the small gravesite, and she smiled when she saw the roses already in bloom on the bush she'd planted. Yellow, of course. She knelt and placed the fresh-cut roses at the base of the headstone. Her fingertips floated across the carving in the stone with a lover's caress. The early spring sun had warmed the marble and sent a ray of warmth through her fingertips.

"I wanted to stop by before leaving town to check on you one more time. I won't be but an hour away, and I'll still bring you flowers when your rosebush is no longer in bloom. I miss you terribly, and there's not a day goes by that I don't reminisce about our life together. I wouldn't change anything, except for having you here with me now on earth.

"Do you remember me telling you about Harley, and how he kicked my ass back into shape after your accident? He was the one who suggested Dr. Cone contact me about taking over his practice." She let out a soft laugh. "Just when I need him most, Harley pops back into my life."

Cam's voice was quivering and she couldn't hold back the tears that silently trailed down her cheeks. "I guess I'll go for now, before I become a total blithering idiot. I love you more today than ever. I'll be seeing you soon, my darling."

She stood and caressed the headstone, brushing away the dust before she returned to her truck. Leaving Sheila was the hardest part of starting over, but Cam was certain she would approve of her actions. She climbed into her truck and pulled slowly out of the cemetery, anxious to start the next chapter of her life.

Before she reached the gate that would lead her to the highway, a battered pickup truck pulled into the drive. Cam smiled when she recognized the driver and brought her truck to a halt.

The truck rolled to a stop beside her, a young man at the wheel. "Hey, Doc Bo."

"Good morning, Tim. How are you?"

"I'm doing good, ma'am." He looked at the boxes in the bed of her truck. "Are you leaving town?"

"I'm going to be taking over a practice about an hour away."

He nodded and a blush rose to his face. "I reckon I should've called to ask your permission, but I bought a rosebush I thought I'd plant across from yours."

"Is it yellow?"

"Yes, it is. Her favorite, right?"

"She loved yellow roses."

Clearly, Tim could see the look of pain cross her face. "I wish I could take that day back." His voice was full of emotion.

"That day is long gone, Tim, and you have suffered enough. Sheila wouldn't have wanted that. She'll love the roses that bush will bear for her."

He nodded, unable to speak.

"Take care of yourself and enjoy your family. Thanks for visiting and caring for the roses."

"It's the least I can do. Good luck, Doc, and don't be a stranger. Drop by anytime you come to town."

"I will, Tim. Take care."

He put his truck in gear, and Cam watched him drive away in her rear-view mirror. She pulled away when he stopped at the grave.

†

Tim Jernigan had been a sixteen-year-old, brand-new driver driving home from football practice when one of Texas's freak rainstorms blew up. The accident report stated his car hit a slick spot and because of his inexperience behind the wheel, he overcorrected when his car began to hydroplane and he lost control, spinning headlong into Sheila's oncoming car. She had died instantly in the impact and he walked away without a scratch. What the report couldn't know was the scars he bore from the emotional trauma the accident brought about.

When notified about the accident, Cam had wanted to hate the kid who had taken her lover, her life, from her. But when she met Tim, she saw his guilt and pain. After the funeral, she took him in her arms and cried with him until no more tears would flow. They sat on a nearby bench and talked while they watched the staff fill the grave and place fresh sod on the raw earth.

Cam remembered the final words she spoke to him that day before she left. "Don't let Sheila's death ruin your life. Make something good of yourself. She would want to see you grow old with dozens of grandkids around you."

Several years passed before she saw Tim again, but she did talk with his mother frequently after the accident to see how he was coping. His mom told her that for several months, he was deeply depressed, but one day after he had taken roses out to Sheila's grave, something in him changed, and she noticed him starting to heal. On many occasions when she visited Sheila, Cam found evidence of fresh-cut roses that had withered and she knew Tim continued to visit.

Seeing him today made her feel better about leaving town. She felt a sense of comfort, knowing Tim would still be around to watch over Sheila's roses, and now Sheila would have even more to enjoy.

A smile grew on her face when she thought of the successful trauma surgeon Tim had become and the lives he touched every day. Cam pulled onto the highway, her gray-streaked hair billowing around her face while the wind blew through the cab of her truck.

Time to move on, she thought as the miles drifted away behind her.

†

Stormy tilted her hat back and watched as Coal and Shadow, her equine partner, raced off to the left, chasing a steer that had broken away from the group they were herding into the cattle pens. Bo and Dolly, the pups Coal had given Gene and Mary Leah for Christmas and who were now six months old, raced after her. They were growing quickly and were turning into smart cattle dogs, learning to herd and assist the ranch hands in moving cattle from field to field. This morning, the crew was rounding up steers to be loaded onto the truck to take them to the feed pens. The first truck would be arriving soon, and they would collect a second group after lunch.

"Get him, cowgirl," Stormy hollered after Coal.

Coal raised her hand in acknowledgment while Shadow thundered after the steer. Stormy knew Coal had been secretly hoping a steer would break free so she and Shadow could take a quick run. Herding cattle was part of their duties, but Coal had never passed on a chance to race at top speed to chase down an errant animal. She obviously loved riding Shadow at a full-out run, and he loved running, so it was a win-win situation for them both.

Gene and Stormy watched them race away. "Such a show-off," Gene hollered with a chuckle.

"You're just mad because she beat you to the punch," Stormy teased.

"Yeah, she did, but that's nothing new. You gotta get up early to get ahead of Coal."

"You got that right. She really loves riding that horse."

"They were made for each other." His face broadened with a grin. "Here we go," he cried when another steer broke ranks. "I got this one." He took off after it, leaving Stormy laughing in his wake.

†

Melissa Conway returned to the MC2 from grocery shopping, and when she walked back into her house, the phone was ringing. She placed the bags on the floor and raced for it.

"Hello."

"Mrs. Conway, this is Roger Tucker in Billings. I was told you might have a few ranch hands I could hire for a two-week cattle drive."

Melissa grinned at the news. Gene, Coal, and Stormy would die if she turned down this opportunity. "I may indeed. What do you have in mind?"

"I'm looking for three more cowboys to move a herd up the mountain pastures in the next few weeks. I've lost a few hands to retirement or relocation and I haven't been able to find decent replacements yet. I've got to get the herd up to better grass."

"When would you need them?"

Tucker chuckled. "Yesterday, but I'll take them whenever they can get here."

"Would you consider a cowboy and two cowgirls?"

"I've heard you have two of the best cowgirls ever, so yes, ma'am, I'd love to have them. My foreman is my daughter Nancy, and she'd probably love some female companions for a change."

"Let me get your number and I'll talk to the crew at lunch and call you back. I can almost guarantee you'll have your cowhands, though. Just don't get any ideas of trying to steal them from me. They're a great crew."

"I wouldn't dream of it. Although I also hear they're great at rodeo events."

"We took top cowboy last year," she said with pride.

"That may make it even tougher to let them go. We have a rodeo coming up soon in these parts."

"Well maybe we'll have to look into entering a few events. I'll talk to you later."

"Thanks, ma'am."

Melissa hung up and returned to the truck for the rest of the groceries. She heard a whistle and turned to see the herd of steers entering the pens. It was turning out to be a great early spring. With the steers off to the feedlot, she could afford to send Gene and the girls off for a few weeks without taking away from the ranch. Harley and the others could keep up with the rest of the work with little problem. She couldn't wipe the smile off her face when she thought of how excited they would be at the news.

†

9

"That's the last of them, boss," Harley told Stan, the ranch foreman, when he closed the gate to the pens. "After we get these loaded we'll go back for the next load."

"The truck should be here shortly after we eat," Stan told them. "Tend to your horses and get ready for lunch. Melissa's cooked up a nice roast and biscuits for you bunch."

"That sounds great. I'm starving," Gene declared.

"When aren't you starving?" Stormy asked.

"I would say when I'm asleep, but I even dream of food."

Harley shook his head. "When I was your age, food was the last thing I dreamed of."

Gene blushed profusely. "I dream of other things too."

"Yeah, I bet. When is Susan coming down for a visit?" Coal asked.

"I don't know yet. Soon, I hope."

"It would be great to see her again and show her our part of the world," Coal told him.

Gene couldn't help but grin. "It'll be a huge difference from Montana, that's for sure."

Susan had been their tour guide when they were in Montana for Christmas. She and Gene had been inseparable. Harley could tell how excited Gene was when their relationship continued after they all returned to Texas. Gene was thrilled when she agreed to come for a visit before summer arrived.

†

Melissa was just finishing setting the food on the table when the crew entered the bunkhouse. "Get cleaned up and back in here before the food gets cold."

When everyone settled around the table and the crew was busy filling their plates, she looked at Harley and winked. She smiled at his cocked head and curious glance.

"I got a call this morning that may be of interest to some of you," she announced.

"Did I finally win the lottery?" Harley asked.

"No, nothing quite that exciting. I got a call from a rancher in Montana who needs some cowboys to go on a cattle drive to take a herd up into the mountains."

The room fell silent, accentuating the clank of Gene's fork falling onto his plate. "Please dear Lord, tell me you told him yes," he said.

"Well, no." She grinned when his face fell. "I told him I'd have to talk to you and the girls first."

His smile returned instantly. "All right!"

"He needs a crew of three for about two weeks. That's including the travel time to get you there since I know you want to take your own horses."

"Oh hell yeah," Gene cried. "Where in Montana?"

"Billings. He also told me there was a rodeo coming up soon, so maybe you could do some events after the drive is over."

Gene's grin grew even wider.

She turned to her two cowgirls. "I would assume you two need to talk this over with your other halves?"

"Yes, but I don't think either of them will have an issue with us going. It's every cowboy's dream to go on a cattle drive," Coal said, unable to restrain her grin.

Harley chuckled. "They aren't quite the romantic adventure you think. Sleeping on the hard, frozen ground, bathing in freezing-cold water, and not having Melissa's cooking to fill your belly. Still, it's an experience you all should have at least once." He grinned at his young friends. "You won't be disappointed."

"I take it you've been on a drive before," Coal stated.

"More than I care to remember. You'll spend a lot of time in the saddle riding from daylight to sundown. Then you get to set up camp for the night."

Unbelievably, Gene's grin grew wider.

"Can you survive without us for a few weeks?" Stormy asked Stan.

"It couldn't come at a better time. Once we get these steers loaded, we'll slow down a bit until the hay season starts. I can work on getting some colts for y'all to train when you get back."

Melissa's grin was almost as big as Gene's. "So it looks like it will happen. I'll call him back this afternoon after you two make your calls."

"A real live cattle drive," Gene remarked as he picked up his fork, then took a bite of roast. "This food is fantastic, by the way, boss."

"Eat up, you may be looking at a lot of beans in your future," Melissa warned.

"That's it, I'm not going if I have to sleep beside him if he's eating beans," Stormy groaned, and the room broke out in laughter.

"I think you and Coal will have your own tent," Melissa replied.

"I'm probably not much better than Gene with beans, though." Coal chuckled.

"Hey, so do we need to buy gear? Sleeping bags and such?" Stormy asked.

"I think you'll want your own sleeping bags, and you definitely need some warmer clothes," Melissa replied. "I'll ask about other supplies when I call him back."

"We'll need to go to town to do some shopping when we get done today," Gene stated. "When will we need to leave?"

Melissa paused. "If Harley will take the cowboy Cadillac in for an oil change and servicing, you could leave tomorrow or the next day. It'll take a few days to get there pulling a trailer."

"This is going to be so much fun." Gene squirmed in his seat like a school kid. "I can't wait to get started."

"I'd also recommend you ask him about firearms since you'll be traveling up the mountains. There will be plenty of hungry wildlife looking for an easy meal," Harley said.

Melissa grinned. "I'll do that. Is there anything else I need to ask?"

"See if he recommends other items he doesn't provide."

†

Gene wolfed down the rest of his meal, barely tasting his food. He was eager to finish work so they could drive into town for supplies for their trip. He, Coal, and Stormy would ride out and start bringing in the rest of the steers while Stan, Harley, and Lucas loaded the truck that would be arriving soon. When he finished, Gene stood and walked out to the barn to saddle the horses.

He heard Lucas rushing to catch up with him as he left the house. "Man, I am so jealous of you guys for getting to go on a cattle drive."

"Yeah, but once that baby boy arrives, you will have forgotten about missing out on this trip."

13

Gene knew Lucas and his girlfriend, Lisa, were expecting a baby in the next few weeks, and nothing could pull him away from the birth of his son.

"I know you're right."

"I just hope one thing, Lucas."

"What's that?"

"I just hope that boy comes out looking like his pretty mama and not his daddy."

Lucas grinned and slapped Gene on his shoulder. "Come on, smart-ass, let's get these horses saddled."

†

After they finished their meals, Coal and Stormy put in calls to Del and Mary Leah to discuss the impending trip.

"Hey, baby, is everything okay?" Mary Leah asked when she answered. "You don't often call me during the day."

Coal smiled at the concern in her lover's voice. "Yeah, darling, it is. I have something I want to talk about with you now, because I have to give Melissa an answer this afternoon."

"That sounds intriguing. What's my sister up to now?"

"She got a call from a rancher up in Montana this morning looking to hire three ranch hands for a cattle drive, and she's asked Gene, Stormy, and I to go."

"They still have real cattle drives?"

"Yes, dear, they do. The rancher wants a large herd moved up into the mountain pastures for the spring grazing. We'd be gone about two weeks, maybe a bit longer, and I didn't want to say yes without talking it over with you first."

"That's so sweet of you, but you know I can't deny you this opportunity. I'll miss the hell out of you, but maybe Del and I can mourn our losses together."

Coal chuckled. "Are you positive?"

"Positive I'm going to miss you? Heck yeah."

"No, silly, that you don't mind me going."

"Yes, I'm sure the three of you will have a grand adventure. Just be sure to pack a camera."

"I'll take lots of photographs for you. That's a promise."

"You have a deal, then, my love."

"I may not be back from town before you get home. We're going into town for supplies so we can get going in the morning."

"Wow, that soon?"

"Sooner we leave, the sooner we get back." Coal was finding it hard to conceal her excitement.

"I'll have to stock up on plenty of kisses tonight to last me two weeks."

"I'm positive that can be arranged. Do you need anything from town?"

"Not that I'm aware of, but thanks for asking. Would you like to meet for dinner somewhere?"

"That sounds like a great idea. Do you want to call Del to see if they want to join us?"

"No, tonight I'm going to be greedy. I want you all to myself."

"Oh really?" Coal purred. "In that case, I'll call when we head to town and we can make arrangements. Bye for now, love you."

"Love you too. Be safe."

†

When Coal stepped out of the main house, Stormy was ending her call with Del, and judging by her smile, she'd also gotten the go-ahead for the trip. Melissa emerged from the bunkhouse just as Coal and Stormy met up in the middle of the yard with a high five.

"I take it you both are going? Like I had any real doubt. Get a move on so you can get your shopping done and get packed. I'll map out a route for y'all to take with you for your trip. I'll also call Mr. Tucker back to let him know y'all will be on the way tomorrow, and to see if there are other supplies you need."

"Thanks, boss. You heard the lady, Coal, let's get a move on."

"I'm right behind you. Thanks for this opportunity, Melissa. It sounds like it'll be hard work but also a great deal of fun."

"I hope you can say that by the time you make it back."

Coal turned and jogged to catch up with Stormy. Gene and Lucas were bringing the horses out of the barn, and Shadow's ears perked when he saw her.

"I hope you're ready for a big adventure, my friend," she told Shadow while she stroked his neck. "You know, we might want to consider taking along blankets for our horses. They don't have a winter coat like the stock up there."

"That's not a bad idea," Harley said when he joined them. "Better get y'all some thermal underwear too. It's going to be wicked cold at night. Be sure to get the heaviest-weight sleeping bags you can find. There's nothing more miserable than trying to sleep on cold, hard ground."

They turned their attention to the driveway as a diesel engine rumbled. The cattle truck was just pulling into the drive as they mounted their horses to bring in the next group of steers.

"Let's do this," Gene called out and took off at a canter, racing ahead of the group with the pups running beside him.

†

When they reached the pasture, the group discussed the supplies they would need for the trip.

"I'm taking my rifle, but it wouldn't hurt to have a few sidearms." Gene patted the scabbard holding his hunting rifle.

"I've got that covered. I have two .9 millimeters with shoulder harnesses," Coal replied.

"Sleeping bags, thermals, horse blankets, canteens, and maybe some dried food items like jerky or trail mix would be good to have as well."

"Well aren't you the regular Boy Scout," Stormy teased.

"Not really, I've just done a bit of hunting is all."

"Are you always going to blush when I tease you?"

He grinned. "Probably so. It's all part of my boyish charm."

Coal chuckled at their banter. "Do I have to listen to this 24/7 for the next two weeks?"

"Probably so," they answered in unison and cracked up laughing.

Behind them, the truck beeped as it backed into the loading chute. It wouldn't take them near the amount of time to load the steers as it would for them to herd the next group to the pens.

"We better get a move on." Coal raced ahead to open the gate to the pasture where the steers were grazing.

"You heard the lady." Gene took off after Coal.

17

"That ain't no lady," Stormy shouted, urging her horse into a canter.

†

Back at the pens, the loading went smoothly as Melissa expected, and within half an hour, the loaded truck was pulling away. Melissa looked across the pasture at the dust stirred up by the herd of steers and knew the last group was on the way.

She watched Lucas walking into the barn for his horse, then turned to Harley. "Do you mind taking the truck in for service once we're done here?"

"No, ma'am, not at all."

She was getting ready to say something else when a shot rang out, and chaos ensued.

"What the hell?" Melissa cried. They shared a look of panic and then raced toward the gate to the pastures.

Chapter Two

They had the steers moving toward the pens, and all was going well until Gene's horse spooked. The movement of the steers had stirred up more than just dust; an angry rattlesnake hissed at Gene's horse, his rattlers shaking angrily, and the horse spooked, nearly unseating Gene. Bo, who had been trotting beside Gene, sprang into action to protect his master. Gene could only watch in horror while Bo raced forward to attack the snake.

"Bo! Get back here!" Gene called out when he realized what was happening. But he was several seconds too late. Bo had already launched himself at the snake.

The snake buried his fangs into Bo's shoulder, releasing the deadly venom while Bo cried out in pain and desperately tried to shake him loose.

Gene was already on the ground, rushing toward his pup. "C'mere, boy, it's going to be all right," he said none too confidently. "Watch out for the snake," he called out to Coal as she arrived, his heart racing with fear.

The snake had released Bo's shoulder and was slowly gliding away when Gene looked up at Coal.

"Hand him up to me and kill that damned snake."

19

Gene carefully passed her the pup with tears running down his face.

"Get the snake and meet me at the truck."

Gene watched Coal race toward the barn holding Bo in her arms.

He rushed back to his horse and pulled out his rifle. It took two shots through his tear-blurred eyes to kill the snake, obliterating the head, which was just fine with him. He didn't need it for a vet to identify what type of rattlesnake it was. He picked the snake up by the tail and raced back to his horse.

†

Coal hurried to the barn, and Lucas met her along the way. She slowed only long enough to say, "Snakebite, help Stormy bring in the steers," before galloping away. She could already feel the young dog shivering as he went into shock.

"Easy, boy, you're going to be just fine," she said, sending up a silent prayer Bo would survive.

Harley and Melissa raced toward the gate, and Coal hoped they would have it open when she arrived. If not, Shadow had cleared that gate many times when following her into the hayfields and she knew they would land safely.

†

As Cam drove her truck down the ranch's driveway, she saw a rider galloping across the field toward the barn and wondered what was going on. She accelerated into the yard toward the pens just as the rider and horse skidded to a halt.

"What in God's name is happening?" Harley shouted as Cam stepped out of the truck.

A woman answered, "Snakebite, Gene's bringing the snake. We've got to get him to Dr. Cone."

"I'll get the truck," another woman said seconds before nearly running Cam over.

Cam held up her hands to steady the startled woman and turned toward the small group as she heard Harley's anxious voice. "Well I'll be damned. I've never been so glad to see you in my life, Doc Bo. Bring your bag, we've got a snakebite."

As Cam raced back to the truck to grab her medical kit, one of the women asked, "What's going on, and who the hell is that?"

"I'll explain everything later. She's a vet and a damned good one." Harley gently took a small dog from the woman's arms. "Doc Bo, this is Coal. Coal, Doc Bo."

"Nice to meet you, Coal. Stretch him out on my tailgate. Can someone get a blanket to cover him? He's already started going into shock, and we need to keep him warm." Cam looked at Harley and Coal. "Rattlesnake?"

"Yes, ma'am. Gene's bringing it with him."

"Did it have a skin pattern that looked like diamond shapes?"

"Yes, ma'am, it did."

Cam rummaged through her kit, looking at labels on several vials before settling on one. She pulled it out and began drawing fluid into a syringe.

The other woman came back with the blanket. "Hi, I'm Melissa. What can we do?"

"Pray," Cam answered bluntly. She looked at Coal. "You got him here quickly, but that's no guarantee. Would you hold this, please?" She handed Coal the filled syringe, then returned to her bag and retrieved a pair of battery-operated clippers. "Can you shave the area around the wound while I get this injection of antivenin started?"

"No problem." Coal traded the syringe for the clippers. "Harley, can you hold his head so he doesn't spook?"

Bo whimpered in pain when Harley placed his large hands on the animal's head.

"Easy, boy, you're in good hands now. I've got him, go ahead and start."

Coal carefully shaved the area around the puncture wound while Cam located a vein in Bo's leg and started pushing the injection. Cam felt Melissa watching her as she inserted the IV line, cooing to the young pup to soothe him.

Moments later, a rider stormed through the gate, barely slowing his horse. He flew out of the saddle and rushed over to the truck, a confused look on his face.

Cam smiled at the young man carrying the remains of a rattlesnake. She took a close look. "Definitely a diamondback."

"Is he going to make it?" the man asked.

"Only time will tell." She looked into his face, touched by the depth of emotion in his eyes as tears trailed down his cheeks. She knew from experience it took a lot to make a cowboy cry.

"This is Gene, Bo's owner. Gene, this is Doc Bo," Harley introduced.

"I'll pay whatever it costs, just make him well again." Gene's voice cracked with emotion.

"I'll do my best, son. Here, you can help by holding this up for me." She handed him a IV bag. "I'm going to give him some fluids and add some antihistamines to sedate him."

She watched with amusement as Gene turned and hurled the snake carcass away from the group with all his might. "How did you get here so fast?" he asked, his hands trembling as he took the bag. "I was actually coming out to meet Mrs. Conway and to see my old friend, Harley Boone. I'm going to be taking over for Dr. Cone when he retires, so I wanted to visit some of the bigger accounts."

"That was very lucky for us," Melissa replied. "You couldn't have arrived at a better time."

Cam looked over to see Harley smiling at her. "I never thought I'd be so happy to see you, Doc Bo."

Another small dog had followed Gene from the pasture, and sat beside Coal, gazing up at her and then back to Bo. She whined when the other dog whimpered in pain and fear. Everyone looked toward her.

"Your brother's going to be fine, Dolly," Coal said softly and reached down to stroke her head. Coal shuffled back and forth, and Cam looked up at her. "If you don't need me, I'm going to help Stormy and Lucas finish bringing in the steers." She turned to Melissa for approval.

"Go ahead, I think we have this situation under control for the moment," Melissa answered.

Coal placed her hand on Cam's shoulder. "Thanks for being here."

"I'm just glad I came out here when I did."

Coal walked over to a beautiful black stallion and swung up onto his back. "Let's get back to work, big boy."

Coal and Dolly raced back through the gate, and then Cam turned to Harley. "Do you think you could find a piece of dowel or some type of stick to hang this IV bag on?"

"I can do that."

"Hang on a second, Harley. Can Bo be moved?" Melissa asked.

"Yes, that won't be an issue if he's carried carefully."

"Gene, go get Bo's bed and put it in Coal's old bedroom, then carry him inside where it's quiet and out of the bright light."

"Yeah, it will be noisy when the steers are driven into the pens, and the next truck should be here soon," Harley agreed. "Let me hold that and you get moving." He took the bag from Gene.

Gene raced toward the bunkhouse.

"You know it'll kill him if Bo doesn't make it, right?" Harley warned Cam.

"I'll do everything I can, but I can't promise anything. He's young and strong, but I don't want to give the young man any false hope. Tonight will tell the story."

"Do you have any place to stay yet?" Melissa asked.

"I was hoping to check in at a local hotel later."

"Would you consider staying here to be close to Bo? I know it's selfish, but I think we'd all feel better if you were around."

Cam smiled warmly. "That would be wonderful. I'd like to stay close to him tonight too. Thank you."

Gene raced across the yard with the bed and into the house, and then emerged from the back of the house breathing hard moments later. "Everything's ready."

"Do you want to carry him?" Harley asked.

"Yes, he's my boy."

Cam sensed Gene was once more on the verge of tears, so she placed a comforting hand on his shoulder. "I know I don't need to tell you, but be as gentle with him as you can. We want him to remain calm. That means you need to stay calm too. Bo will sense your distress, and he needs your comforting strength right now."

"Yes, ma'am." He nodded, wiping away his tears, and then carefully lifted Bo from the tailgate. Harley walked beside him carrying the IV bag.

Melissa picked up the trash from the vet supplies while Cam reloaded her bag. "Would you like me to take your bag so you can bring in your suitcase?"

"Sure," she answered and handed her medical bag to Melissa.

†

"How's Bo?" Stormy asked when Coal returned to the herd.

"Too soon to tell, so keep praying. Gene's a hot mess, but I can image how he's feeling." She looked down at Dolly trotting beside them. "Mary Leah would kill me if anything happened to Dolly."

"I doubt that, but let's not test your theory."

The steers were moving quickly, and when the pens came into view, Stan rushed out from the house to open the gates.

"He made it back quickly from town," Stormy replied.

"We'll have a truckload of feed to unload when we're done here," Lucas reminded them. "I can handle it if you two want to head into town to get your shopping done."

"Crap, I completely forgot about that when everything went to hell," Stormy remarked. "Do you think we need to delay a few days?"

"I don't know. We'll have to ask Melissa what she thinks. It depends on what happens with Bo tonight. There's no way we're dragging Gene away until he's stable, even for a cattle drive."

"I don't think another day or two will make that much difference," Stormy answered.

"I agree. But we can go ahead and do the shopping tonight anyway if you want."

"That might be better than pacing around waiting to see what's going to happen with Bo. Gene will be nervous enough already. Man, he's got to be all right for Gene's sake."

†

Coal raised the bandana around her neck to cover her mouth. The steers were kicking up dust while they moved from field to field on the way to the pens. They'd just finished driving the last of the steers into the pens when a diesel engine approached.

"We did just arrive in time," Stormy stated when Harley slammed the gate closed.

"How is Bo doing?" Coal asked.

"He's holding his own so far. If anyone can save him, it'll be Doc Bo. She's the best vet I've ever met."

Curious, Coal asked, "Where did y'all meet?"

"Years ago, before I came to MC2, I did a bit of rodeo. I was working for a cattle company that provided animals for rodeo stock. One night, she came out to handle an emergency case for us, and our friendship grew from there. Years later, she suffered a personal tragedy, and I convinced her to come to work for the company. It's been about three years since we've seen each other."

"Well I'm glad she chose today to track you down. I don't think Bo would have stood much of a chance of surviving if she wasn't here."

Always the curious one, Stormy asked, "So was this more than a friendship?"

Harley broke out in a laugh. "I would have jumped on that opportunity if I could have, but Doc Bo bats for your team."

"She's a lesbian?" Stormy asked.

"Much to my chagrin, yes. We love each other as friends, but nothing more."

Coal smiled at the obvious admiration Harley felt toward the vet. She had never heard him speak of a woman with such excitement, or with the bright smile that twinkled in his eyes.

The truck arrived to haul the cattle. Coal and Stormy cared for the horses while Stan, Lucas, and Harley loaded the steers.

"Let's go check on everyone, and then we can come back to unload this feed," Coal told her.

†

Gene sat beside Bo, running his hand down the dog's flank. "What do we have to watch out for, Doc?"

"We need to keep him warm until the threat of shock is gone. We also need to watch the wound closely. The snake's venom carries enzymes that destroy flesh, so I need to know if the skin around the wound blisters or begins to turn black."

Gene swallowed hard, fearful of asking the obvious question. "Will he lose his leg?" he asked, his voice cracking.

"I certainly hope not, but that is a possibility if the venom damage starts to spread. I've added some antibiotics to the IV to ward off infection, and the antihistamines will help keep him calm."

27

The back door opened and footsteps came down the hall. Stormy and Coal entered the room.

"How's he doing?" Coal asked.

Cam looked at her. "He's holding his own so far."

"This is Stormy." Coal nodded toward her friend.

"Nice to meet you, I'm Cameron Bohannon, but most folks call me Doc Bo or Cam."

"Just like my boy," Gene replied and forced a smile.

"Yes, just like your boy, so I'm going to take that as a good sign."

Melissa was propped against the wall watching. "Unless you need us, we're going to unload the feed from the truck and head into town to get our shopping done," Coal told her.

"I think we can handle things here. I've got lasagna in the oven if you want to have dinner when you come back," Melissa said.

"Thanks, but I promised to meet Mary Leah in town for dinner. When she hears you've made lasagna, she may change her mind, though."

"Do you want me to call and ask her while you unload the truck?"

"Yeah, that would be fine with me. Nobody beats your lasagna. Do you think you could also call Mr. Tucker and let him know we'll be delayed a couple of days? We can still make it by Monday if that suits him."

Gene looked up at them. "You two would risk losing out on a chance for a cattle drive for me?"

"Hell yeah, you and Bo are family. If he can't wait until Monday, then that's too bad," Stormy answered.

†

Cam watched the interaction between them and smiled at the genuine feel of family radiating from them. She knew they weren't relatives, but she could feel the love they had for one another. *This is just the kind of place I was hoping to find.*

"Thanks, you two. Do you want me to help with the feed?"

"Stay where you are. Bo needs you right now, and I think with Lucas's help we can handle the truck."

Cam smiled at them as Gene nodded and resumed stroking down Bo's side.

"You'll call Mary Leah for me, Melissa?" Coal asked.

"I'm all over it."

"I've got my fingers crossed, then. Will you let her know what's going on here?"

"Of course I will. Now get to it so you can be back in time for dinner."

"Yes, boss." Coal smirked, and they left the room.

†

Stan, Harley, and Lucas were already working on unloading the feed when Coal and Stormy arrived at the barn.

"How are the boys doing?" Stan asked.

"As well as could be expected, I think, given the circumstances. Gene seems to be holding up," Coal answered.

"I sure hope Bo pulls through. That boy loves him dearly," Stan replied.

"Yeah, he does. Where do you want us?"

29

"Why don't you climb up on the truck and hand the bags down to Stormy. We can form a line and Lucas can stack for us," Stan instructed.

"Not a problem." Coal climbed onto the truck.

†

Melissa called Mary Leah to fill her in on the afternoon's events.

"Hey, sis, is everything alright? Both you and Coal have called today."

"We've had a crazy afternoon. Bo got bitten by a snake while out in the pasture with Gene."

"Oh my goodness, is he going to be okay?"

"As luck would have it, an old friend of Harley's arrived just when it happened and she's a vet, so we were able to get him prompt medical attention, but he's not out of the woods yet."

"I bet Gene is distraught. How's he holding up?"

"He's having a rough time but trying to be strong for Bo. I've moved them both into the house for the night, and Doc Bo is staying the night too."

"That's wonderful. I'm thankful she showed up when she did."

"She's going to be taking over Dr. Cone's practice. Seems really nice and has been great with Gene and Bo."

"I appreciate you calling to let me know what's going on."

"I also wanted to see if you and Coal would join us for dinner. We're having lasagna, but she'll still meet you for dinner if you want, so it's your call."

"That's probably the easiest decision I've had all day. We'd be crazy to pass up on that. Is there anything I can bring?"

"Just bring a hearty appetite. I'll let Coal know you're joining us. She and Stormy are going to get their shopping done tonight. The trip will be delayed a day or so, but hopefully they'll still go."

"I sure hope Bo pulls through. I know how I'd feel if it was Dolly."

"Just keep them both in your prayers."

Melissa ended the call and dialed Tucker's number. He was considerate when she told him about Bo and agreed another day or two wouldn't make that much difference. He also gave her a small list of supplies he recommended they bring with them before they hung up.

†

When they finished unloading the feed, Coal turned to Harley. "Will you be able to take the truck in for an oil change and inspection?"

"I'll be on my way in just a few minutes. I want to check on Bo and see if Melissa needs anything from town before I go."

"Tell her we'll be back as quick as we can. The young'un here's going to drive me to town so we can shop." She punched Stormy's shoulder.

"Well then, come on, old woman."

Coal chuckled. "We'll see you for dinner," she said, and they left the barn.

"Good luck with your shopping," Harley called after them.

31

Melissa stopped them before they made it to Stormy's truck. "Mr. Tucker understands the delay and recommended a few other supplies. Are you two okay for money?"

"We've got it covered, boss," Coal replied, and then she slipped the additional list Melissa handed her into her pocket.

†

The shopping trip went quickly and they were well equipped by the time they started back to the ranch.

"I don't know if it was the shopping or unloading the feed, but I'm hungry," Stormy announced when they left town.

"Is Del coming out to eat with us?"

"No, she had a late session tonight. I'll take her some leftovers when we finish."

"You're assuming there will be leftovers," Coal said.

"You didn't see the number of trays of lasagna Melissa was preparing to bake. Even on his best days, Gene couldn't eat all that."

Stormy's comment brought the painful reality back to them. "I sure hope Bo makes it. I don't know what we'll do with Gene if he dies."

"I know. It's an unfortunate part of living on a ranch. We just have to have faith Doc Bo started treatment in time."

Coal felt a need to lighten the somber mood. She gave Stormy a playful look. "What did you think about Harley's comment?"

"About her being a lesbian? She's a handsome woman, for sure."

"Yeah, I was thinking that too. I wonder what the rest of her story is."

"I have a feeling we will be seeing a lot of her in the future, and I'm sure Harley can give us the scoop."

"He sure seemed smitten by her." Coal chuckled.

"Yeah, he did." Stormy turned down the long drive to the ranch.

"Can we drop off my supplies before we head over to the MC2?"

"Sure, that won't take but a few minutes."

†

When Coal entered the house, Melissa and Mary Leah were bustling around the kitchen. Stormy volunteered to carry Gene's supplies to his room in the bunkhouse.

"I'll be right back to help after I check on Gene." Coal passed through the kitchen. "That smells great, by the way." She stopped long enough to kiss Mary Leah and continued to the back of the house. When she entered the bedroom, Gene was sitting on the floor with Bo's head in his lap, and Doc Bo was adding medicine to the IV bag hanging from the bed's headboard.

Gene looked up when she entered, and Coal's heart lodged in her throat at the redness in his eyes and the scowl on his face. She sat across from him. "How's he doing?"

Gene looked up at Doc Bo.

"He's taking in a little water, and the threat of shock has passed at least for now, but he's still got an uphill battle ahead of him."

Gene flinched at Doc's warning, and Coal felt the worry he was experiencing. "Is there anything I can do to help here?"

"Why don't you stay with Bo and I will encourage Gene to shower and grab a bite to eat."

"I'll go shower, but I'm not hungry."

"That has to be a first. You need to eat to keep up your strength too," Coal reminded him.

"Maybe later. I'll be back in a few minutes." He carefully placed Bo's head on a pillow.

"Take your time. I won't leave him," Coal promised.

"I'll be here too," Doc Bo added.

After Gene left, Stormy entered the room. "Gene looks horrible. Is there any change?"

"He's fighting hard and making slow progress. His youth and strength have allowed him to make it this far, so I'm hopeful he'll last the night. If he does, his chances of survival improve tremendously."

"Is there anything I can get you?" Stormy asked.

"No thanks, I'm good." She finished the injection and sat on the edge of the bed.

Coal sat next to Bo and buried her hand in his coat, stroking him softly. "Where's Dolly?"

"She's over in the bunkhouse with Harley. She kept pacing the room, so he took her away to see if he could distract her," Doc Bo answered.

Stormy shuffled her feet nervously. "I'm going to go see if the ladies need my help in the kitchen."

Doc Bo watched her leave, then turned to find Coal looking at her. Coal smiled and continued to stroke Bo's head. "Have you two been friends long?"

"A little over a year now, I think. We met at a rodeo where we were both competing."

"I worked as a rodeo vet until just recently when I learned of Dr. Cone's retirement. I really enjoyed the work, but I dreamed of putting down some roots again."

"I can understand that. I left Dallas for the serenity of working on a ranch after my military service was complete."

"Wasn't Melissa's husband also in the military?"

"Yes, we served in the same unit. I was there when he died." Coal grimaced at the painful memory.

"What rodeo events do you compete in?"

Coal breathed a sigh of relief and gratitude for the change of subject. Her therapy sessions with Del had helped her greatly, but talking about her time in the desert was still difficult. "Barrel racing, pole bending, and team roping with Gene," she answered.

"Are you a header or a heeler?"

"I can do both, but I'm a better heeler than Gene, so I heel most of the time. He's improving, though."

"He seems like a fine young man and he sure loves this pup." She bent down to listen to Bo's heart.

"I gave Bo to him as a puppy last Christmas. They have been inseparable since. I gave his sister, Dolly, to my lover, Mary Leah. Have you met yet?"

"Yes, Melissa introduced us earlier. Have you been together long?"

"Almost four years now. We live just across the first pasture."

"I saw that. Nice house, and that's one fine stud you were riding today."

"That's Shadow. We paired up when I first arrived here. If an animal can be a best friend, then he'd have to be mine."

"I believe they can. Gene and Bo are prime examples," she pointed out, then returned to her feet and sat on the edge of the bed.

"That's for sure."

Mary Leah arrived at the door. "We'll be ready to eat in just a few if you want to get washed up."

"I'm going to stay with Bo, so see if you can get Melissa to convince Gene to eat something when he returns."

"I'm sure she'll try her best. Can I bring you something to drink at least?"

Coal smiled at her lover. "I'd love a tea, baby."

Mary Leah shifted her gaze to the handsome woman sitting on the bed. "May I bring you something?"

"Thanks, but I'm starving, and Coal has everything under control here, so I think I'll get cleaned up and join y'all for dinner." Doc Bo disappeared into the bathroom.

Mary Leah watched her leave and turned back to Coal. "I'll be right back with your tea."

Coal heard the back door open and then the clicking of dog nails on the hardwood floor. Seconds later, Dolly trotted into the room to lie down beside Bo and propped her head on Coal's thigh.

"Hey, girl." Coal petted the dog's head. "Coming to check on your brother?"

"She's been pacing the bunkhouse floor," Harley replied, then leaned against the doorframe. "Are you going to eat with us?"

"I'm going to give Gene a break so hopefully he can eat something. I'm afraid he's going to have a long night. I'll eat later. I'm sure if he eats, he'll rush through the meal to get back here."

"I know that's right. Did you get all your shopping done?"

"Yeah, we did. I think we're all set. I'm glad Melissa was able to get us a few extra days."

"There's no way you're going to get Gene to leave until he knows Bo will be all right."

"I can understand that. I'd be the same if something happened to Shadow."

Dolly lifted her head when Bo whimpered in his sleep, then replaced it on Coal's thigh, looking up at her with worry in her expression. Coal stroked her head. "Easy, girl. Bo is strong and is going to be okay," she said softly.

Harley smiled down at them sitting on the floor together. "I heard a commotion in the kitchen on my way in, so I'm going to help the ladies carry food to the bunkhouse. You need anything?"

"Mary Leah's going to bring me some tea, but thanks."

"I'll see you in a bit, then." He disappeared down the hall.

"I hope you didn't think I forgot your tea." Mary Leah entered the room and knelt to hand Coal the drink.

Coal smiled up at her. "I knew you'd bring it when you got a chance. Thanks."

"Are you sure I can't bring you a plate?"

"No, I'm sure Gene will be here as soon as he finishes eating."

The back door opened and Gene entered. "I'll take over now, Coal, so you can go eat."

Coal shook her head. "We've all agreed I'll stay while you help take the food out and eat first. You're going to have a long night ahead of you, so eat a good meal. Bo's resting well, so we'll be fine until you get back."

Gene looked like he wanted to argue, but Melissa called from the kitchen, "Gene, I need you in here."

"I'll be back quick."

Coal turned back to Mary Leah. "Try to get him to eat."

"I'll do my best. Love you." She smiled and leaned down to kiss Coal.

"I love you too."

†

When Gene returned, Coal went to the bunkhouse and ate a quick meal.

"Melissa outdid herself again with that lasagna, didn't she?" Harley asked when he sat down across from Coal.

"I swear it gets better every time she cooks it."

"She had an idea at supper,"

"Really? What's up?"

"Doc Bo will be looking for a place to stay and a spot for an office to set up her practice, since Doc Cone worked out of his home. Melissa asked me what I thought of Doc Bo staying at her place and using Mitch's old office at the rear of the barn for her practice."

Coal lifted a brow, surprised by his comments. Since Coal's arrival at the ranch, no one had spent much time in the office that had been Mitch's haven when he was alive. It seemed odd that Melissa would consider letting the vet use it, but then Melissa often surprised Coal with her acts of kindness. Having a vet on-site would benefit the ranch, and since she specialized in large animals, Doc Bo would travel to treat most of her clientele. "That could be really good for us," she agreed and continued eating.

"I think that's what the boss is thinking too. I also think she's been lonesome in the house since you and Mary Leah moved into your own place, and then Stormy moved in with Del."

"I can see that too. It would be nice to have some company for her."

Harley sat with her until she finished her meal, then he stood and stretched. "I'm going to check on Gene and Bo and then drag my tail to bed."

"Come on, then. I'll walk back to the house with you."

The night air was a bit chilly as they left the bunkhouse and walked to the house. Coal and Harley entered the back door and stopped by the bedroom to check on Gene. After finding Bo's condition hadn't changed, Coal walked into the kitchen.

"Your lasagna is still the best ever, boss," Coal told Melissa. She poured a cup of coffee and joined them at the kitchen table.

"I'm glad you enjoyed it. You always appreciate my cooking."

"That I do," Coal said.

Mary Leah was resting her hand on Doc Bo's arm while they talked about the town. The intimacy of the gesture gave Coal a twinge of jealousy. She tried unsuccessfully to push the feeling out of her mind and looked back at Melissa to clear her thoughts.

†

Melissa saw the pained look cross Coal's face and was relieved when Cam moved her arm away from Mary Leah and stood. "I think I'll check on the boys."

Melissa waited until Cam had left, then turned to Coal. "I've offered for Cam to stay here and use Mitch's office to start her practice. What do you think of the idea?"

"I think it's a good move for her and the ranch."

Coal's voice lacked emotion when she answered, and Melissa cocked her head, looking at Coal with curiosity. This was a business decision that would benefit both parties, and

Coal's lack of enthusiasm left her confused. Maybe it was her imagination or the strain of the day, but she was surprised Coal wasn't as excited to have an on-site vet as she was.

Coal looked back at her and then turned away from direct eye contact. Coal's dark eyes were windows to her emotions, and Melissa had learned that when Coal was upset, she would avoid eye contact until she had her emotions under control. Melissa wouldn't press the issue right away, but she would talk to Coal in private before the night ended.

†

Cam fled from the kitchen and the spark of anger in Coal's eyes. The last thing she wanted was to cause problems for anyone at the MC2. When she entered the room, she smiled. Bo was resting quietly, and Gene had curled up next to him on the floor, also sleeping soundly. Harley sat on the bed watching them and smiled up at her while she checked the IV, adding another dose of antibiotics to the bag. She took a blanket from the bed, spread it over the two sleeping forms, and then followed Harley out the door, dimming the lights in the room as she left.

"He seems to be resting peacefully. Is that a good sign?"

"I think the worst is over for him, but he will be sore for several days," she answered while they stood in the hall.

"We were very lucky you showed up when you did."

Cam nodded. "I don't think he would have made it to Dr. Cone's office."

"I don't think so either. I'm going to call it a night, but let me know if anything changes tonight."

"I will. It's good to see you again, my friend."

40

"Yes, it is. Maybe we can catch up some tomorrow if things stay calm."

"I'd like that." She stepped forward to hug Harley. "You okay with me staying here and using the office in the barn?"

"Do you really have to ask? I'm happy to have you here, and you'll be a great addition to this crew."

She smiled warmly at him. "Good night, Harley."

"Night, Doc. See you tomorrow."

†

When Cam reentered the kitchen, Coal stood and announced she was going to saddle Shadow for the ride home.

"Do you mind if I walk out with you?" Cam asked.

"Not at all," she replied.

"You can help me pick up the kitchen," Melissa told Mary Leah, who stood, presumably to go to the barn also.

"All right," she answered while the two women left the kitchen and walked across the yard.

†

They walked to the barn in silence, and Coal stepped into Shadow's stall to lead him out.

"He's a beautiful animal."

"The best horse I've ever had. He's smart, fast, and is loyal to me."

"I get the impression you're not pleased with Melissa's offer for me to live at the ranch and set up an office here."

"I'm very pleased with that. I think it's a good business decision for both of you. If you hadn't been here today, Bo would be dead and Gene would be shattered." She slipped

41

Shadow's bridle over his head and took the saddle blanket Cam held out to her.

"Is there something else, then? I sensed anger from you back in the kitchen, and I don't want us to start badly. I'd like for us to be friends."

Coal placed the blanket across Shadow's back and turned to look at Cam. "It's probably irrational of me, but I didn't like the way Mary Leah had her hand resting on your arm. I reckon I got bit by the green-eyed monster."

"I'm sorry you felt jealousy, but let me assure you, I'm not interested in pursuing any type of relationship with Mary Leah or her sister other than friendship. I've had the love of my life, and that will never be replaced."

Coal recognized the familiar look of a painful loss on Cam's face and emotionally kicked herself for coming off like a jerk. "I should be the one apologizing for my insecurity. You have been nothing short of a miracle for us since you arrived, and I should give you the respect you deserve." She lifted the saddle, placed it gently on Shadow's back, and tightened the cinch.

"I was just doing what I was trained to do. I do hope we can be friends."

"I'd like that too." Coal finally smiled. "Do you ride much?"

"Whenever I get the chance."

"I'll give you a tour of the spread tomorrow if you're interested."

"That would be great. I have a morning appointment, but my afternoon is free."

"That will work out well. Stormy and I'll get our supplies loaded in the morning for our trip."

"I'm envious of you going on a cattle drive. I think getting a taste of life on the trail would be an incredible experience."

"Too good for us to pass up," Coal agreed, taking Shadow's reins in her hand.

"How long will you be gone?"

"Probably about two weeks."

"You'll be ready for a hot shower and a soft bed when you get back to civilization."

"That's for sure." Coal grinned. "Some of Melissa's cooking too."

She draped the reins over a hitching post outside the bunkhouse. "We'll be headed home soon, big boy," she told him while she stroked the horse's neck. She turned back to Cam. "I really am glad for you to be joining us out here. We need a good vet nearby, and Melissa will enjoy having company in the house again. The boys are close by, but she says there's nothing like having another female under the roof."

"I can appreciate that. She will never remarry, will she?"

"No, Mitch was her one and only. She's had numerous offers for dates, but she's not been interested in any of them."

"I can understand that. Some relationships can never be repeated or improved, so why not stop with memories of the best?"

"I reckon that's how she sees it too. I'm not sure I'm strong enough to do that," Coal admitted.

"When you've had the one, you'll know how it feels."

"I did, but I guess it's just not meant for me to be alone. I think I need someone to keep me out of trouble," she answered with a smirk.

"A bit of a troublemaker, are ya?"

"I don't make it, but I'll be damned if I don't seem to attract more than my share. When I first arrived, there was a bully of a cowboy in town that I had several run-ins with, and when he was killed by a jealous husband, I was a suspect briefly."

Cam raised an eyebrow. "I have great respect for a woman who stands her ground."

Coal chuckled. "Billy Ray was too dumb to realize that, and he died before I could convince him all women wouldn't cower in fear of him. I gave him a few good lessons, though." She grinned.

"I'm sure you did. I don't think I want to get on your bad side."

"I don't think you will. I'm pretty easygoing unless you treat my family badly, then my patience wears thin quickly."

"I'll keep that in mind. I just do my work and help out where I can."

"Better be careful or Stan will put you to work around here."

"Hard work doesn't bother me, and I'd gladly help."

Melissa and Mary Leah were finished washing dishes when Cam and Coal returned to the kitchen. "I'm going to check on Gene and then ride for home," Coal told them.

"I'll go with you. It's probably time for another bag of fluids."

†

Gene was still sleeping soundly with an arm draped over Bo. Cam replaced the IV bag and bent down to listen to Bo's heart.

"He's still beating strong, and the flesh around the wound looks bruised but healthy. I think he's going to be just fine."

"That's great news," Coal whispered.

Gene stirred and opened his eyes to see the two women watching over him. "Is everything okay?"

"Bo's doing well. I just changed his IV bag and checked his heart and the wound. You have one strong pup there. He may wake up during the night to get rid of some of these fluids we've been pumping into him."

"Can he go outside?"

Cam knelt in front of Bo and showed Gene how to disconnect and cap off the IV line. "If he's strong enough to go outside, I think it's safe to remove the IV, so wake me when you come back in and I'll reconnect him after checking him over. Carry him, though, so we can keep him off that leg whenever possible."

Gene smiled for the first time since earlier in the day. "Thanks, Doc. I knew you'd save him."

"It was Bo's strong heart and your love that brought him this far. He should be fine, but if he starts running a fever, wake me immediately."

"I will."

"Get some sleep and I'll see you in the morning," Coal replied.

"Good night, ladies."

"Come, Dolly," Coal called.

Dolly refused to get up and crawled closer to Bo. "Can she stay the night?" Gene asked.

Coal smiled at the dog's behavior. "I think that will be just fine. I'll let Mary Leah know."

"Thanks."

They left the room and went back to the kitchen. "Dolly's spending the night with Bo and Gene," she told Mary Leah.

"Is everything alright?"

"Yes, she just doesn't want to leave her brother right now."

"I can understand that," Melissa replied.

Coal smiled at her. "Thanks for another great meal, boss."

"Yes, that was terrific. I can see I'm going to have to start exercising if I'm going to be living here." Cam grinned.

"No worries, we'll work it off you," Melissa promised.

"Shadow and I are going to start for home." Coal excused herself.

"I won't be far behind you," Mary Leah said.

"Good night, then, ladies."

"Come along, Cam, and I'll show you where the towels and supplies are. You have to be exhausted after today's events," Melissa said.

"I'm definitely in need of a hot shower."

"I'll see you tomorrow," Mary Leah told them.

†

Shadow plodded down the drive while Coal enjoyed the cool evening breeze and the sky filled with brilliant stars. Little light came from the house and bunkhouse to affect the view.

"Soon we'll be sleeping under this blanket of stars every night," she told Shadow. "I hope we're up for it."

Shadow moved steadily along as Coal contemplated speaking with Mary Leah about Cam and her moment of jealousy. One part of her wanted to be honest about her feelings, but instead she decided not to mention how she felt about the intimacy her lover showed toward a total stranger.

"I'm just being silly," she told herself and urged Shadow into a trot.

She watched the lights of their home come on after Mary Leah arrived.

"Home," she whispered. Shadow's ears flicked at the sound of her voice. "Let's get home."

†

Coal got Shadow settled in the barn and walked toward the house. She hadn't realized just how tired she was until she entered and heard the shower running in the master bath.

A nice hot shower would be heavenly, she thought while she stripped out of her work clothes. Dust flew from her jeans when she tossed them in the hamper. It seemed like days since they'd moved the steers from the dusty pastures into the pens. The long, emotionally draining day had taken its toll on her body and psyche.

She entered the bathroom and found Mary Leah already bathing. "Would you mind some company?"

"I'd love some company," she called from the steamy shower.

Coal pulled the curtain back and stepped inside. Mary Leah was busy washing her hair. It had grown back curly after the chemotherapy, and the shampoo's thick lather covered her head. She stepped from the flow of the shower, allowing Coal to rinse in the hot water.

"Oh my God, this feels terrific."

"You had a crazy day today. You look like you're worn out."

"I didn't think so until I rode home. Now I feel like I've been drained of what little energy I had left."

47

"Let me rinse my hair and I'll help you bathe," she offered.

"I'm not so tired I can't bathe myself, but you could scrub my back. I feel like I have a few extra pounds of dust on me tonight."

"Hopefully we'll get some rain soon." Mary Leah moved into the flow of the water while Coal lathered her hair. "Are you going to get a haircut before you go?"

Coal pondered her question. "I think I'm going to let it grow a bit while we're on the trail. I might need it to keep my head warm."

"I've never seen you with long hair."

"I haven't let it grow out in a long time."

"I'm sure it will be beautiful. You have such nice hair," she commented while she added soap to a washcloth. "Turn around so I can get to your back."

†

Mary Leah watched the muscles of Coal's arms ripple as Coal scrubbed her scalp. She followed the line of muscles down past Coal's shoulder to the fading scars from her injuries in the desert. Shrapnel from the car bomb that had killed Mitch and Tessa had embedded in her side, and it had taken hours of surgery and dozens of stitches to repair the damage. She stroked lightly across the scars, still sensitive to touch after several years, reminding Mary Leah of her own permanent scars. Her gaze moved to her own chest and the scars her ex had found so repulsive that she'd abandoned her when emotionally Mary Leah had needed her most. Coal had never flinched at the scars marring Mary Leah's chest from the double mastectomy she'd survived. A smile came to her face when she remembered Coal telling her that breasts did not make her any more beautiful in her eyes. She stroked her hand down Coal's narrow hip and knelt to wash Coal's legs.

"That feels really good," Coal moaned.

"Turn around and I'll take care of your front."

"Let me rinse my hair first."

Mary Leah moved aside while Coal opened an eye and stepped under the flow of the shower to rinse her hair.

Coal turned to face Mary Leah and leaned her head back. Mary Leah appreciated the sight while the lather floated down Coal's front.

This is the view of my dreams. She reached out to caress the soapy cloth against Coal's firm body.

"I could get used to that." Coal grinned when she looked into her lover's eyes.

"Don't get spoiled by the hot water and special attention," she warned. "You've got freezing-cold water to look forward to for the next two weeks."

"Ugh, don't remind me of that part. At least it'll be too cold to work up much of a sweat."

Mary Leah swirled the soapy cloth over Coal's breasts and smiled when she saw that Coal's nipples had grown hard under the touch. "Are you thinking of the cold water or are you enjoying my hands on you?"

"Do you even have to ask?" Coal guided Mary Leah's hand down her stomach between her thighs while her other hand pulled her close for a kiss.

†

Mary Leah dropped the cloth on the floor of the shower and teased Coal's opening with her fingertips.

"Damn, that feels good," she groaned when Mary Leah's fingers entered her silky wetness.

"I thought you were exhausted."

"I've gotten a second wind," Coal murmured while Mary Leah trailed her lips down her neck. Coal's hips rocked in rhythm with Mary Leah's thrusts and she trembled with need.

Mary Leah's teeth grazed across her swollen nipples, causing Coal to shudder with pleasure. Electric currents ran through her while Mary Leah's fingers plunged deeper. She leaned down to plant a feverish kiss on Mary Leah's lips, and Coal exploded with pleasure.

"Oh God, yes, baby" echoed in the shower. Her legs felt like rubber and her muscles quivered as she held on to Mary Leah for support.

"That was intense. Where have you been hiding that one?"

"I don't know, but it felt like it ripped from my soul. Now I'm truly exhausted."

"You won't get that on a cattle drive either." Mary Leah chuckled. "Let's get you clean and we'll hit the sheets."

†

The cool sheets felt like heaven against her skin when Coal stretched out on the bed and closed her eyes. She heard Mary Leah shutting down the house for the night. Moments later, the mattress depressed as Mary Leah climbed into bed beside her.

"Are you asleep yet, Romeo?" she asked as she snuggled in behind Coal.

"Not yet, but well on my way," she responded.

"Sweet dreams. I love you."
"Love you too."

Chapter Three

Storm clouds hung ominously overhead while Coal saddled Shadow for the short ride to the MC2, and she prayed it wasn't an omen of bad things to come today. Her sleep was fractured by dreams of Bo thrashing in pain while Gene looked on helplessly at his side, and then of Mary Leah and Doc Bo in a lovers' embrace. Her eyes were raw from lack of sleep, so at five o'clock she gave up, deciding to head off to work early, leaving Mary Leah sleeping soundly, wearing a soft smile on her face.

Coal could tell Shadow also felt the moisture in the air from the way he stomped his hooves impatiently when she placed the saddle on his back.

"I know, big boy. We might just get wet before we arrive." With a sense of dread weighing heavily on her shoulders, Coal mounted Shadow and they cantered toward the ranch.

If there's bad news on the horizon, we might as well face it right off.

The wind picked up, causing branches to sway with a moan. A chill raced through her, making her shiver even though the temperature was already in the low eighties.

†

Coal spotted Gene outside, and when she saw his smile, she knew her fear of Bo's death was unwarranted. When they got closer, she could see Bo sniffing the ground. When he heard them, he lifted his head to see who was approaching. The weight lifted off her shoulders and she found herself grinning wide when she pulled Shadow to a stop a few feet away from her friends.

"I am so relieved to see Bo upright and doing so well."

"Me too. He really had me worried, but Doc Bo told me he'll be back to his puppy self in just a few days. I think she was surprised by how well he's doing."

"Bo knows how much you love him and that you never left his side last night. That pup would move mountains for you if he could."

Gene smiled broadly at Coal's comment. "He's a good boy."

"Are you going to be comfortable leaving him behind?"

"Harley promised to keep him out of trouble while I'm gone, and Doc Bo assured me she'd keep a close eye on him. You know she won't let me pay her, not even for the supplies."

Coal smiled. *She really is remarkable.* "That's great news and very generous of her."

"Yeah, it is. I've been studying the map Melissa printed out for us. If we take turns sleeping and driving in shifts, we can make it to Billings in about twenty-four hours."

"Does that take into consideration some breaks for the horses?"

"No, so I guess we'd better add a few hours."

"Still, that's not bad at all. I think we could do it with no problem." Coal turned her head at the sound of Stormy's truck rattling down the drive. "Seems like we're not the only ones up early this morning," she noted with a nod.

"Harley's cooking breakfast. Better go tell him to add two more plates."

"I will. Are you coming over?"

"Yeah, just let me get Bo back in bed."

"I'll see you in a few."

Coal rode Shadow to the barn and dismounted. She was removing his tack when Stormy walked in.

"I didn't think you'd be here so early. Is everything okay?"

"Yeah, I wasn't sleeping well, so I got up so Mary Leah could sleep."

"Dreams?"

"Yeah, I was worried about Bo and Gene." She didn't add that Doc Bo was also on her mind.

"Well it looks like your worry was unnecessary. Bo looks good."

"Yes, he does. I'm very happy for them both."

Thunder rumbled in the distance.

"It sounds like we may get a bit of rain. Let's grab some breakfast, and if it starts, we can spend the morning loading the trailer," Stormy said.

"I was thinking the same thing. Gene says we can make it to Billings in about twenty-four hours if we share the driving and take turns sleeping. That will even give us some break time for the horses."

"That sounds good to me. I don't think I'll get much sleep tonight."

"Maybe Del will wear you out."

"Maybe so." Stormy blushed. "Gene better take the first round of driving. I bet Mary Leah keeps you up tonight."

A look of pain crossed Coal's face.

"Is everything all right between you two?" Stormy asked.

"I'm just dealing with a bit of jealousy."

"You, jealous? What's gotten into you?"

"Mary Leah seems a bit enamored with Doc Bo."

"That's a big word for a cowgirl."

Coal shrugged.

"You're serious. Girl, you know Mary Leah is totally in love with you, right?"

"I thought so. I realize I'm being irrational, but I just can't help myself."

"Has Doc Bo done anything to encourage Mary Leah?"

"No, not at all. She must have sensed my mood last night and we had a brief talk. She assured me she wasn't interested in a relationship with anyone. She lost the love of her life too."

"Damn, that sucks."

"Yes, it does. I just can't shake the dread of losing Mary Leah."

"Ain't gonna happen, my friend. Come on, let's go get some food in you so your brain starts working again."

Coal chuckled. "I'm right behind you."

Coal stored Shadow's tack and stepped into the gray morning just as raindrops began to fall. They felt cool against her face and slid down her cheeks like silent tears as she looked up into the heavy clouds. The drops raised puffs of dust as they struck the dry ground, which tried in vain to capture the sought-after moisture. The grass crunched beneath her boots when she started for the bunkhouse.

Bring on the rain, she thought when she reached the porch. A lazy rainy day is just what we need today.

†

Harley looked up from the stove as Coal entered the bunkhouse. "How do you want your eggs?"

Coal surveyed the table, and most of the crew was eating scrambled. "Scrambled is fine with me."

"Drop some toast and I'll have your eggs ready in a few minutes." He cracked half a dozen eggs he would share with her.

"Harley suggested we pull the trailer into the barn so we can load it without getting soaked," Stormy mentioned between bites.

Coal turned to face Stormy after dropping the toast. "It shouldn't take us long to load the tack and the supplies for the horses. Did you bring your camping supplies with you?"

"Yes, ma'am, I did. I'll run you back to the house to get yours once we've finished loading the rest so all we have to do tomorrow is toss in our last minute bags and load the horses." Stormy grinned and took another bite.

"It would be great to be on the road early," Gene tossed into the conversation. "Do you think we can drive straight through?"

"You guys have plenty of time to make it there if you want to spend a night in a hotel," Harley reminded them.

"I think we're all pretty eager to get this adventure underway," Coal replied with a grin.

"Suit yourself, but you may regret not getting a last hot shower and good night's sleep."

Coal looked at Gene and shot an eyebrow up in thought. "He does have a good point about the shower."

"Yeah, I hadn't considered that. Maybe we can put a long day of driving in and find a spot to settle in for the night before driving the rest of the way into Billings."

"Mr. Tucker will put us up in his bunkhouse Sunday night too, but I doubt that's going to be a luxury suite," Coal said.

Harley brought a skillet with scrambled eggs to the table and divided them between his and Coal's plate. "Last call for seconds," he announced.

"I think we're all good," Gene answered. "Eat before yours get cold."

Stan entered the bunkhouse just as Harley took his seat. "You need some breakfast, boss?"

"I'm good, thanks, Harley. I'll grab a cup of coffee, though. I want everyone to pitch in and help load the supplies for the trip and then take the rest of the day off. The weatherman says we'll have rain all day. I can't complain, with as bad as we need it for the hayfields."

"I told Doc Bo I'd show her around town and guide her to some of her accounts this morning, but it can wait until we finish."

"Go ahead, Harley. We have plenty of help to get loaded. We may even have to break out a deck of cards for some poker when we're done." Gene grinned.

"That sounds like fun. I may have to stick around for that," Stan replied. "Besides, if I go back home now, the missus is going to put me to work on her honey-do list."

The crew broke out in laughter, which a burst of thunder interrupted.

"A nice steady rain all day will do us good," Stan added while he poured sugar into his mug.

†

Coal and the younger members of the crew loaded the trailer with hay, feed, tack, and other supplies they would need for the horses. Harley supervised the operation while waiting for Doc Bo so he could take her to see the town.

"Tell Doc Bo we'll have to take a rain check on the tour of the ranch. I don't think this weather will clear by afternoon," Coal told him.

"I'll gladly give her the grand tour while you guys are gone."

"I just hope you don't go soft on us while we're away," Stormy teased.

"I'm sure we'll find plenty to keep us busy. It will certainly be a lot quieter with you three gone," he shot back.

Lucas was handing off the last of the hay bales to Gene when his cell phone chimed. He pulled it from his shirt pocket and blanched.

"What's wrong?" Coal asked.

"Lisa just sent a text. She's on her way to the hospital; her water just broke."

Gene slapped his friend on the back. "Here we go. You're going to be a baby daddy soon."

"So why are you still standing here?" Coal asked. "Get a move on. You okay to drive?"

"Yeah," he answered as a smile grew on his face. "My son's on the way!"

"Keep us posted and congratulations. You're going to make a great dad," Coal assured him while she slapped him

58

on the back. "Be careful driving. It's probably going to be several hours yet, so don't wreck your truck trying to get there in record time."

"I hear ya. Have a great time on the drive," he told them before rushing out of the barn.

†

The crew finished loading just as Melissa and Doc Bo arrived.

"I just saw Lucas fly out of here like a scalded cat. What's going on?" Melissa asked.

"Lisa's in labor," Harley answered.

"Good grief, she's early. I wonder if it's a false alarm."

"Her water broke, so I reckon it's the real thing," Coal replied.

"Ready or not, he's going to be a daddy soon," Gene added.

"I don't think anyone is ever truly prepared." Doc Bo grinned.

"Are you set to head into town?" Harley asked her.

"Whenever you're finished here," she answered.

"I think the kids can finish up."

"All we have left is our camp supplies. Stormy is going to run me back to the house to pick up my goods." Coal tossed Gene the last bag of feed.

"Go ahead and I'll finish up here," Gene told her.

"Race you to the truck?" Coal challenged Stormy, and they dashed from the barn.

"Is everything a competition between the two of them?" Doc Bo asked.

"Pretty much," Gene and Harley answered in unison and broke out laughing.

"Well, I guess we better get a move on too, but I ain't racing you to my truck," she remarked. "We'll see you later. Try to keep Bo out of this weather," she added.

"Yes, ma'am," Gene answered and watched them dash out into the rain.

"Anything I can do to help?" Melissa asked.

"No, ma'am, I've got this."

†

Melissa wandered back through the barn to the small office that had been Mitch's when he was alive, and would now become Doc Bo's office. Memories of Mitch filled the space, and for a moment, Melissa was overwhelmed with sorrow. She could still hear his voice while he spoke over the phone and the ringing of his deep laughter when one of the crew cracked a joke. Her nostrils flared at the scent of his cologne still lingering in the air of her imagination.

"God, I miss you, Mitch," she whispered when she sat in his leather desk chair. She surveyed the photos on the walls taken across the years at rodeos, working on the ranch, and on their numerous vacations. When her gaze landed on their wedding photo, Melissa was reminded of how young they'd been and the fun they'd shared on their honeymoon in the Grand Caymans. A tear slipped through her restraint and she quickly wiped it away from her cheek. She hoped Mitch would approve of Doc Bo taking over his office and putting it to good use.

"That's silly. Of course he would approve," she spoke to the empty room.

†

Gene watched Melissa enter the office and was becoming concerned when she hadn't left by the time Coal and Stormy returned with Coal's supplies.

"What's wrong?" Coal asked.

"Melissa's been in the office a long time, and I'm worried about her."

"Go check on her while Stormy and I finish loading."

Gene dropped down from the tailgate of the truck and walked back toward the office. When he entered the doorway, Melissa was sitting at the desk, so he knocked lightly on the doorframe. She looked at him, and Gene could see the sadness in her eyes.

"Are you all right, ma'am?"

"Just reminiscing. I don't think it will take much to turn this into an office for Doc Bo."

"No, ma'am, it should be pretty easy. Is there anything you want me to help you with?"

"Thanks, but I'll wait until Doc Bo decides if she wants the office, and then Harley can help us after you three get on the road. There won't be much to do for the next two weeks, so that will give us something to focus on."

"I wanted to thank you for offering to take care of Bo while I'm gone. Harley offered, but I think he and Dolly will be good company for you right now. I'm sure going to miss him, though."

Melissa chuckled. "I promise I won't spoil him too badly while you're gone."

Gene cracked a smile. "I appreciate that, ma'am. He's spoiled enough already."

"You've got a great pup."

"Yes, I do. I'm so thankful he's going to be healthy again."

"We certainly dodged a bullet there. It will be nice having a vet so close at hand."

Gene nodded and grinned. "Yes, it will."

"Are you all loaded?"

"Coal and Stormy are adding the last of her supplies."

"Let's go check on them. Did I hear someone mention poker?"

"Yes, you did indeed. Care to join us?"

"Don't mind if I do." Melissa stood and walked around the desk. With a final look, she smiled and closed the door behind her.

Chapter Four

"So what do you think of the MC2?" Harley asked Cam.

"It looks like a really nice spread, and the folks seem like fine people to be around."

"It's quite the mixed bag, but I think we make a great team. Are you okay with the plans we seem to be making for you?" He chuckled.

"To be honest I don't think I could ask for better accommodations, and having an office there is almost too good to be true."

Harley listened to the windshield wipers whisk the water away for several seconds before continuing. "How are you doing, Doc? You look great, but I know looks can sometimes be deceiving."

"I'm in a really good place right now. I'm ready to settle in and put down some roots. I'm tired of the constant travel, and I've run long enough to wear down the pain of Sheila's death." Cam stared straight ahead, fearing to take her eyes off the road and to allow Harley to see the hurt in them still when she mentioned Sheila. She couldn't fool herself, much less Harley, into believing she was over the loss, and she was thankful he refused to question her further. "The crew seems to be very excited about the cattle drive."

"Man, is that an understatement. They are beyond excited, and I can't say I blame them. It'll be a good experience for them."

"Do you wish you were going?"

"Only if I were thirty years younger. I've gotten spoiled sleeping in a bed every night."

"I completely understand that. It sounds like a lot of fun, but I know it's going to be hard work and less than pleasant living conditions for a while."

"Those three don't shy away from hard work, Coal in particular. I think the Good Lord broke the mold when he made that one."

"You like her that much, do you?"

"She's been a blessing for the MC2 since she arrived. None of the younger men can outwork her, and she has a way with horses that's almost magical," he said with true admiration.

"She does appear to be cut from a special mold. I have the feeling she's suffered a great deal of loss in her young life."

Harley ran his hand through his graying hair. "She experienced hell in the desert when her lover and Mitch, Melissa's husband, were killed. Tessa, her partner, died in her arms, and she blames herself for their deaths. She's been seeing Del, Stormy's partner and a damned good therapist, professionally to help with PTSD, and she's made good progress."

"I can't believe anyone could think she'd commit murder. She told me about the bully she had run-ins with when she first arrived."

"Billy Ray was a real mean SOB and eventually got what he deserved, but make no mistake, Coal was trained to be a killing machine by good old Uncle Sam. She's done some damage to the menfolk around here, but only when pushed beyond her tolerance."

"So I definitely don't want to get on her bad side."

"I'm not sure you could, Doc. She's pretty easygoing unless you mess with her family or her horse."

"I think I came pretty close last night without even knowing it. Coal was a bit jealous of the attention Mary Leah was giving me after dinner. We had a talk, though, and I assured her I wasn't interested in a relationship with anyone."

"That seems odd. Coal doesn't seem that type."

"I guess with everything that went on yesterday nerves may have been a bit frayed."

"Maybe so. I'm sure you don't need to worry about Coal."

"I hope not. I bet she would make a great friend."

"You won't find one more loyal." He grinned. "Except for me, of course."

"Harley Boone, you should know by now you're beyond a friend to me. You're my guardian angel. Just when I need you most, you crop back up in my life."

"Stop or you're gonna make me blush. Oh crap, you were supposed to turn left there." He burst out laughing.

"No worries, I've mastered the art of U-turns."

†

"I do believe I'll take this hand," Melissa bragged, then she spread her cards on the table.

"Dang, that's four hands in a row," Gene cried. "Are you sure you're not hiding cards up your sleeves, boss?"

Melissa made a production out of shaking her arms, just for his benefit. "Just my lucky day, I guess."

Gene was thinking up a comeback when their phones chimed with a new text message. They all reached for them. Stormy was the fastest and exclaimed, "Aww, what a cutie."

Coal smiled as she read the message aloud. "'Meet Mathew Lucas.'" Attached were a trio of photographs with Lucas, Lisa, and their son. "What a beautiful family."

"She was lucky to have such a short labor," Melissa stated.

"Well it is almost four, so she's been in labor over eight hours," Stormy replied.

"Four?" Melissa cried. "You mean we've been playing cards over four hours?"

"Time flies when you're having fun, boss," Coal stated.

"I reckon, but that means dinner will be late."

"So why don't we ride into town and bring something back?" Gene suggested.

"That works for me. How about a couple buckets of fried chicken and sides?" Melissa asked.

Bo whined from across the room.

"I think it's time for Bo to go outside. Stormy and I will drive to town for dinner," Coal volunteered.

"I'll buy, then," Melissa said.

The rain had turned into a light mist when they reached the door.

"It looks like the worst has passed," Melissa said.

"Come on, Bo," Gene called, and the dog followed them outside.

Doc Bo and Harley returned as they started across the yard.

"What's up?" Harley asked.

"We played cards right through starting dinner, so Stormy and I are going to head to town for some chicken."

"Hop in and I'll drive you."

Stormy shrugged. "Fine with me."

Coal climbed in behind Doc Bo and moved over for Stormy to have a spot.

"Hang on, let me grab my card," Melissa said.

"No worries, I've got this," Doc Bo stated. "You've fed me plenty since I arrived, so let me get this one."

Melissa nodded. "Hurry back, but drive safe."

"Yes, boss," Doc Bo replied with a wink and put the truck in gear.

"Any big winners from the poker games?" Harley asked from the front seat.

"Melissa wiped us all out like usual," Coal complained. "One person should not be that lucky all the time."

"Maybe she should go to Vegas," Doc Bo suggested.

"That's not a bad idea," Stormy replied. "Maybe we can hit a rodeo there."

Harley grinned. "Is that all you ever think of these days?"

"No—well, mostly," Stormy admitted. "It's in my blood."

"Are y'all all set to leave in the morning?" he asked.

"Just our last minute bags and we'll be ready to roll. Gene wants to try to drive it straight through," Coal shared.

"Trust me, you'll need to spend a night along the way. Get a good day's drive in, but don't jeopardize yourselves or the horses by driving tired. There's plenty of time for y'all to get there."

"That's what I'm thinking too. We're going to take your recommendation. One last night for a nice bed and a hot shower won't hurt us either," Coal answered.

"How long will the cattle drive last?" Doc Bo asked.

"We'll be on the trail for about ten days," Stormy answered.

"Have you ever been to Montana?"

"Stormy is from there and we spent a week there last Christmas. It was beautiful in the winter, and I can only imagine what it'll look like this time of year." Coal was nearly breathless with excitement. "We'll be heading into the Pryor Mountains according to Mr. Tucker. It's beautiful there, especially in the spring."

"Nice," Doc Bo replied. "Isn't there a reservation near there?"

"Yes," Coal replied. "The Crow Reservation is there and so is Custer National Forest."

"Wild mustangs roam freely across the range there. I think there's a wild horse refuge designation there now too," Doc Bo said.

"Mustangs," Coal whispered in a dreamy voice. "I hope we get to see them."

"Chances are pretty good for that," Stormy answered.

†

When they returned with the fried chicken feast, Mary Leah had arrived at the MC2.

"I missed you this morning," she whispered to Coal while she filled a plate.

"I was tossing and turning and didn't want to wake you."

"You can wake me anytime, darling," Mary Leah purred. "Were you dreaming?"

"Yeah, I think I fell asleep worrying about Bo, and the stress followed me into my dreams. I couldn't sleep, so I came to check on him myself."

"At least you won't have to worry about him tonight. He looks great."

"Just a slight limp that will go away, but other than that, you'd never know he was on death's doorstep."

"That has to be a huge relief for Gene."

"Yes, it is. He was a hot mess last night."

Mary Leah chuckled. "Where did you learn such language?"

Coal grinned. "I think I heard it on MTV, but it fit the situation."

"Are you two going to hover over the food all night or join us at the table?" Melissa called out.

"Someone must be hungry," Mary Leah tossed back at her sister.

"I'm starving, so quit gabbing and come on to the table."

"Yes, Mom," Mary Leah teased, instigating a round of snickers from the crew.

†

Del hung up the phone and went into action. Mary Leah had given her a call when Stormy left the MC2 for home, just the way they'd planned. She placed a chilled bottle of wine in an ice bucket next to the garden tub, then lit an array of candles. She wanted Stormy's last night here to be memorable and make her eager to get back home.

†

Mary Leah also had plans for Coal, but she worried Coal wouldn't be up for a night of loving. Her lack of sleep the previous night was weighing heavily on her while she helped clean up after the delicious meal.

"Do you want to ride home with me tonight?"

"Yeah, I'll leave Shadow here for the night since we're pulling out early in the morning. I better go check on him before we go, though."

"Do you really think he'll stay here?" Melissa replied.

"He will if I leave him in a stall. Gene's promised to load the horses, and Stormy will pick me up on her way."

"I know Harley's going to prepare breakfast, but would you like me to send some sandwiches along?"

"Would it be too much to ask for some of your egg salad?"

Melissa smiled. Coal loved her egg salad. "I'll make up a big bowl for the cooler and send a fresh loaf of bread and some chips with you."

"Thanks, boss. I'll be right back," she answered and left the house. Gene and Bo were out in the yard for the puppy's final bathroom break of the night.

†

"Are you getting ready to head out?" Gene asked.

"Yeah, in just a few after I check on Shadow."

"Just think, this time tomorrow night we'll be over halfway to Montana."

"Do you think you'll be able to sleep tonight?"

"Like a baby."

Coal chuckled. "You realize babies wake up for feedings at night, right?"

"Dang, you're right. Like a rock, then."

"I guess Lucas will be learning about that real soon. I bet he's on cloud nine tonight."

"I talked to him earlier and he was babbling like a schoolgirl. I bet he won't be getting any rest tonight," Gene said.

"That has to be so exciting to hold your baby in your arms."

"Did you ever think of having kids?"

"Tessa and I talked about it. She planned on having artificial insemination when we returned from the desert," Coal's voice cracked with emotion. She looked away to hide the tears forming.

"You would make a great mom."

"Thanks, I thought so too, but now it will never happen."

"Never say never, my friend. We never know what the future may hold."

Coal shrugged. "Mary Leah isn't interested in having children."

"I'm sorry. Maybe I'll have a houseful and you can get your mommy fix."

Coal shook her head and chuckled. "Thanks, Gene, I'll look forward to that. See you in the morning."

Shadow lifted his head over the stall door as Coal approached. "I guess you'll always be my baby, big boy." She stroked down his face. "Are you ready for our big adventure?"

He placed his head on her shoulder and she encircled his neck with her arms. "It's going to be cold and hard work, but it'll be fun, I promise. I'll see you in the morning." She planted a soft kiss on his muzzle.

†

Melissa and Mary Leah were waiting for Coal on the front porch as she approached.

"I've got your eggs on to boil. Get a good night's sleep. You look exhausted," Melissa said.

"No doubt I will, boss. It's been a long day."

"Are you ready?"

"Right behind you," she told Mary Leah. "Good night, boss."

"Good night, ladies," Melissa called and watched them walk to the car, a frown forming on her face. Something was off between them, but she couldn't put a finger on what it was. She turned back to the door and joined Doc Bo for a cup of coffee before they called it a night.

†

Del met Stormy at the door with a deep kiss.

"Wow, let me go back out and come back in for another of those," she replied when Del broke the kiss.

"No worries, I have many more of them planned for you. Come with me." She held her hand out.

Del led her into the bathroom and slowly peeled off Stormy's clothing, kissing her way down her body.

Her bathrobe fell open and Stormy pulled Del to her feet and brushed the robe off her shoulders. Her hands encircled Del's waist, pulling her close.

"My eyes never tire of looking at you," Stormy whispered while she ran her hands up Del's sides.

"I want to show you how much I'm going to miss you while you're gone."

"This all looks fantastic." Stormy looked at the bubble bath awaiting them, the scented candles, and the two glasses of wine resting on the edge of the tub. "You've been busy."

"Let's take advantage of the hot water before it starts to cool." Del smiled and then dropped her robe onto the pile of clothes she had taken off Stormy.

She watched the liquid movement of Stormy's body as she stepped into the tub and turned to offer her hand. Stormy took Del's hand and stepped into the steamy water. Del turned so she could sit facing Stormy, draping her legs over Stormy's much longer ones. She picked up the two wineglasses and handed one to her lover.

"To a grand adventure and safe travels home." She touched glasses with Stormy.

"I'll be back before you know it."

"Not soon enough for me, Stormy. You've gotten me spoiled sleeping next to your warm body every night."

"I will definitely miss that too." Stormy took a sip of wine. "Sleeping on the ground is something I'm not looking forward to."

"Maybe Coal will let you snuggle in so y'all can share some warmth. Mind you, that's all you can share."

Stormy chuckled. "No worries, Coal would kick my ass if I tried anything with her."

"Yes, she would." Del grinned. "What time are y'all planning to head out in the morning?"

"I told Coal I'd pick her up at five. Harley's cooking breakfast, so we should be on the road by six."

"I better get busy, then, if you intend to get any sleep tonight." Del reached for a cloth and body wash.

"Sleep is overrated." Stormy leaned forward to kiss Del.

"That may be true, but this water won't stay hot forever and I do have plans for you."

"I do like the sound of that."

After bathing, Del dried them and looked up at Stormy. "Grab that bottle of wine and follow me."

"Yes, ma'am." She picked it up and followed Del into their bedroom.

†

Candles lit the bedroom when Stormy entered.

"Put the wine on the table and lie down on your stomach, please," Del instructed. "I'll be right back."

"Sure thing, Doc." She took a final sip of her wine.

Stormy could hear the microwave in the kitchen and she spied the sheet Del had draped over the bed. "Looks interesting," she said and then stretched out on it. Stormy heard Del return, turned, and saw the massage oil in her hands. As Del stopped in the doorway, Stormy could see the need and love on her face.

"Welcome back, Doc." She closed her eyes and was completely relaxed. Or so she thought. Then the warm oil flowed across her shoulders as Del straddled her hips. Stormy felt the moisture growing between Del's thighs when she made contact with Stormy's back and knew her lover had naughty plans for them.

"Take the pillow from under your head and stretch your arms out, please," Del requested as she smoothed the oil across Stormy's skin and began to knead the taut muscles.

"Umm, that feels great. Do you think I can hide you away in my bags and take you with me?"

"Sorry, but I don't relish sleeping in a tent on the cold ground for even a week. Make it a luxury hotel and I'm all over it."

"Ah, 'tis the life of a cowgirl to sleep under the stars on the cold, hard ground," Stormy lamented.

"These magical hands will be waiting for you when you return from your journey, so enjoy them tonight."

"I'm very much enjoying them so far."

"Your pleasure is just beginning," Del promised with a chuckle.

"Oh, Doc, I love it when you get naughty."

"Hush or I might have to gag you."

Stormy looked over her shoulder and opened her mouth for a comeback, but then closed it. Sometimes she had a hard time discerning when Del was joking, so she played it safe and lay back down, enjoying Del's magic hands.

Del's hands moved farther down her body, and Stormy moaned softly as her back muscles rippled beneath Del's fingers. When Del kneaded her firm buttocks, a quiver of pleasure ran through her body.

Del was getting so soaked, Stormy wondered if she could hold off long enough for her to finish the massage. Del finished rubbing the oil into Stormy's long legs and then climbed back up to whisper in her ear. "Roll over."

She moved to allow Stormy to roll onto her back, and Del's eyes sparkled with arousal when Stormy reached up to pull Del onto her.

"Lean down and kiss me, please, Doc."

Del smiled and lowered her face to Stormy's. She trailed her tongue across her lover's lips, teasing them open, and then covering her mouth with a passionate kiss. Stormy urged her hips lower with her hands until they were mound to mound.

Del's wetness grew as Stormy slowly ground her hips into her lover. The movement brought forth a moan from Del that vibrated through the kiss, urging Stormy to move her hips faster. She held Stormy's hips firmly and ground more urgently.

"Damn, Stormy," Del moaned between gasps for breath. "That feels so good, baby."

"Come with me, darling," Stormy groaned between thrusts, locking eyes with Del.

Del erupted, the rush of juices running down her thighs adding to the lubrication already flowing between them. Stormy went rigid as the orgasm seized her, and her eyes slammed shut as she rode the wave of passion. Del cried out in ecstasy, and Stormy opened her eyes and smiled up at her.

"Where has that been hiding?" Stormy asked.

"I don't know, but damn, that felt good."

"I'll definitely agree with that."

"I didn't get to finish your massage, though," Del stated with a pout.

Stormy laughed and pulled Del onto her chest. "My God, woman, I think you exercised every muscle in my body. I will definitely need another massage when I return, though."

"I'll be more than happy to fill that order, ma'am," Del promised, then caressed Stormy's jawline with her lips.

Sensing Del needed more, Stormy rolled her onto her back and pinned Del's arms above her head. Her hot breath caressed Del's ear while she suckled her earlobe. "This cowgirl still wants to ride."

"Ride 'em, cowgirl." Del locked her legs around Stormy's hips.

After another ear-shattering round of orgasms, Stormy and Del rinsed off in the shower and collapsed onto the bed to finish the bottle of wine.

Del finished her glass and handed it to Stormy with a serious look. "You know, I think I'm reconsidering this cattle-drive venture."

"What? You don't want me to go now?" Stormy cried and sat up in bed.

"Oh no, I was thinking you should go more often if it gets me this kind of loving."

Stormy laughed and fell back onto the mattress. "C'mere, you. I'll give you this kind of lovin' anytime you want it."

Del rolled over onto her side and placed her hand on Stormy's chest. "I never thought I'd say this about anyone, but I just can't get enough of you."

"I'm all yours, anytime you want me, Doc." Stormy lifted Del's hand to her lips for a tender kiss.

"Don't say that now or you won't get any sleep tonight. You have a long trip ahead of you, remember."

"Yes, ma'am. I'll be missing you."

"I'll be right here." Del placed her hand over Stormy's heart. "Always."

Stormy blew out the last candle and pulled Del into her arms with a huge grin. "Good night Doc, I love you."

"Love you too, so hurry home to me."

†

"This will be my last opportunity to sleep in the buff for a while," Coal stated with a grin when she climbed into bed.

"I imagine you'll be sleeping in most everything you take with you."

"Probably so. I'll look like the Stay Puft Marshmallow Man I'll have so much on."

"I'm going to miss you badly, but I understand how much you want to go."

"I'm going to miss you too, and this bed, hot showers, and good food, but I won't be gone for any longer than necessary."

"Just enjoy this trip. It may be the last time I let you out of my sight."

"Aw now, what trouble can I get into in the middle of nowhere?"

"Plenty, I'm sure, but next time make sure there's room for me."

"You are more than welcome to join us. I can load another horse and supplies in no time at all."

"Thanks, but my butt gets sore after an hour in the saddle. I can only imagine what it would feel like all day long, day after day. Promise me you won't come back bowlegged," she teased.

"I can't promise, but I'll try my best. I'll get Stormy or Gene to pull on my legs every night if that will make you happy."

"The only thing that will make me happy is to see you walk back through the door safe and sound, bowlegged too if that's what it takes."

"That's the most romantic thing I've heard all day."

"Come here, then, and let me whisper in your ear. Maybe I can come up with something better."

Coal turned out the light and rolled over on top of Mary Leah. "You were saying?"

"How much I want to make love to you right now."

Coal leaned down and kissed her, gently at first, then with more passion when Mary Leah's hands made their way between her thighs. Coal was surprised at how quickly she responded to her lover's teasing, then Mary Leah's fingers slid gently inside her. A fire ignited within her, and her body took command as she relaxed and enjoyed the feel of Mary Leah inside her body.

Mary Leah moved down until she could suck one of Coal's breasts while her fingers caressed Coal's most intimate spots. Her being inside Coal was like coming home, her fingers sliding easily in the silky wetness as Coal reacted to her gentle exploration. The sensation was clearly as pleasurable for her as it was for Coal, and Coal felt her quivering with need. Sensing her lover's desire, Coal slipped a hand between their bodies to enter her, and together they rode the wave of passion until they came as one, gasping for air, their bodies coated in a sheen of sweat and totally spent.

The last thing Coal remembered before falling asleep was Mary Leah snuggling against her and whispering, "I love you."

†

"Man, what a day," Melissa said as she stirred sugar into her coffee.

"It sounded like you had a pretty lucky day, though. The kids said you wiped them out in poker," Cam said.

"Sometimes I think they just let me win."

"As competitive as they are? I seriously doubt that."

"Did you and Harley have a good day?"

Melissa watched Cam's fingertip trace the rim of her coffee cup. For some reason, that simple motion sent a chill through her.

79

Cam looked up at her. "Yeah, we did. He showed me around the county. There's quite a few large spreads here, which surprised me. It was also good to spend time catching up with him."

"It's been pretty crazy since you showed up. It's not normally that exciting around here."

"Let's try to keep it that way." Cam smiled.

"I hear that. Are you starting to feel settled in?"

Her eyes sparkled. "Yes, I am. Are you still okay with me using the office?"

"Absolutely, it's a great location for you, and Mitch would be happy to know his little haven is being used."

Cam covered Melissa's hand with her own. "I can't tell you how much I appreciate your generosity. Taking over a practice is stressful enough, so having a home and office taken care of is a godsend."

Melissa was pleased Cam didn't move her hand away after she finished speaking. Her offering was such an intimate touch, one Melissa hadn't felt in a long time, and she enjoyed the feeling.

Where are all these feelings coming from? "It's been great having some company in the house again too. I didn't realize how lonesome it could be. I got used to having Coal, Mary Leah, or Stormy here. The silence, especially at night, can get unbearable at times."

"I can relate to that. I think that's why I stayed on the road so long. The walls of my tiny apartment closed in fast when I came home."

"You've got hundreds of wide-open acres to enjoy here."

Cam lifted the cup to take a sip. "That is exactly what I need."

"With the kids gone this week, I'll have some extra time if you want some help setting up your new office."

"I'd like that." Cam smiled.

Chapter Five

The sun was beginning to peek through the trees as Coal waited for the coffee to finish brewing. She'd woken early, refreshed from a good night's sleep, and had showered and dressed before starting the coffee. When it finished, she poured two cups and carried them into the bedroom to wake Mary Leah. She placed them on the nightstand and sat on the edge of the bed. Coal rested her hand on her lover's forehead and brushed the unruly hair from her eyes, then whispered, "It's time to wake up, my love."

"Is it morning already?" Mary Leah groaned. "It feels like we just went to sleep."

"Sorry, love, but that was hours ago. I can let you go back to sleep if you want."

"Don't you dare even think of sneaking out without a proper good-bye, Coal Bryan."

"I wouldn't think of it, but if you need more sleep, I'd understand."

"Stop, you big tease. I'm getting up."

"Just sit up in bed. I brought our coffee in here."

"You're so sweet. You're already dressed, what time is it?"

"A few minutes before five. Stormy will be here soon, but I wanted to share a cup with you before I go."

"Aw, honey, you should have woken me sooner."

"You were sleeping so peacefully, I couldn't bear to wake you just to watch me get dressed and pack my final bag."

"Oh, but how I love to watch you dress."

"To think all this time I thought you liked me naked."

"Naked is best, but, girl, you do fill out those jeans nicely."

"Why thanks, ma'am." Coal stretched and said with a grin, "I slept like a rock last night."

"You look refreshed this morning. Are you excited?"

"Yeah, I can't wait to get there. I bet it's going to be so beautiful."

"Did you remember to pack your camera?"

"I did, and also a power pack so I can recharge the battery a few times if needed. I'll call until we lose towers and then again when we make it back."

"I'm missing you already." Mary Leah took a sip of coffee. "Damn, you make the best coffee. Why doesn't mine turn out this good?"

Coal grinned. "I've just got coffee magic, I reckon."

†

A few minutes later, someone knocked on the door. Coal glanced at the clock and chuckled. "Stormy's right on schedule. Do you want to put a robe on so you can see us off?"

Coal went to the front door to let Stormy in. "Good morning, you're right on time."

"Morning, I had to drive painfully slow to arrive at five. I drove past the turnoff and busted a U-turn just to give you a few more minutes. Are you all set?"

"Yes, I am, let me get my bag."

"Don't be in such a hurry, Stormy Braxton. May I at least get a kiss good-bye?"

"I'm sorry, Mary Leah. I didn't mean to rush her."

"Relax, I'm just teasing you. I know you're both excited about the trip. You keep her safe and get back here as fast as you can, you hear me?"

"Yes, ma'am, I'll do my best."

"I know you will."

"Take this." Coal tossed a small duffle to Stormy. "I'll be out in just a minute."

"See you later, Mary Leah."

"Good-bye, Stormy, have fun."

Stormy carried the bag out to the truck, and Coal embraced Mary Leah and kissed her sweetly. "I love you and will be home soon."

"Not soon enough," Mary Leah pouted. "Go have a great time and call me when you can. I love you."

"I will. See you soon," she promised and walked out to climb into Stormy's truck. Coal looked back at the house to see Mary Leah still standing in the doorway to watch them leave. She waved and smiled when Stormy pulled away from the house.

"Let's do this," Coal said, turning back to a wildly grinning Stormy.

†

Gene was carrying a small cooler and a bag of groceries to the truck when they arrived.

"I've got everybody loaded except Shadow. He won't budge for me," he told them.

"I'll get him after we eat." Coal grinned. "Promise me you'll at least make an attempt to chew."

"Yes, Mom."

The sun was rising, making it a beautiful morning.

"Looks like we'll have a great day for travel," Stormy commented while she stretched.

"It's clear all the way to Montana," Melissa told them as she and Doc Bo joined them in the yard.

Harley opened the door to the bunkhouse. "Breakfast is served."

Coal was shocked when she walked in. This was no mere breakfast. Harley had cooked up a feast to send them off on their adventure. "Good Lord, where do we start?"

Harley chuckled. "I thought I'd send some ham biscuits with you if there are leftovers."

"I would certainly think there would be," Stormy commented and took a seat. "This looks terrific, Harley."

"I know y'all are eager to leave, but I wanted you to have one last good meal in your bellies."

"This will definitely qualify," Gene replied while scooping a large serving of eggs onto his plate.

Harley poured a tray of juices and coffee and joined them at the table.

Coal smiled at him. "You must have been up at the crack of dawn to cook all this."

"I had a helper." Harley grinned and nodded toward Doc Bo. "You know I still can't make gravy as good as yours, Coal, but Cam's a pretty decent cook."

"I'm pleased to hear you approve, Harley."

†

After everyone ate their fill, there was still enough to send a dozen biscuits filled with country ham with the "young'uns," as Harley called them.

When they'd loaded Shadow and were preparing to leave, he said, "Wait just one minute. I have something else for you to take," and rushed back into the bunkhouse. Coal looked at Melissa, who shrugged, just as clueless as the rest of them.

Moments later, Harley returned carrying two rifles in scabbards and handed one to Stormy and the other to Coal. "I thought you both needed to carry a rifle in addition to your sidearms. They will be much better at a longer distance, and there might be critters up there you don't want to get close."

"I'm glad Mary Leah isn't here to hear that," Coal stated.

"They're .30-30s and fully loaded. There's a box of shells in the outside storage in case you need more." He looked at Coal and Stormy. "Coal, I know you can handle this, but have you ever shot a rifle, Stormy?"

"It's kind of like a using a camera. Just point and shoot, right?"

Harley chuckled. "Okay, smart-ass, just be careful of what you're pointing at."

"I'll make sure she doesn't shoot off any vital body parts," Gene commented with a grin.

"Thanks, Harley." Coal hugged him. "I guess we'd better get moving before Mary Leah changes her mind."

The group broke out in laughter and exchanged hugs. Melissa embraced Coal last, whispering in her ear, "Have a great time and bring them home safe."

"I will, boss. Thanks for everything."

"Enjoy those biscuits and egg salad," she said and let her go.

"I got shotgun," Coal called as they started toward the truck.

"Fine, I'll take the whole backseat," Stormy shot back.

"Be safe and let us know when you get to the hotel tonight," Melissa requested.

Coal looked at Gene. "Yeah, she's booked us at a nice country hotel equipped with stables. Already paid for too, so we can't drive straight through," he added.

Coal chuckled and gave Melissa a thumbs up. "Let's roll."

†

Mary Leah stood at the front window of their home watching the truck and trailer pull down the drive with a tear sliding down her cheek. "Be safe and come home soon," she whispered.

†

Coal looked toward her home and thought she saw Mary Leah standing in front of the window. She smiled, turned back to her friends, and broke out in a chorus of "On the Road Again."

Gene and Stormy joined her as they pulled onto the paved road to begin their new adventure.

Chapter Six

The miles passed quickly, and the crew chatted excitedly about the cattle drive and what they hoped their journey would bring them. When they tired of talking, Stormy stretched out across the backseat, settling in for a nap. Gene pulled his sunglasses down to keep the blinding glare from reaching his eyes while he drove, and Coal watched the landscape pass by her window.

The rock formations in the distance across the arid desert plains reminded her of Afghanistan. Memories of Tessa flooded back and her heart raced as panic threatened to seize her. Her fingers found the button to lower the window, and she leaned her head out for a rush of fresh air.

"You okay, Coal?" Gene asked.

"Yeah, just needing some fresh air." She pulled her face back in and raised the window.

"You're not going to get carsick, are you?"

"No—at least I don't think so," she answered to mess with him. "This terrain"—she pointed out the windshield—"brought up memories of Afghanistan."

"Do you want to talk about them?"

"Yeah, if you don't mind. Del says it will help the panic go away."

Coal opened a bottle of water and took a long drink of the refreshing liquid. "My first tour of duty in Afghanistan, I was a sniper. I was still an army ranger, and my partner Charlie and I registered twelve kills together in a little over a year."

Coal knew Gene adored her, and she imagined he struggled to envision her as a killer, even though he had witnessed her fighting skills firsthand. The news she had been a party to killing twelve people probably astonished him, even if it was in the service of her country. He remained silent while Coal gathered her thoughts.

"Every time we went out on a mission, we'd gear up in our Ghillie suits and rappel from a low-flying helicopter. We'd run for miles and then crawl for hundreds of yards to get into our final positions. Our suits were the color of desert sand and the rocks of the surrounding mountain range, and God were they hot."

"Is the sound of the helicopter rotors one of your triggers?"

"Yes, the sound brings up painful memories, especially the deaths of Tessa and Mitch."

"Is it true nights in the desert can be unbearably cold?"

"Even the suits that cooked us during the day weren't enough to keep us warm." She picked up the bottle of water and drained it, then stared at it. "Sometimes we'd be in position for days, waiting, barely moving a muscle to prevent detection from advance security details sent out to secure the meeting areas. Only at night could we stretch our muscles or relieve our aching bladders. Whenever we returned from a mission, we'd have to rehab for three to four days to get rehydrated and recuperate from exhaustion."

"That sounds painful. I'd never be able to do that."

"I'd say you get used to it, but it would only be a lie. It was torture lying so still all day while trying desperately to not think about having to pee." Coal cracked a smile.

"Who were they?"

"The kills, you mean?"

"Yes."

"Terrorists and high-level arms dealers. I don't remember the names, but I'll always remember the faces. I could probably get in deep shit for telling you this, but it doesn't matter any longer."

"So your targets were top secret?"

"I don't think we were told their real names, just code names and photographs. They were enemy targets of the United States, and that's all that mattered to us. We had orders and we followed them."

"Do you ever regret signing up?"

Coal pondered his question for several long moments. She had asked herself that many times. "No, I had a particular skill set that was helpful to my country's mission during wartime. I fulfilled my duty like a good soldier and left my sacrifices on the field of battle."

"What happened to Charlie? Do you stay in touch?"

"When I rotated back to the States, Charlie still had another month to go on his tour. A mission he was assigned was compromised, and the chopper he was on was shot down with no survivors. It took days to find the wreckage and recover the bodies."

"I'm sorry to hear that."

"It's a hazard of the job, one that is drilled into us from day one of training. We all knew the inherent risk going in, and no one left the program."

"So when you went back, with Tessa and Mitch that time, why didn't you have sniper duty?"

"I wish I had. Maybe things would have turned out differently. All the slots for snipers were full when I got called back up."

"I don't think it would have mattered in the long run. Mitch and Tessa would have faced their destiny even if you weren't there to intervene. At least you got the chance to say good-bye. If you were embedded in the desert, you wouldn't have had that chance."

Coal grinned over at him. "When did you get so philosophical?"

"It must be the company I've been keeping."

"Whatever you say."

"We need some gas, so I'm taking the next exit."

"That's good. I need to get rid of some water."

"You want to wake up Sleeping Beauty back there?" He nodded toward the backseat.

"The princess is awake," Coal answered as Stormy sat up and stretched.

"Are we there yet?"

"No, we're just twenty minutes from the ranch."

"No way, Gene, I know I slept longer than that."

"We've been on the road almost four hours with another five until we stop for the night," he answered.

"Have I missed much?"

"Not in the way of scenery. It's been bland so far. We're stopping for gas and a break. I don't know about y'all, but I need to stretch my legs."

"Amen to that," Gene agreed and he pulled off the highway.

"Do you want me to drive awhile?" Coal asked.

"Naw, I'm good. I don't make a very good passenger. I'll let you know if I get tired."

"Knock your socks off, then," she said.

†

A few minutes after they returned to the road, they crossed into Colorado and mountains came into view.

"They are gorgeous," Gene declared.

"The Rockies," Stormy replied. "Bigger than the Pryor Range, but no less beautiful."

"That's for sure. I think I would find it very difficult to leave here if that's where I'd grown up. Do you miss them?" Coal asked Stormy.

"I love the mountains. They're a part of me like the blood in my veins. I miss them every day, but the memories I have of living up here overshadow their beauty. I'll always love to visit, but I don't think I could ever live here again. Besides, Texas has really grown on me."

"I'm sure Del will be glad to hear that," Gene teased.

"What about you, Gene, would you leave Texas to move up here with Susan?"

Gene pondered the question for a few long moments. "I'm not sure. Texas is all I've ever known."

"Do you think you'll get to see her while we're up here?" Coal asked.

Gene blushed. "We've already made arrangements for her to drive in when we get back from the trail."

"I think the boss and the others may drive up too if we can get entered into the rodeo," Coal said.

"We may be sick of being on a horse by then," Stormy replied.

Gene and Coal whipped their heads around to look at her.

"Are you serious?" Coal asked.

"Watch the road, cowboy. I was just teasing."

"Damn, girl, you about gave me a heart attack," Gene cried.

"After herding cattle for a week, we're going to need something a lot faster paced," Coal said. "Maybe we can get some practice roping along the way. I'm feeling a bit rusty."

"That's not a bad idea," Gene agreed.

"No broncs to ride, though," Stormy added with a sigh.

"Maybe sitting all day in a saddle will make your butt sore enough you don't want to hit the ground." Gene chuckled.

"You're probably right about that."

Coal pulled out the printout Melissa had given them that had information on the hotel where they would be spending the night. "This is too cool to have a hotel with stables and a riding ring," she commented. "Are you guys up for a ride when we get checked in?"

"Oh yeah," Stormy replied. "I feel so cramped up in here."

"Maybe the ring will be lit. It's going to be pushing dark before we arrive."

"We're in luck. The picture clearly shows lights," Coal said.

"Awesome," Gene said.

Coal pulled out her camera and snapped shots of Gene and Stormy, then of the mountains that loomed closer as they drove.

†

Melissa was boxing up file folders from Mitch's office when the door creaked softly open. Seconds later, a solid-black tomcat jumped onto the desk.

"Well hello there, Hank." She stroked the purring cat. "I haven't seen you in days. Have you been out catting around?"

His soft meow was her only answer.

Cam knocked on the doorframe. "Would you mind if I joined you?"

"No, please come in, Doc." Melissa pointed to a seat across from the desk.

Cam sat. "Who is this handsome fellow?" she asked as Hank strolled over to her.

"That would be Hank. He's about the tenth generation of our original mouser, Harry, and father of most of the barn cats around here."

"I can see why. He's quite the charmer." Cam stroked under his chin and his purring filled the room. "He's got a strong motor under his hood too."

"That he has. You know, Mitch always told me black cats have a unique personality, and I'll admit I have to agree with that."

"I agree. It's too bad they get such a bad rap from superstitious people. Some of the best I've had were black."

"Get used to seeing him, then. Hank will visit often. He has his own bed here." She nodded to a small cat bed in the corner.

"I don't have any problem sharing with Hank. Are you sure this is what you really want? I'm certain this was a special place for Mitch."

"He would be happy you're using it. You'll need to have the phone lines reactivated, though. I let them drop last year since we never used them."

"Would you mind if I have Internet run in here?"

"Not at all, make whatever changes you need to make it work for you."

Hank curled up in Cam's lap and she stroked him.

"I think you have a new best friend."

"He does seem rather comfortable with me." Cam smiled up at Melissa. "We need to discuss payment for the office and the bedroom."

"My vet bill with Dr. Cone runs about eight hundred a month. Are you interested in fee exchanges for rent? If we go above that, I can write a check."

"That is very generous of you, if drastically underpriced. Once I get settled into the practice, I'll look for a place of my own and we can renegotiate."

"That sounds like a deal, but there's no rush. It's nice having someone else in the house with me."

"Thanks for all your generosity. I really like it out here."

Melissa smiled at the sparkle in Cam's eyes and knew she was telling the truth. "We have quite the crew assembled."

"That you do. Harley was giving me some background on them earlier today. Quite a diverse group, but they blend well together."

"Like they have been working together forever, and they get along so well."

"Have you heard from the new dad today?"

"Oh yes, he's sent me a dozen shots of the baby."

"That's got to be so exciting."

"I would imagine. Did you have any children?"

"Goodness no. At one point Sheila and I discussed having a child, but that dream was cut short."

"I'm sorry. I didn't mean to bring you sadness."

"That's okay. We've both suffered painful loses. I can talk about her finally without getting choked up."

"Do you mind telling me what happened?"

Cam hesitated for a short moment and shook her head. "She was coming home one afternoon, when a freak thunderstorm popped up and the rain came down in buckets. A young man named Tim Jernigan was going home from football practice. He'd only had his license a few weeks," she added with pain in her voice. "His car hit a slick spot on the road and it spun headlong into Sheila's car, killing her instantly, and he walked away without a scratch."

"Oh my goodness, I'm sorry."

"It was quick and painless, according to the doctors. Tim was emotionally shattered for a while afterward, and I was worried he would end his suffering in suicide."

"You had to hate him for destroying your life."

"I can't say I hated him, but I was crushed. Sheila wouldn't have wanted me to harbor ill feelings over an unpreventable accident, so I reached out to him at her funeral and we shared our grief. It was rough for him for some time afterward, but he went on to become a trauma surgeon, a damned good one too."

"You keep in touch with him, then?"

"Only when our paths cross. We don't seek each other out, but I did see him the morning I left town. He came to the cemetery to plant a rosebush by her grave."

"He sounds like he's grown into a good man."

"He has, and he's touched so many lives in a positive way, I just can't resent him for living when she died."

"I'm not so sure I could be that strong."

"But you are. You've resolved a similar situation with Coal, if my information is correct. She was there when your husband was killed, right?"

"I never thought of it like that, but yes, you're correct. Coal still blames herself for his death, although not nearly as vehemently as before. She's undergone extensive therapy for PTSD, and it's helped her a great deal."

"Del is her therapist, right?"

"Yeah, she and Mary Leah went to college together, and I saw Del for a time after Mitch's death. She's a fantastic therapist."

"So how did she and Stormy end up together?"

"Coal and Stormy became friends during rodeo season, and when Del saw Stormy, it was lights-out." She chuckled. "Stormy is a sexy woman."

"That she is, but she had a reputation of being a player, so Del made her work for her attention, and fortunately Stormy stepped up to the plate."

"With Stormy's looks, I could see that."

"Stormy had her own hurt she was running from. She's originally from Montana and got screwed over by an ex."

"I wonder if she'll be okay heading back into the area."

"She'll be fine, or Coal will kick her ass."

"Ah, the brawler rules." Cam grinned.

"Gene and Stormy adore Coal and will do anything she asks of them. Coal's a good friend to her, so I'm sure she'll keep a close eye on Stormy. We were in Montana over Christmas and she seemed just fine."

"They are quite a trio."

"Just wait until you see them at a rodeo. They all kick ass."

"I look forward to that. Did I hear someone mention a rodeo while they're in Montana?"

"Yeah, they're going to try to enter when they get done with the cattle drive."

Harley stepped into the office. "Here you both are. You have a visitor," he told Melissa.

"Who on earth?"

"You'll have to come see for yourself."

They followed Harley out of the barn into a brilliant late afternoon. Melissa smiled when she saw Lucas's truck parked in front of the bunkhouse.

He grinned up at her, holding a bundle in his arms. "Hey, boss, I wanted you to meet our newest little cowboy, Mathew Lucas."

"I can't believe they've already been released from the hospital," Melissa commented as she walked closer and looked in on the sleeping baby.

"They released her at lunchtime, and I wanted to bring him out before we head home."

"He's adorable. Is Lisa doing well?"

"She's sore as you would imagine," he said and turned toward his truck where she was waiting.

Melissa waved to Lisa. "You've got a beautiful baby."

"Thanks, Melissa. Our folks haven't even seen him yet. Lucas insisted on bringing him here first."

"He's going to be a handsome one," Cam said, looking over Melissa's shoulder at the boy.

"Yes, he is, but you two move along. You'll want to keep him out of public for a while until his immune system is built up."

"Yes, Mom." Lucas grinned at Melissa.

"Thanks for bringing him out. I hope he'll visit often," Melissa said.

"You can count on it," Lisa promised.

"Be safe and we'll see you all soon, then."

Lucas placed his son back into the car seat, and with a wave, they were on their way home.

They watched Lucas pull away, and then Melissa turned to Harley. "So what should we cook for supper?"

"Oh, I forgot to tell you. Harley and I picked up steaks while we were out. Harley's cooking for us tonight," Cam said.

"That sounds terrific. Anything I can do?"

"Sit back and keep us in cold drinks," Harley instructed.

"I can do that," Melissa said.

"The potatoes are in the oven and salads are chilling. I'll start the grill if you and Doc will pull out a few chairs from the barn and grab us a cold one."

"Consider it done," Cam stated and went for the chairs while Melissa went to the bunkhouse for some cold brews.

†

"Only fifty miles to go," Gene said while he wiped egg salad from the corner of his mouth. "I think we should hunt down a hot meal after we get the horses settled for the night."

"You won't get any argument from me," Stormy said. "These sandwiches are good, but I need some red meat, especially if we're gonna be living on beans the next few weeks."

"We have a cook traveling with us, so I think we'll be having more than beans," Coal said.

"I sure hope so. I get hungrier when it's cold out," Gene replied.

"You mean you can get hungrier than you usually are?" Stormy teased.

"What can I say, I'm a growing boy," he shot back.

"That you are, my friend," Coal agreed, then snapped a shot of the setting sun. "It's really beautiful up here," she remarked, and when Gene turned toward her, she got a shot of him with the sunset in the background. "That's gonna be a good one." She grinned.

†

"I wonder if the crew has made it to the hotel yet," Melissa said before she took a bite of the juicy steak. "Harley, you've outdone yourself on the steaks."

"Thanks. I hope the kids get a good meal in their stomachs."

"They are way beyond kids," Cam reminded him.

"They will always be kids to me." He grinned with a twinkle in his eyes.

"I'm sure Gene's appetite will drive them to get a hearty meal tonight. If I had to guess, though, I bet they're riding in the ring about now," Melissa said.

"Let's see about that." Harley pulled out his cell. After several long moments with no answer, he ended the call. "I bet you're right. No answer."

"Maybe one of them will call to check in tonight," Melissa said hopefully.

"Are you worried about them, boss?"

"I'll just rest better when I know they're settled for the night."

"Give them a call in a bit. After they ride, they'll probably grab a hot meal."

"I will, Harley."

†

"That felt good." Coal dismounted Shadow and started to remove his tack. "Just what the doctor ordered."

"Speaking of doctors, are you two going to call home before we eat?" Gene asked.

Stormy looked at Coal and shook her head. "Let's eat first, and then we can all check in. Will you call Melissa and let her know we're safely tucked in for the night?"

"Yeah, I can do that," he answered as he filled feed bins for all three horses. "Will one of you get the water?"

"I'll get it if you'll load the tack back in the trailer," Coal said to Stormy.

"I'm all over it," Stormy replied and picked up two saddles and left the stables.

†

Melissa and Cam were sitting at the kitchen table sharing a cup of coffee when Melissa's cell phone rang. She pushed the Speaker button. "Hello."

"Hey, boss, it's Gene. I just wanted to let you know we're settled in for the night."

"I'm glad you called. I was beginning to worry."

"We got checked into our rooms and decided to ride for a few minutes before getting some supper."

"I hope you got something good."

"A decent steak, but not nearly like one of Harley's."

"I'll be sure to let Harley know. He cooked steaks for us tonight, and they were delicious."

"I bet they were. That man can cook some meat. I keep hoping his talent will rub off on me."

"Give it some time and you'll be grilling delicious meals like him."

"Thanks for the vote of confidence."

"Did you have any issues traveling today?"

"Not a one, and the rooms are nice. Great stables too."

"I'm glad you've made it and can get a good night's rest. What time do you plan to head out tomorrow?"

"Early, hopefully around six if we can."

"That should put you at Tucker's place before nightfall."

"That's what we're hoping for. That'll give us a day to get our stuff packed into the wagon and ready to move out early Monday morning."

"Call again tomorrow to let me know you've made it. Have the girls called home yet?"

"That's what they're doing now."

"Tell them good night and have safe travels tomorrow."

"I will, ma'am."

"Gene?"

"Yes?"

"I'm very proud of y'all."

"Thanks, boss, and thanks for giving us this opportunity."

"Enjoy it and come back with many stories. Good night."

"Good night."

Melissa ended the call and found Cam smiling at her. "What?"

"They are like your children, aren't they?"

"Family, yes, but not children. Each of them has grown up in a hard way."

"What's Gene's story?" she asked and took a sip of coffee.

"From what I've heard, his father was a real bastard, physically abusive to his wife and kids. Kicked him out when he graduated and told him it was time to grow up. That's when he showed up on my doorstep, nothing to his name but a beat-up truck and several outfits." Melissa paused to sip her coffee. "He was starving half to death for proper nutrition, and love, and we were able to provide both. He's grown into a fine young man, and I couldn't ask for a harder worker."

"I agree with you. He's strong, yet sensitive, and he loves working here."

"The MC2 is the home he longed for growing up."

"This seems to be a great place for broken hearts and spirits."

Melissa chuckled. "That it is, my friend."

†

Gene passed Coal in the hallway of the hotel. "The boss says to tell everyone good night. Everything okay at home?"

"Yep, Mary Leah says the house is way too quiet without me there. You all set for the night?"

"I'm good, and y'all?"

"Good too. See you in the morning. Try to get some sleep. May be the last decent bed we have for a while."

Gene laughed. "See you in the morning."

Coal watched him enter his room, then went into the room she and Stormy were sharing to find Stormy stretched out on her bed. "How's Del?"

"Lonesome, but I think she'll survive. I think she's going to call Mary Leah to go to a movie or something this week to break up the monotony."

"I didn't know we were so lively."

"Me either. Good to hear we're missed, though."

"Yeah, it is. Gene checked in with Melissa, who told him to tell us good night. I think she misses us too," Coal said.

"We'll be home before they know it." Stormy turned on the television. "You mind a bit of noise?"

"Not at all, just set the sleep timer." Coal kicked off her tennis shoes and entered the bathroom to brush her teeth.

Stormy had curled up under the covers of her bed when Coal returned and appeared to be fast asleep.

"Good night, my friend," Coal whispered, then turned off the lamp and climbed between clean, crisp sheets.

Chapter Seven

Coal woke early, showered, and woke Stormy before carrying her bag out to the truck. The Colorado sunrise filled the horizon with orange-and-purple rays, and the air smelled fresh and crisp with the scent of evergreens. She tossed her bag into the backseat of the truck, pulled out her camera, and collected several shots of the sunrise. When finished, she turned toward the stables to see Gene emerging.

"Good morning."

"You too," he answered with an excited grin. "I've fed the horses, so we can get going right after we have some breakfast."

"Let me go tell Stormy to meet us at the restaurant next door. Go ahead and get us a table and a pot of coffee."

"Yes, ma'am." He tipped his hat.

Coal shook her head and chuckled at his antics, then returned to the hotel. She entered the room just as the shower turned off. "Hey, Stormy."

"Yeah, I'm out."

"Meet Gene and me next door for breakfast when you're done."

"All right, I won't be long."

"Good. I'm starving,"

"So what else is new?"

"Get a move on, smart-ass," Coal prompted her and left the room.

†

The sun had fully risen when they pulled out onto the highway. Coal reviewed the shots she had taken of the sunrise and hotel while Gene drove. He fiddled with the radio until he found a country station with a strong signal.

"Now we're in business," he stated and then began singing along with the radio. His excitement was contagious, and soon Coal and Stormy joined in as the remaining miles elapsed.

†

Mary Leah wandered through the house, her footsteps echoing through the rooms.

"I never realized how much you bring this place alive," she spoke into the empty room while she paced. The kitchen still smelled of the toast she'd burned while she was getting dressed.

She finally gave up and drove to Melissa's house.

When Mary Leah arrived, the house was empty. She walked into the bunkhouse and found her sister and Doc Bo seated at the table while Harley cooked breakfast.

"You have room for one more?" she asked.

Harley turned and smiled at her. "There's always room for you."

"Is the house too quiet for you?" Melissa asked.

106

"Yeah, and I even burned my toast. I've gotten so used to Coal cooking me breakfast that it seems I've forgotten how."

"Are you going to survive the next two weeks?" Melissa asked.

"Yeah, I have a feeling they will be miserable, though."

"Would you like to come stay at the house?"

"No, I just need to put my big-girl panties on and deal with Coal's absence, and remind myself I used to live alone. Thanks for the offer, though."

"You're welcome anytime if you change your mind."

"Would you like some bacon, eggs, and toast?" Harley asked.

"You're a lifesaver, Harley. That would be wonderful. What can I do to help?" Mary Leah asked.

"You can pour yourself a cup of coffee and juice for everyone."

"That I know I can handle."

†

"Good morning," Del said as she answered her phone.

"It's a glorious morning up here, sweetie," Stormy told her. "How are you?"

"Missing you, but otherwise I'm okay. The bed sure was cold without you in it."

"I miss you too. I'll know what you mean when I'm sleeping on the cold, hard ground."

"Awww," came the chorus from the front seat, making Stormy regret putting her phone on speaker.

"Hush, you two," Stormy growled and took it off speaker.

"No sympathy from your cohorts, I take it?"

"None at all from this lot. We're having a blast together, though, so I reckon I'll forgive them."

"That's mighty kind of you, Ms. Braxton."

"So what are you going to do today?"

"Probably just mope around the house. I'll give Mary Leah a call later to ask her to a movie and dinner this week."

"That's a good idea. I'm sure she's probably lonesome too."

"I've got some files to work on this morning, but I'll give her a call later. Has Coal talked to her yet today?"

"Dunno, let me ask. Hey, Coal, have you talked to Mary Leah this morning?"

"Not yet, I thought I'd let her sleep in a bit."

"Nope, she's letting her sleep in."

"Okay, then, I'll wait until midafternoon to give her a call. How much longer do you have until y'all get to Montana?"

Stormy looked at the GPS stuck on the windshield. "The GPS says our ETA is six more hours."

"You're making good time. What's the weather like?"

"It's a beautiful sunny day, a bit on the cool side. I think it's about sixty right now."

"That doesn't sound too awful. I think it's already eighty here."

"We may be wishing for some hot Texas sun before this trip is over to help thaw us out."

"Maybe it won't be too terribly cold."

"I'll just have to think of you to get warm."

"That is so sweet," Gene called to Stormy.

Del laughed. "I hear the peanut gallery on your end."

"Yeah, they're a laugh a minute. I won't give them any more ammunition. I'll call you later when we can have some measure of privacy."

"Good luck with that." Del chuckled. "It's good to hear your voice."

"Love you, Doc."

"Love you too. Call me later."

"I will," Stormy promised. She ended the call with a sigh. "You guys are nuts."

"Yeah, but you love us," Gene quipped.

"I don't know why, but yeah, I do."

†

"I think I'll drown some worms later today if y'all want to join me," Harley offered while he picked up the kitchen.

"Maybe," Cam answered. "You know, Coal promised me a ride to show me around the place, but we got rained out. Melissa, would you mind a ride?"

"That sounds like a good idea. Mary Leah, would you like to join us?"

"No thanks, I don't share Coal's love for riding. I think I'll drive to town and work a few hours."

"Give me just a few and I'll saddle a couple of horses for you." Harley left the bunkhouse.

Cam and Melissa escorted Mary Leah out to her car.

"You sure you won't join us?" Melissa asked.

"Thanks, but it will just make me long for Coal more than ever."

"You've got it bad, don't you?" Melissa asked.

"This is the first time since we've been together that we'll be apart so long. I feel like a part of me is missing already, and it's only been a day," she answered with tears filling her eyes. "I'll just have to keep busy to occupy myself."

Melissa hugged her baby sister. "Come over for dinner. I bet Harley will catch some fresh fish we can cook up."

"That sounds good. I'll see you both later." She turned and climbed into her car.

They watched her drive away and then walked to the barn.

"I have a feeling it's going to be a long two weeks," Melissa said.

"I'm afraid you're right."

†

Harley brought the saddled horses over to them and watched them mount.

"Have a great ride."

"We will. Try to catch enough for supper. Mary Leah's coming over to eat with us."

"I'll do my best, boss. I wish Coal were here to make the hush puppies."

"Is there anything Coal doesn't do well?" Cam asked.

Harley seemed to think for several long moments. "If there is, I can't think of it," he answered with a grin.

"I can't think of anything either," Melissa added.

"A great woman to have on the payroll," Cam replied.

"That she is. Are you ready to ride?" Melissa said.

"Yes, I am."

"Hang on and I'll get the gate open for you." Harley walked beside them. "Keep an eye out for Hector. I've heard him howling at night, so he must be back in our territory."

"We will," Melissa promised.

Cam looked at Harley. "Wolf or coyote?"

"A Mexican wolf that ranges up this far in early spring," Harley answered.

"Does he cause you any problem?"

"Naw, he's been traveling these parts about four years now. He's never attacked one of the herd, but he's cleaned us out of jackrabbits a time to two."

"Good thing they reproduce quickly." She chuckled.

"That they do. Be careful," he told them and swung the gate wide to allow them to pass through.

"See you soon," Melissa called.

They rode through the gate and started down the trail after the gate clanged shut behind them.

†

Gene pulled the truck into a gas station for a fill up. Coal grabbed her camera and walked to the edge of the parking lot to take shots of the mountains across an open field. The mountains loomed closer the farther north they drove, and snow topped several peaks, even in the full sun.

"Beautiful, aren't they?" Stormy asked as she appeared beside her.

"Yeah, they are. Stand over by that fence and let me get a shot of you for Del."

"All right, just make sure you get my best side."

"You better turn around then," Coal teased. She took several shots and was pleased with her efforts.

"You want me to take a shot with you and Stormy?" Gene asked as he joined them.

"Sure, then I'd like to get one with you, and one of you and Stormy."

111

"I think we can handle that," he replied as he took the camera.

They took several photos, and when the break was over, Coal walked between her friends as they headed back to the truck. "I need a pit stop and I'll be ready when y'all are."

"I thought we might grab a bite to eat at the barbeque joint over there. The smell's been killing me since we pulled in," Gene said.

"Sounds good to me," Stormy replied.

"I'm always up for some pulled pork," Coal added.

"Hurry back, then." Gene grinned.

†

Coal entered the small store and walked through the aisles to get to the restroom. On her way back through the store, she spotted travel mugs on a display rack and bought one for each of them. An array of wolves, bears, and the Rockies covered each of the mugs. She got matching designs so there would be no fighting over who got which one. Besides, the mugs were a matched set, just like Gene, Stormy, and her. She paid for her purchases and returned to the truck.

She opened the bag after she climbed inside and handed each of them a mug. "Our first souvenirs." She grinned.

"Thanks, Coal." Gene smiled, examining the mug as if it were a priceless relic.

"These are great," Stormy added.

"You're both welcome. They should come in handy on our journey too."

"I can just taste the coffee now. It'll probably be strong enough to grow hair on your chest," Stormy said, sounding worried.

"I sure hope not," she answered, laughing. "I don't think Mary Leah wanted me to turn into Bigfoot while I was away."

"I was thinking more like Chewbacca," Stormy teased.

"Good grief, let's go eat so we can get back on the road." Gene chuckled and then put the truck in gear.

†

"It's so beautiful here," Cam said as she rode beside Melissa. "I can understand why your crew loves this place."

"It's home," she answered.

"That it is. How many acres do you have here?"

"With a little over five hundred acres, we're one of the largest spreads still active in the area. We manage to get a few hundred steers off to the feed lots a couple times a year, sell a few thousand bales of hay, and train a few horses in our downtime."

"Sounds like you stay pretty busy."

"There's rarely a dull moment around here."

"I can understand that."

They rode together for another half an hour before Cam's cell phone rang. She fished it out of the case on her hip and answered. "This is Doc Bohannon," she said, then listened for several minutes. "The Hollister place, you say? Okay, I'll get there as soon as I can."

Melissa watched her with a growing worry. "You'll need someone to show you how to get out there," she said when Cam hung up.

"Are you available? He's got a mare in trouble birthing her foal."

"Sure, we better pick up the pace here, though," she answered.

"Let's go, then," Cam replied and urged her horse into a canter.

†

Harley was landing a fish when he heard hoof beats hurrying toward him, and turned to see Cam and Melissa racing across the field. He stored the fish and his gear in the back of the gator and drove to the gate.

"What's going on?" he asked as they pulled the horses to a stop.

"There's a breach foal over at the Hollister place. Melissa is going to guide me over there," Cam answered.

"Do you need my help?"

"I think I've got this covered, but keep your cell close if you don't mind."

"No problem. Call if you need me. I'll get these ready for cooking later when y'all return."

"Thanks, Harley."

"No problem. Just leave the horses at the hitching post and I'll tend to them so y'all can get on the road."

Cam nodded and trotted her horse over to the hitching post and dismounted.

"Be careful," he called to Melissa.

"See you soon, I hope," she answered.

She seemed genuinely excited to be helping out, which brought a smile to Harley's face.

Cam rushed to the office and returned with a bag, which she placed it in the backseat of her truck. "Ready?"

Dust kicked up behind her truck as Cam sped down the driveway and made a right turn onto the paved road. Harley smiled as he watched them disappear and then led the horses into the barn.

†

"Only five miles to go," Gene told them, his grin broad across his face.

"I don't know about y'all, but I'm ready to be out of this truck," Coal groaned.

"Amen to that, sister," Stormy chimed in from the backseat. "No matter how I've shifted, I think my butt is permanently imprinted into this seat."

"We'll be there soon," Gene assured them as he took a right turn onto the final road they would travel.

†

"Easy, girl," Cam soothed as she stroked down the mare's side.

"Thanks for getting here so quickly. This girl's one of my best mares and she's bred to the top cutting horse in the state of Texas. There's a lot riding on this foal."

"Let's see if we can bring it into the world safely, then," Cam replied as she slipped a full arm-length glove onto her right arm and spread lubricant across it. She caressed the mare's lower belly with her left hand and felt the foal struggling to turn into birthing position. "Hang in there, little one, and we'll have you out soon."

115

The mare stamped her front hoof when a labor convulsion raced through her. "Will you stand at her head, Melissa, and see if you can comfort her?"

"You got it." She moved over and stroked the horse's face.

"Here we go, Mama." Cam began the tedious process of turning the foal into position to safely birth. The panic-stricken foal struggled against her efforts, and Cam's face was coated with sweat in a manner of minutes.

"Work with me, baby," she whispered and struggled to wipe the sweat out of her eyes.

"Can I wipe your face?" Mr. Hollister asked.

"I'd very much appreciate that."

Cam worked for several more minutes before the foal finally relaxed and she was able to get it moving in the right direction.

"Here we go now, Mama, work with me." She could feel the mare's muscles contract as she worked to push the foal from her body. "Oh yes, Mama, that's it, girl. I need your help, Mr. Hollister," she called out when the foal's front hooves emerged. "I've got the front half, if you'll catch the rear end when the foal arrives so we can get it to the ground."

"Yes, ma'am," he answered and moved into place.

"It's coming quickly now," Cam stated through gritted teeth while she gently pulled the foal through the birth canal.

She used her left hand to clear the afterbirth from its face, and they lowered the colt to the ground.

"We did it, Mama," she told the mare as she carefully removed the remainder of the afterbirth and cut the colt's umbilical cord. "The rest of the job's all yours. You can let her go now, Melissa."

Cam stepped backward several paces and pulled the soiled glove from her arm, her gaze never leaving the beautiful colt lying on the straw covering the floor of the stall.

Mr. Hollister stood there grinning at her. "That was a great job."

"Thanks," Cam answered and wiped her face. "Could I trouble you for a bottle of water?"

"Sure thing, pardon my bad manners." He raced from the stall.

She knelt and watched the mare lick her newborn colt. "He's a beauty, Mama. You did well," she said softly.

Hollister returned with three bottles water. "Here you go, Doc."

"Thanks." Cam twisted the top from the icy-cold bottle and took a long drink. "Man, that's good. You have a beautiful new colt," she told him while they watched the foal struggle to his feet.

The mare used her muzzle to steady the colt on his wobbly legs, and after several minutes, she stepped forward and the colt instinctively began to nurse.

"That's what I was waiting to see," Cam replied with a broad smile. "I do believe you are good to go. I'll come back out in a few days to give them both a checkup, but don't hesitate to call me if needed."

"Thanks, Doc," Hollister said. "Can you send me a bill?"

"I'll bring it out with me when I return."

"I was afraid I'd lose both of them," he answered with tears sparkling in his eyes.

"You could have if you hadn't realized the colt was in distress."

"Thanks again," he replied and picked up Cam's bag to walk them out.

"I've got this. Stay and enjoy the new family." She took the bag from him. "I'll see you soon."

Melissa smiled at her as they left. "That was amazing."

"Just helping Mother Nature to do her thing. I'm whipped, though. Would you mind driving home?"

"Not at all," Melissa answered, taking the keys from her.

Cam turned the air conditioner on high and then settled back in the passenger seat.

Melissa looked at her. "You were fantastic. That was really exciting and miraculous to watch. I've seen hundreds of animals born, but that was just incredible."

"That was a tough one, but I'm glad to see him arrive safely. He had me worried."

"You'd never know that from the way you responded. You made it look easy, and I'm sure it was anything but easy."

"The heat in that barn didn't help matters. Being inside the mare and trying to maneuver the foal was quite a workout already. I'm definitely in need of a hot shower."

Melissa watched her bathe her face in the cold air. "You can shower while I check to see if Harley needs any help."

"You have a deal." Cam slumped back into the seat and closed her eyes.

†

Melissa glanced over at the dozing woman with growing admiration. The way Cam tended the mare, soothing the animal with her voice and touch had been amazing. Melissa had found herself mesmerized by the sound of Cam's voice as she spoke softly to the animal to keep her calm.

What an incredible woman.

†

Melissa pulled into the yard to find Mary Leah tagging along after Harley as he prepared the outdoor fish fryer to cook. She parked the truck and looked over at the groggy woman sitting beside her. "Do you want your bag back in the office?"

"Yes, I'll take it. Thanks for driving home."

"I'll take the bag while you hit the shower and get refreshed."

"Thanks."

Cam climbed out of the truck and walked through the front door while Melissa carried her bag toward the barn.

Harley and Mary Leah had pulled out a table, and Harley poured oil in the cooker to fry the fish he had soaking in a pan.

"What can I do to help?" Melissa asked.

"I've got the fish covered if you want to finish the corn on the cob that's cooking in the bunkhouse and help Mary Leah with the hush puppies. There's some salad left over that's still cold in the fridge. Where did Doc Bo go?"

"To hit the shower. That birthing took a lot out of her. You should've seen her, Harley. She was amazing."

He grinned. "I told you she was a great vet."

†

"Man, will you look at this spread," Gene remarked as he pulled the trailer through a huge wooden arch covering the drive into the Circle T ranch. The large spread of barns and outbuildings framed in the distance by the Pryor Mountains looked truly picturesque.

"Nice," Stormy agreed as she leaned forward between the front seats to get a better look.

"Look at that house." Coal pointed to a large log home, complete with a plethora of windows to accentuate the view.

Gene pulled the truck to a halt in front of a large barn and turned off the engine. His gaze landed on a competition-sized riding ring with barrels already in place, and he grinned. "Looks like they're ready for you to run," he told Coal.

"Maybe we can get a few runs in once we're settled."

"I'm sure your boy is ready to stretch his legs," Stormy said.

"Probably so," Coal agreed before her attention turned to the woman striding across the yard toward them. She turned to look at Gene and grinned when she saw him watching her. The woman's blonde ponytail swayed from side to side beneath a black Stetson as she approached.

"Stan sure doesn't look that good in Wranglers," Gene stated when he caught Coal's grin.

"I will have to second that," Stormy agreed with a low whistle. "This trip is getting better by the minute."

"Easy, Trigger, that's our boss for the next two weeks, so put your tongue back in your mouth."

"It never hurts to look," Stormy came back.

"Look but don't touch," Gene reminded her. "Don't get us kicked off the cattle drive before we get started."

"Oh ye of little faith." Stormy clutched her chest, feigning hurt. "Del would kick my ass and you both know it."

"If she didn't, I would," Coal replied without smiling. She opened her door and stepped out of the truck.

The woman held her hand out to Coal with a smile as her blue eyes sparkled. "Welcome to the Circle T. I'm Nancy Tucker."

"Coal Bryan," she replied. "These two ruffians are Gene and Stormy." She nodded toward them.

Nancy chuckled. "You three come highly recommended. Dad and I are pleased to have you if even for a few short weeks. Follow me and I'll show you the bunkhouse, and then we can get your horses settled in."

They followed her inside a smaller version of the log house. They would each have a private room, and the den and kitchen were fully equipped.

"The other four members of our crew will be here by six in the morning so we can get the herd moving north."

"Your dad mentioned a wagon that will carry our supplies. Can we go ahead and load our gear tonight?" Coal asked.

Nancy smiled. "I was just about to suggest that. We've got a couple hours to get you settled before supper will be ready. Georgia, our cook, has a feast planned for us."

"That sounds great," Gene replied. "If you two will get the horses settled, I'll load our gear onto the wagon."

Coal was about to agree when the bunkhouse door opened and a tall, slender man entered. She knew instantly where Nancy had gotten her long legs. She was the spitting image of her dad, but his hair had gone to gray. He smiled at Coal with the same sparkle in his sky-blue eyes.

"You must be Coal," he stated. "I'm Roger Tucker."

"Nice to meet you, sir," she answered. "Gene and Stormy," she said, nodding to her companions.

"I heard y'all might like to do a bit of rodeo while you're up here." He smiled.

"Oh yes, sir," Gene replied. "We hope to make it back in time to enter some events."

"That shouldn't be a problem, and I've told our local sponsor to save us three more slots."

"Thank you, sir." Coal smiled.

"I have one request, though. I'll pay your entry fees if you'll agree to ride for the Circle T. I'd love to pull top cowboy from Silver Crescent, and I hear y'all are just the crew to do that."

"That's very generous of you," Coal replied.

"It's a fair price to pay to wipe the smug look off Charlie Wilson's face when he doesn't get to take the trophy home for the first time in a dozen years." He chuckled.

Coal looked at Gene and Stormy, who were both grinning like Cheshire cats. "You've got yourself three more on your team," she answered.

They spent several minutes discussing the various events they would enter, and Nancy was excited that she, Stormy, and Coal would be competing in several speed events together.

"We can rack up a lot of points if we run well," she told them.

"Would you mind if we take a few runs at the barrels tonight?" Coal asked.

"Absolutely not," Roger answered. "We can even round up a few steers if you want to do a bit of roping."

"Now we're talking," Gene replied. "I'm going to start loading our gear if you'll show me where to go," he told Nancy.

"Come with me, Gene, and I'll give you a hand," Roger stated and slapped him on the back.

"I'll show you the stables, and once you get your horses and bags settled, we can make a few runs," Nancy told them.

"Let's do it." Coal grinned, and they followed her outside.

†

"That's one beautiful stallion," Nancy remarked when Shadow backed out of the trailer.

"My boy, Shadow," Coal stated with pride. "He runs like the wind and has turned into a great cow pony."

Nancy led Gene's horse into the barn ahead of Coal and Stormy.

"Wow, these are nice digs," Stormy replied upon entering the immaculately kept barn. "Is that really heat I feel?"

"Yeah, Dad believes in treating our horses like family," she answered with a grin.

"Don't you get too spoiled," Coal told Shadow.

Stormy laughed. "Who are you kidding? He'd chase you all the way back to Texas and you know it."

"Yeah, he would," Coal replied as she hugged his neck. "Ready for a run?" she asked while she stroked down his neck.

Shadow tossed his head.

"I think he understood what you asked," Nancy remarked.

"Sometimes I think he's smarter than me," she said, shutting the stall gate behind her. "Let's grab the tack and some feed for later."

"I'll get saddled while I'm waiting for you to get settled." Nancy disappeared into a stall.

Stormy and Coal returned carrying their tack as Nancy led a palomino mare from a stall.

"She's a beauty," Coal said.

Shadow poked his head over the gate, his ears perked.

"Shadow, meet Athena." Nancy chuckled as her mare stretched her neck to explore muzzles with Shadow.

"This could be interesting," Stormy replied.

"Yeah, it could. You want a girlfriend, big boy?"

Shadow breathed in deeply, his nostrils flaring as he took in Athena's scent.

"Too bad she won't be in her cycle while we're on the drive. I bet they'd make a beautiful foal," Nancy remarked.

"He's got a few offspring, and they are fine specimens," Coal stated proudly.

"Athena has had one colt Dad is trying to spoil to death."

"I am certainly not doing that," her father replied as he entered the barn with Gene. "Just because he follows me around like a pup doesn't mean he's spoiled."

"Oh geez, that sounds like Shadow," Gene commented.

"Saddle up, Gene, and you can help Nancy round up a few steers while Coal and Stormy warm up a bit."

"Yes, sir," Gene answered and saddled his horse.

Coal tucked her roping gloves in her back pocket and mounted Shadow.

Roger opened the gate to the ring to allow them to enter. He watched them lope smoothly around the ring to loosen up muscles cramped during the long ride from Texas. When Gene and Nancy had penned a half dozen steers, Stormy and Coal joined them in the ring.

"Who's running first?" Gene asked.

Roger had climbed up onto the top rail, stopwatch in hand. "Guests first," he called out to them.

"Go ahead, Coal, I know he's chomping at the bit," Stormy stated as they left the ring.

"I can't argue with that. I won't open him up fully on the first run."

"Good luck with that," Gene called as he pulled up next to where Roger sat on the rail.

"I'm ready when you are, Coal," Roger told her.

Each of the three women made several runs at the barrels, and their times improved with each run while the grin on Roger's face grew.

"These are great times, ladies," he remarked after Coal made a final run. "We should run the table on the barrel racing with the three of you."

Coal pulled out her gloves. "Are you ready to do some roping, Gene?"

"Heck yeah!"

"I'll work the chute for y'all. Will you two pen the released steers for us?" Roger asked Nancy and Stormy.

"Sure thing, Dad."

†

They practiced roping for nearly an hour before Georgia called them for dinner. After caring for the animals and washing up, the crew followed Nancy into the ranch house. The feast was indeed incredible, and when they returned to the bunkhouse to retire for the night, Gene was moaning in pleasure.

"I don't think I have eaten like that in a long time," he groaned.

"It was a great last meal before hitting the trail," Coal agreed. "I don't think I could've eaten another bite."

"I was glad to learn Georgia would be joining us on the drive," Stormy added. "Somehow I can't see her cooking beans every night."

"It certainly won't be the feast we had tonight, but I'm sure she'll fill our bellies before we hit the sack," Coal said.

"Speaking of which, I'm outta here," Gene told them. "I'll see you in the morning."

"Bright and early, I'm sure." Stormy smiled.

"Let's all get a good night's sleep and enjoy a comfortable bed one more time before we hit the ground." Coal followed her friends down the hall to the sleeping quarters.

Chapter Eight

Coal needed no alarm the next morning. Gene's singing in the shower woke her with a grin. His excitement about starting the cattle drive was obvious. She pulled out her hygiene bag and headed to a shower of her own. When she stepped out of her room, Stormy and Gene were waiting for her.

"Georgia has breakfast ready. We can saddle up and be ready to ride right after breakfast," Gene said, barely pausing for a breath.

"Let's toss our bags in the wagon on the way to breakfast, then," Coal suggested.

†

Coal pulled on a light jacket and they left the bunkhouse. The morning air was crisp and had a slight chill, raising the skin on her arms.

"I hope it warms up when the sun comes out."

"It'll be fine once we get moving around a bit," Gene said.

"I'm going to hold you to that."

"My personal guarantee." He winked.

They dropped their overnight bags into the wagon and continued on to the house. Focusing on food was difficult when they were excited to be on the trail.

"Eat up and fill your canteens before you saddle up. It'll be dusty riding behind the herd," Nancy informed them.

Gene was the first to finish, barely chewing his food before swallowing. Coal and Stormy grinned at him while they took time to savor the rich coffee and country ham. Gene squirmed in his seat until Coal chuckled. "Go ahead and we'll catch up with you soon."

"Thanks," he replied and stopped long enough to thank Georgia for the meal before he flew out of the house headed to the barn.

"I hope he's still that excited a week from now." Nancy grinned.

"He will be," they answered in unison and cracked up laughing.

"I'm surprised he slept at all last night. Did Georgia slip something in his food?" Coal questioned, stifling her laughter.

"Nope, I just sent him to bed with a full stomach," Georgia hollered from the kitchen.

"That you did," Stormy replied. "I slept like a rock."

"Me too," Coal agreed.

"Hopefully the weather will warm up and the nights won't be too bad," Roger said. "I don't envy y'all sleeping on the ground, though."

"It's not too late to join us," Nancy replied.

"Someone's got to keep this place running, especially since Georgia's going with you."

"Try not to burn down my kitchen while I'm gone," Georgia warned as she walked out with a pot of coffee. "Refills, anyone?"

"Thanks, but I'm stuffed," Coal answered.

"We better get moving before Gene comes after us," Stormy replied.

"Thanks, Georgia. We'll see you at the barn, Nancy."

"Hang on a sec and we'll walk out with you." Roger waited while Georgia poured him another cup of coffee.

"It's going to take me a week to find my way around the kitchen again after you move everything," Georgia complained.

"You know you love it when I rearrange for you," Roger teased back.

"Out now, before I change my mind and stay behind," she threatened.

Nancy grabbed her father by the arm and led him out of the dining room. "Let's go before I end up cooking."

Roger laughed and allowed her to walk him outside to the barn, which was buzzing with activity now that the rest of the crew had arrived.

When they got there, Gene had his horse saddled and their canteens filled. He helped Stormy with her tack and secured the rifle to Coal's saddle while she tied her range coat across the back of her saddle. She stopped to breathe in one final breath of the familiar scent of hay and manure, then, with a smile, led Shadow from the barn.

When Stormy arrived and everyone mounted, Nancy gave out assignments. Roger thanked the crew and wished them luck and safe travels, then he got Georgia settled onto the wagon bench.

"Let's go get 'em," Nancy hollered, and the riders trotted ahead of the wagon.

129

Nancy turned to look at Roger watching the group while they disappeared and lifted her hand to wave a final good-bye. Coal glimpsed a brief look of sadness on Nancy's face. She had felt that sadness several times in her life when she left a loved one behind, and she sympathized with her temporary boss. She turned her attention to Gene and Stormy, who had looks of excitement on their faces and her heart swelled with love for her friends. She felt Shadow's muscles quivering as he danced with excitement, eager to run.

This is going to be a great day, she thought, then pulled the brim of her hat down to shelter her eyes from the rays of the rising sun.

†

As the morning faded into early afternoon, the herd was moved fluidly and the crew chased back any attempts to stray from it. Coal pulled a bandana around her face to cover her mouth from the dust the cattle kicked up.

Georgia had pulled ahead of the herd hours ago, and when they saw the wagon again at the day's stopping point, Coal was ready to be on the ground moving to stretch out tired muscles.

Georgia had made several piles of tents and camping equipment. She had raised one tent and was working on a second when the crew circled the herd to stop their forward movement. The cattle were also eager to stop and began grazing in the sweet grass and drinking from a slow-moving creek.

"Let's get the horses settled and tents raised. We can relax for a bit before supper and discuss shifts for tending the herd tonight," Nancy instructed.

Coal dismounted and stretched her arms and legs. She tied Shadow off to a small tree and began removing his tack and brushing him down. "You did great today, Shadow," she praised while brushing his back with loving strokes.

"Being in the saddle all day like this is different from what we're used to, isn't it?" Stormy asked.

"Yeah, I didn't think I'd be this stiff," Coal admitted. "Getting that tent up and our gear settled will hopefully loosen us up."

"I hope you're right."

Coal refrained from chuckling at the groan Stormy let out when she lowered her saddle to the ground.

Gene partnered up with another ranch hand named Tony, and they went to work raising their tent and had it up in no time.

"You gals need some help?" Tony asked, shooting a grin at Coal.

"Sure," Coal replied. "We never turn away an offer of help."

With everyone working together, they quickly set camp up for the night and fed and watered the horses. The crew settled in on a couple of fallen logs to await supper, and Coal gazed at her surroundings.

"I take it you've used this site before, Nancy," she said.

"We have campsites arranged for the end of each day. We've made this trip each of the last ten years."

"That's awesome," Gene mused. "I can't imagine doing this every year."

"I'm sure Dad would keep a spot open for y'all if you enjoy it this year. You really can't have too many hands on a drive."

Gene looked at Coal. "Do you think Melissa would allow us to do this again?"

"We won't know until we ask her, but it is a good time of the year for us and a nice break before the hellish hay-baling season begins."

"I bet it does get hot down there," Tony stated.

"You could two-step with the heat waves coming up off the ground," Gene told him with a grin.

"Do you do a lot of baling?" Nancy asked.

"We usually sell about ten thousand bales and keep another ten on hand for our stock," Coal answered. "We do two or three cuttings a season, depending on how much rain we get."

"Man, do we pray for rain," Stormy added. "We get an extra share of the profits off a third cutting that usually pays for our rodeo season."

"Dad would gladly pay your fees if you wanted to come up for some events once your season ended."

"You're making this way too tempting," Coal replied.

"Just think about it," Nancy offered before she stretched and went to check on dinner.

†

The night fell quickly after the sun set in brilliant oranges and reds. Coal was thankful for the campfire that burned hot for an extra bit of warmth while they ate dinner.

†

"If you have someone to call, I'd suggest you do it tonight. We won't have cell service again until we return," Nancy told them.

Coal looked at her phone. "I've got a signal." She smiled.

"Me too," Stormy said.

"Are you going to call Susan?" Coal asked Gene.

"I called earlier and promised to let her know when we make it back in so she can join us for the rodeo." He blushed.

"Is she your girlfriend?" Nancy asked.

"Yeah, we met over Christmas here in Montana."

"I look forward to meeting her. She must be really special from the way you're blushing."

"Oh God, not you too. Coal and Stormy tease me bad enough already."

"I think it's sweet," Nancy replied.

"We got a sweet one on our trip, boys." Tony chuckled, and the group broke out in laughter.

Gene rolled his eyes. "C'mon, Tony, we have first guard duty."

Tony carried his plate to Georgia and followed Gene to the area where the horses were tethered. Two riders would ride around the herd in four-hour shifts. Stormy and Coal would take the next shift, then retire to get some sleep.

"Do you want to get a nap in?" Stormy asked.

"Naw, that'll just make me sleepier. I think I'll grab a cup of coffee and a slice of that cake and enjoy the beautiful night."

"Mind if I join you, then?"

"Not at all."

They returned to the wagon, where Georgia was cleaning up from supper.

"Do you need some help?" Coal asked.

"I've got this. I'm almost done anyhow. Can I get you ladies something else?"

"We were hoping to get a slice of cake and some coffee if you have some left," Coal said.

"Cut yourselves some cake and I'll pour coffee. Serve up an extra slice and I'll join you in a few. You sitting by the fire?"

"Yes'm," Stormy replied and cut three slices of cake and placed them on paper towels. "We're next shift on guard duty and not interested in a nap."

"You interested in some poker? We only play for braggin' rights, though," she explained.

"That sounds like fun," Stormy replied.

"Grab that card table and set it up for us. See if any of the boys want to join in."

Coal unloaded the small table and carried it over to the fire, while Stormy carried the cake over and went back for coffee. John, one of the other hands, decided to join them while the rest opted for a chance to crawl into their sleeping bags until their shift to guard the herd.

†

Poker wasn't one of Coal's better skills, but she did surprise herself by winning several hands. They played for nearly two hours before John and Georgia decided to turn in for the night. Nancy, who disappeared after supper, made an appearance at the fire.

"John and I will relieve you at the end of your shift. Stay alert and I'll see you later," she said, then bid them good night.

†

"Just you and me now," Stormy said.

"Is everything okay with Del?"

"Yeah, she and the girls are going out to the movies tomorrow night after a dinner in town."

"Hmm, Mary Leah didn't mention that when I talked to her," Coal said and stared out into the deep blackness.

"She was probably so excited to hear from you she forgot."

"Maybe so," Coal replied and let her thoughts drift off into the stillness.

Hearing a dark mood creeping into Coal's voice, Stormy sighed. "It's really beautiful out here, isn't it?"

"Yes, it is," she agreed, and they fell into a comfortable silence listening to the wood crackling in the fire ring.

The sky filled with streaks of green and yellow as meteors sliced through the night on their way to earth. Stormy felt Coal shudder as she sat next to her. "Are you cold?"

"No, I'm warm."

"What was that shudder, then?"

"Those." Coal nodded toward the sky and looking up as the storm continued.

"They are beautiful, aren't they?"

"Yes, but they remind me of the tracers used at night in the desert to help locate enemy targets. They would fill the skies for hours, until you forgot the sounds of gunfire."

Stormy draped an arm around Coal's shoulders. "I'm here if you want to talk about it."

"It's ridiculous; they're just damned meteors."

"Yes, they are, but they triggered a painful memory for you. You're safe and far away from the desert."

135

"I know," Coal responded with a haunted look.

The tears glistening in her friend's eyes made Stormy's heart lodge in her throat. Coal was the epitome of strength and bravery in her eyes, and seeing her hurting like this was almost unbearable. "You know, before I came to Texas, I'd stretch out in the bed of my truck and watch these storms for hours in the early spring. Once I even think I found a fragment of a meteor buried in a pasture."

Coal let out a deep breath. "What did you do with it?"

"The meteor was about a four-pound chunk of what looked like iron and granite mixed together. Rather ugly, but it made a great doorstop." She grinned. "Too bad I left in such a hurry and didn't bring it with me."

"Maybe you'll find another piece. Some of it looks like it's headed in the direction we're traveling."

"I'll keep my eyes open for sure," Stormy replied.

"Thanks."

"For what?"

"For being here to remind me there are beautiful memories to outshine the bad. Tessa and I used to drive out to the plains to watch them too. The excitement in her eyes set me on fire, and we'd end up making love in a sleeping bag until the sun came up before climbing back in the cab to drive home."

"That sounds like some great memories," Stormy replied. "You think I can get Del in the bed of my truck like that?"

Coal laughed, and it was a pleasant sound. "If anyone could, I know it'll be you, my friend. Doc has loosened up so much since you two got together."

"You saying Del's a loose woman?"

"With you, hell yes."

"It's good to see you smile."

Coal looked up into the starry night. "They're just fucking meteors."

"That's right, they are." She stood and stretched. "I'm going to go relieve my bladder and get saddled up."

"Watch out for poison ivy."

Coal stared into the sky, watching the streaking meteors. She shook her head, shattering the memory of the desert and stood to walk over to where Shadow was tethered. He turned his head at her approach, and she slid her hand down his side.

"Are you ready to do some work?" She reached down to pick up her saddle blanket and stretch it across his back.

"Have I told you lately how much I hate peeing in the woods?" Stormy growled when she joined Coal.

"Better get used to it. That's all we have for the next ten days or so."

"Maybe next year we can bargain for a porta potty if we get to return." She grinned. "Or even an outhouse."

"Keep dreaming, my friend." Coal chuckled while she cinched the saddle. "I guess you didn't see the potty chair in the back of the wagon."

"What are you talking about?"

"The aluminum chair with a toilet seat on it." She chuckled again.

"Damn, so why didn't you tell me?"

"Cause I like to hear you bitch about peeing in the woods."

"I see how you are." Stormy grinned. "Did you grab a spotlight?"

"Yeah, I did." Coal swung up into her saddle and raised the spotlight hanging from her saddle horn to show Stormy.

†

They left camp and rendezvoused with Gene and Tony ten minutes later.

"How's the herd doing?" Coal asked Gene.

"All settled in for the night. I have a feeling it won't take me long to settle in either."

"Get some sleep and we'll see you in the morning."

"G'night, boys," Stormy called.

"Stay safe," Tony replied and they turned toward camp.

†

Stormy and Coal rode in a large circle around the herd. The night was relatively quiet, except for the chirping crickets and the occasional lowing of one of the cattle. The rhythmic creaking of the leather beneath her threatened to lull Coal to sleep.

"It's almost too quiet out here," she said to initiate a conversation with Stormy, who had also fallen silent.

Stormy jerked awake. "Damn, I think I actually drifted off in the saddle."

The moon had risen high before the meteor storm faded, creating a glow above the resting cattle. A cool breeze had picked up, so Coal slipped her coat over her shoulders, and a distant howl broke the eerie silence.

Stormy looked over at her. "Wolf or coyote?"

"I'd guess wolf in this area. Let's see if he gets an answer to his call."

They sat in silence for several minutes with no answering call. "I guess we have a lone wolf in the area, probably a young male looking for a mate." Coal gazed into the dense night.

"I hope that's all he's looking for."

"He's miles away from us," Coal assured her. "A solo wolf would never attack a creature the size of one of the cattle alone. A pack could easily take one down, but one wolf will prey on smaller game."

"I'll take your word on that. I heard them in the distance growing up, but never saw one while working the herds. Plenty of bears, though, and I pray we don't run up against one hungry from the long winter hibernation. They can be terrifying."

"I hope we don't either," Coal agreed before they resumed circling the herd.

†

Nancy and Tom arrived to relieve them, and Coal was eager to climb into her sleeping bag. She tended to Shadow, placing a warm blanket over him and fresh food and water in his buckets.

"I don't know about you, but I'm whipped," she admitted when she and Stormy entered their tent.

"My body feels like it's been up for days," Stormy groaned while she kicked off her boots.

Coal piled her clothes in the corner and entered her sleeping bag wearing thermal underwear. The bag was cool, and the pad they had placed between them and the ground did little to soften their beds. Exhaustion crept in quickly, and thoughts of the hard ground drifted away as Coal slipped into a deep sleep.

Chapter Nine

Coal woke early from the cold creeping into her bones. She checked her watch and saw it was five o'clock. She could hear movement around the camp and she prayed it was Georgia with a pot of coffee ready to get her blood pumping again. She slipped on her clothes and boots, then left the tent where Stormy remained curled up in a shivering ball.

Outside, a light ground fog limited her vision. The herd softly lowed in the distance, and Coal smiled when she saw the roaring fire someone had built. Gene was sitting on a log bench, sipping coffee with Georgia. He smiled at her when she approached.

"Good morning," he welcomed a bit too cheerfully for the early hour. "How did you sleep?"

Coal stretched. "Good until the cold crept in and woke me."

"It was colder than usual last night," Georgia said. "You ready for some coffee?"

"More than ready."

"Sit tight and I'll grab a cup for you," Gene offered, smiling at her while she moved toward the fire to warm her hands.

"Thanks, Gene."

"Mind if I make a suggestion?" Georgia asked.

"Not at all."

"Zip your sleeping bags together and share your warmth with Stormy. Two bodies are always warmer than one."

"I'll suggest that tonight. That does make good sense. My bones hurt from being so cold."

"I'd gladly offer to heat y'all up," Gene stated as he handed her a steamy cup of coffee.

"Eww, boy cooties in our tent?" she cried with a grin.

Gene broke out in a grin of his own.

"Don't laugh, a few more nights like last night and I may take you up on your offer."

His laughter stuck in his throat. "Yeah right."

"What offer is that?" Stormy croaked as she joined them at the fire.

"Gene's volunteered to keep us warm at night."

"Oh really, you think you could keep up with us, big boy?" Stormy asked and Gene blushed furiously. "Man, I love it when you blush."

"Stop it," Gene cried out. "You want coffee?" he asked and headed off to the cook wagon to escape her teasing.

"Do y'all always tease him like this?" Georgia asked.

"Always," they replied in unison.

"We love to watch him blush," Coal told her.

"He's a cutie," Georgia admitted.

"Good Lord, don't let him hear that or his hat won't fit his swollen head," Stormy warned.

Georgia chuckled. "Are you bunch ready for some breakfast?"

"We're always ready to eat," Gene remarked, then passed Stormy her coffee.

"Can we do anything to help?" Coal asked.

"Nope, I've got this. You can go ahead and break down your campsite when you finish your coffee."

"Relax a bit and I'll get your sleeping bags and tent stored," Gene offered. "I've already had two cups, so it's not safe to give me more."

"I'll help you, Gene." Coal set her cup on the log.

†

Working together, they soon broke down their campsite, and Gene packed away the equipment while Coal and Stormy tended the horses. They placed feedbags over their heads and removed the blankets.

"I hope you stayed warm last night, big boy," Coal told Shadow and stroked down his flank. She looked over at Stormy. "Ya know, Georgia recommends we zip our sleeping bags together and snuggle to keep ourselves warm. You okay with that?"

"To keep from freezing my ass off for another night? Heck yeah."

"Let's try it, then." She checked Shadow's hooves, picking out a few clumps of packed mud.

†

The rest of the crew started arriving while Stormy, Gene, and Coal feasted on eggs, bacon, and cheese grits. When Nancy showed up, they were nearly finished eating.

142

"When you three are done eating, will you ride out to replace the crew guarding the cattle and get any stragglers back with the herd? We usually have one or two wander off in the dark. This danged fog gets them confused too."

"No problem." Coal stood and carried her dishes to the cook wagon. "Thanks, Georgia."

"Welcome." Georgia nodded and continued to stir the next batch of scrambled eggs.

†

They soon reached the pair of cowboys circling the herd.

"Go grab some coffee and breakfast," Coal said when they arrived. "We'll take it from here."

"You won't get an argument from us. I'm ready to toast my buns at that fire. I lost feeling in my butt an hour ago." Tony groaned.

"I can understand that." Coal watched as they moved off toward camp. "Let's check the herd," she said to Gene and Stormy, and they spread out to circle the cattle and pick up any stragglers.

†

When Nancy and the rest of the crew joined them, they began moving the herd north. The ground fog had burned off with the rising sun, and the dew kept the dust down until midmorning. The clean scent of evergreens filled her nostrils while Shadow plodded along behind the herd. The mountain peaks in the distance drew her attention. A white blanket of snow created a glare when the sunshine glowed off them.

This is gorgeous. Coal pulled out her camera and took several shots of the scenery before Stormy and Gene filled

143

her lens. She took pictures of her friends while they concentrated on moving the herd. Stormy must have felt eyes on her and turned to find Coal's camera pointed at her. She smiled and then nodded to Coal when she lowered the camera.

†

They ate a brief lunch in the saddle to keep the herd moving and by late afternoon had moved the cattle into a fertile valley where they would stop for the day. Georgia had parked the cook wagon against a stand of evergreens and was looking off in the distance. When Coal turned her head to see what she was looking at, she saw a large cloud of dust over the stand of trees. She cocked her head, curious about what was causing it. Moments later, the sound of thundering hooves filled her ears.

The first of the wild horses burst through the forest, threatening to startle the herd of cattle. Shadow quivered beneath Coal, eager to join in the run.

"Easy, big boy."

"Hold tight, everyone," Nancy called out while a herd of a hundred wild horses galloped by, tended by two young Native Americans. The young woman of the pair peeled off from the racing herd and rode toward Nancy, a jet-black braid flying through the air behind her head. She pulled to a stop close to Nancy and spoke in a strong voice.

"Sorry, Ms. Tucker, I didn't realize you were moving the herd through today."

"No problem, Tanya. I guess Dad forgot to call the rez again."

Stormy and Gene raced after the group that had bolted at the sudden appearance of the horses, leaving Coal and Nancy within earshot of the horse wrangler.

"The herd looks like it's growing," Nancy said to Tanya.

"We've been lucky to add two dozen foals this year. Geronimo, the stallion leader, has been a busy boy." Her gaze wandered to Coal.

Nancy grinned at the obvious attraction. "Coal Bryan, this young rascal is Tanya Bearclaw. The other daredevil is her younger brother, Thomas."

"Nice to meet you, Tanya."

"Likewise. You aren't one of the usual Tucker hands, are you?"

"No, Coal and two of her fellow hands are on loan from a rancher in Texas," Nancy said.

"Wow, Texas. That must be a great place. I'd love to visit there one day."

"It's much hotter and not as beautiful as this place."

"It gets hot here in the dead of summer, but I'm sure nothing to compare to Texas." Tanya's gaze never left Coal's.

"Would you and Thomas like to join us for dinner tonight?" Nancy asked, a smile twinkling in her eyes.

"Yeah, that would be great. Let me help him get the herd settled for the night and we'll ride over."

"I'll let Georgia know we have two more for dinner."

"Cool." With a final smile at Coal, Tanya galloped off to catch up with the herd.

"Energetic young woman." Coal grinned.

"Smitten with you, apparently. She and Thomas are in charge of the herd each summer when they're home from college. Tanya is studying to be a vet, and Thomas is in business administration. They are the pride of the rez."

"Cute and smart." Coal chuckled, then urged Shadow forward, leaving a smiling Nancy behind.

†

Coal tended the horses while Gene and Stormy set up camp with the rest of the crew. She spent a few extra minutes brushing down Shadow before placing his blanket on for the evening.

"We've got the midnight shift tonight, big boy, so stay warm. Maybe tomorrow we can get a good run in." She stroked down his flank. "I know you wanted to run with the mustangs today, and I did too, but that's not what we're being paid to do." She chuckled softly and whispered, "Maybe we'll get a chance on the return trip."

†

The aroma of fried pork chops filled the air as she returned to camp. Georgia had been busy since she arrived to set up camp, and dinner was almost ready. Thomas and Tanya had joined them and were sitting around the campfire talking with the group when Coal walked over. Tanya introduced her brother and smiled brightly when Coal sat beside her.

"Nancy says you're in vet school."

"If I'm lucky I'll finish next year and can sit for the boards."

"What then?"

"I plan to come back here to start a practice. I've spent my youth growing up with these mustangs, and I don't think I could ever leave them."

"That's a very honorable plan. Will there be other opportunities to practice in the area?"

"I hope she will become our vet," Nancy chimed in.

Tanya beamed. "I would love that."

"The job is yours when you're ready."

"Thanks, Ms. Tucker."

"Please call me Nancy, like everyone else."

"Yes, ma'am."

"Dinner's ready," Georgia called.

"Damn I'm starved," Gene groaned.

†

Gene was disappointed he and Tony had pulled the first shift of guard duty again. He was enjoying listening to Tanya and Thomas talk about running with the mustangs.

"We'll see you guys later," he told them and went to saddle his horse.

"I guess we should be moving on too, before it gets too dark to find our camp. When do you think you'll come back through?" Tanya asked Nancy.

"We should be back in five days. It'll take us three more to get to the summer pastures and another day to make sure the herd is set, then another day's ride to make it back here."

"It might be fun to have the Texas crew experience running with the mustangs. Do you think you could take some time out for that?"

"Absolutely," Nancy replied. "That's the least we can do for our Texas crew."

"Oh hell yeah." Coal grinned. "That would be a blast."

"We'll meet you back here then," Tanya told them. "Thanks for a great meal."

"Thanks for the great company. We'll see you in five days," Nancy replied.

"Good night, ladies." She tipped her hat to Coal with a warm smile.

"Stay safe," Coal said.

"You too." Tanya disappeared into the dark.

"Are you two going to catch a few hours of sleep?" Nancy asked, nodding toward Stormy.

"I think it'd be a good idea. I don't know about Stormy, but I'm whipped."

"You okay for guard duty tonight? We can always substitute if needed."

"No, ma'am, I'll be good to go by midnight," Coal assured her.

†

"I wonder how our crew is doing on the cattle drive," Harley said to Melissa and Doc Bo while they shared coffee on the front porch that evening.

"I hope they're having the time of their lives. I made reservations for hotel rooms in Billings for the rodeo today. Stan assured me he can handle anything that might come up while we're gone, so pack your bags."

Harley grinned. "I can't wait. I haven't been to Montana in the spring for a long time. I wish you could go, Doc."

"Me too, but I need to get settled into the practice. I'll be ready to go to the Texas rodeos, though."

"It's a lot of fun watching the kids, but I sure don't miss the bruises and sore muscles." He grinned.

"I can understand that."

148

"Speaking of old bones and sore muscles, I think I'll call it a night, ladies. See you in the morning." He tipped his hat to them and stepped off the porch.

"Good night, Harley," Melissa called.

"See you for breakfast." Cam watched Harley step into the night. When she turned around, Melissa was looking at her.

"Do you want to stay out for another cup?"

"I'd like that; it's such a nice night."

"We won't get many of these, especially with a nice breeze. Sit tight and I'll get us some more." Melissa carried their cups inside the house.

Cam sat in one of the cane-bottomed rockers and gazed out at the fireflies, their yellow-and-green flashes glowing against the blackness of the night. Memories of nights spent watching the fireflies with Sheila flooded back to her and silent tears slid down her cheeks.

Melissa pushed through the screen door and Cam rushed to wipe her tears before Melissa could see them, but her efforts came too late. "Is something wrong?"

Cam continued to dab at her eyes. "A memory just took me by surprise. Sheila and I used to cuddle up on our porch swing and watch the fireflies. Seeing these tonight brought that rushing back to me and it caught me off guard."

"That happens to me sometimes. Something happens and for a moment I forget Mitch is no longer here with me."

"I know exactly how that feels. The hurt comes rushing back all at once and overwhelms you for a moment."

"Sometimes longer." Melissa sat on the porch swing and took a sip of coffee. "There are times when I think this is all a bad dream and one day I'll wake up and the world will be right again."

Cam stood and went over to sit beside Melissa. "I've been there and damn near drank myself to death trying to end that nightmare. Then I realized, the world can be right, and I had to move on. I mostly have Harley to thank for that."

"He's a good man and an even better friend."

"I'm glad to have crossed paths with him again."

They sipped their coffee in silence for several minutes. Melissa turned on the swing and placed her hand on Cam's thigh. "I realize how much hurt and loss we share, and I'm glad you've come to us and I'm proud to have you for a friend."

Cam smiled at her. "I feel at home and enjoy the feeling of family I get from everyone here."

"We are one big happy family, and I'm grateful to add you to our motley crew."

Cam chuckled softy and looked down to see Melissa's hand still resting on her thigh. She understood it was nothing more than a friendly gesture and lowered her arm to cover Melissa's hand.

Melissa made no effort to move away. "Thank you for taking in a broken-down old vet," Cam said as the tears returned.

"You're not broken down or old to us. We each have our perceived flaws, and the way we accept them in ourselves and others is what makes us such a cohesive group."

Her answer lodged in her throat, so Cam nodded her agreement.

"Come, let's call it a night and get some sleep," Melissa said.

Cam followed her into the house, and when Melissa stopped outside her bedroom door, she turned back to her. "Good night, Cam. Sleep well, my friend."

"You too," she answered and walked past Melissa to her room.

†

The full moon was high in the sky when Coal and Stormy rode out to relieve the other riders. The few hours of sleep had refreshed Coal, and the night air felt chilled but good against her cheeks as she leaned down to pick through her saddlebags until her hands landed on the item she sought. She pulled out her flute and brought it to her lips. She hadn't played in some time, and the beautiful sound floated across the crisp air while they circled the herd. Even the cattle seemed to enjoy the soothing music while they chewed their cuds and eyed her curiously as she and Stormy passed by.

Coal played for an hour until she saw the beam of a flashlight coming through the forest ahead of them. She stopped playing, curious to see who was approaching.

"Don't stop playing or I won't find you," Tanya said.

Coal resumed playing while she and Stormy rode toward the approaching light.

When Tanya finally stepped into the clearing, she looked up at Coal. "I knew that had to be you playing. My grandfather used to play to the herds too to soothe the tired or stressed animals."

"What are you doing out this late?" Coal asked.

"I heard you playing and thought I'd bring you some hot coffee to warm you," she answered holding up a thermos and two empty cups.

"That's very kind of you. I apologize if my music disturbed your sleep."

"Quite the contrary, it soothed me like it does the animals and brought back fond memories of my grandfather when I

151

was young. I hope you take cream and sugar." She grinned up at Coal.

"That sounds perfect." Coal rewarded her with a smile, and Tanya removed the lid from the thermos and poured a cup for each of them. Coal looked over at Stormy, her smile evident in the low light.

"Thanks," Stormy replied as she took the cup from Tanya. "Ah, that feels good already."

"It's been a chilly night. Even the campfire does little against the cold breeze," Tanya commented. "It's usually not this cool this time of year."

"I have to admit, I didn't think it was going to be like this," Coal told her.

"A late cold front is moving through, but this should be the last of it after tonight according to the weatherman."

Stormy chuckled. "I need a job like that."

"Why would you want that?" Tanya asked.

"What other job do you know where you can be so wrong and still keep your job?"

"Ah, gotcha." Tanya laughed softly. "Well, this is Montana, and the weather's been known to change in a matter of minutes. I hope he's wrong later in the week. He's predicting rain in two days."

"Aw now, I could've gone all night without hearing that," Stormy cried.

Stormy stopped moaning when the stillness of the night erupted with a mournful howl. Coal looked off in the direction of the sound while sliding her hand down to the butt of her rifle.

"You can relax, Coal, that's just Gimp. He won't attack the herd."

"Gimp?" she asked.

"My nickname for him. He's a timber wolf I found injured a few years ago in a poacher's trap. I couldn't save several of his toes, so he walks with a limp. Therefore, I called him Gimp. He's been in the area ever since but has never attacked cattle or horse." She grinned up at Coal. "He's played hell on the rabbit population, though, and every now and then he downs a small deer."

"You sound as if you know him well," Coal said.

"He follows us while we move the herd. Thomas teases me about Gimp being my guardian angel."

"I'd say it was probably the other way around if you saved him from a trap. That took a great deal of courage to approach an injured wild animal."

"My mother would agree with you, but I couldn't stand to hear his cries of pain, and I didn't have the heart to shoot him, so I doctored him the best I could and left his fate to Mother Nature."

"You're gonna make a great vet," Stormy said. "You've got a good heart."

"Thanks." Tanya ducked her head shyly.

Coal was sure if there had been more light she would have seen a blush on Tanya's cheeks. She was about to agree with Stormy's statement when she heard two riders approach. She turned in her saddle as Nancy and Tom, another cowboy on the ride, emerged from the darkness.

"Hey, boss."

"Hey, ladies, I didn't know coffee service was on the menu for tonight," she teased Tanya.

"It's all Coal's fault. I heard her playing her flute, so I thought I'd bring her something to warm her up."

"Can you make a repeat performance in about an hour?" Tom asked.

"The best I can do is leave you the rest of the coffee in the thermos."

"Tom's just teasing you, Tanya. You need to get your rest too."

"I'm so ready for my sleeping bag," Stormy replied, stifling a yawn.

"Thanks for the coffee, Tanya." Coal nodded to Stormy. "Come along, Sleeping Beauty. See y'all in a few hours for breakfast." She turned Shadow toward camp.

"Good night," Nancy called after them. "Rest well."

†

They unsaddled and tended to the horses before entering the tent. Coal sat on the sleeping bag, and began removing her boots and outer shirt. "Even this hard ground is going to feel good tonight," she groaned when she lay back.

Stormy hurried to climb into the sleeping bag after pulling off her boots and outer layers. "I can almost see my breath in here. You mind if I snuggle with you?"

"Are you really that cold?"

"Yeah, I am."

"C'mon, then, just watch those wandering hands of yours," she warned and turned onto her side away from her friend.

She felt Stormy snuggle into her back and carefully drape her arm across her hip. Coal smiled until she felt the coolness of Stormy's body. "Damn, you are cold." She reached back to pull Stormy closer.

"Yeah, and you're warm. Thanks. How do you deal with the temperature change so much better than me?"

154

"I guess I just have a different metabolism, or maybe it's just from the exposure in the desert. It was scorching-hot in the daylight, but freezing cold at night."

"I'll take advantage of your metabolism, then. I sure don't want to go to the desert."

"Good night, Stormy."

"Night, Coal. Thanks for getting me warm."

Coal quickly drifted off to sleep, Stormy's warm breath puffing against her neck.

†

Stormy grew warmer while she snuggled into Coal. A grin spread across her face when she thought of Nancy and Tanya, who would both jump at the chance to snuggle with Coal. She buried her face in Coal's hair, where the fragrance of her shampoo still lingered, and slipped into a deep, restful sleep.

Chapter Ten

Nancy kept glancing at the angry, dark sky forming ahead, the clouds roiling as they grew heavy with moisture. "I'd really like to get the herd across the river ahead of that rainstorm," Nancy told them around breakfast.

"I have to go south several miles to find a place I can safely cross," Georgia replied. "I'll arrive when I can, but it may be a late dinner tonight. It will take me most of the day to catch up with the herd."

"We've all got jerky and other snack items in our saddlebags," Nancy told her. "If we beat you to the campsite, we'll go ahead and get a fire started. Let's finish breakfast and get the camp gear stored on the wagon so Georgia can get underway," she instructed the crew.

"I'm done, so I'll get started breaking down the tents," Gene replied, then took his dishes to the wagon.

"Hang on, Romeo, and I'll help you," Stormy called after him.

Coal smiled at her friends. "If you two can get us packed, I'll start saddling the horses."

†

Once Georgia was safely on her way, Nancy called the crew together. "I'd like to have the herd across the river by early afternoon if possible. That will allow us to reach the campsite before the sun goes down."

"Let's get them up and moving," Tony told Gene.

"We'll spread out once we're moving if you and Gene want to take point," Nancy told them.

"Sounds good to me, boss. When we get close do you want me to ride ahead to scout out a river crossing?"

"Pick us a good spot. Hopefully the water's not too deep or fast moving yet. This is the part of the drive I dread each time," she told Coal and Stormy. "Hopefully we won't lose any of the herd this year."

Gene and Tony caught up with Tom and Joe while they circled the herd. "Let's get them moving," Tony called out to the men.

Tom let out a whistle and made a circular motion with his hand to Joe. Joe nodded and they began pushing the herd forward while Gene and Tony circled around to retrieve stragglers that had drifted during the night.

Within the hour, the herd was moving steadily north. The crew was strategically spaced around the edge of the herd, watching for breakaways. Coal took up the rear position, and Stormy rode ahead of her with Nancy off to her right. Gene and Tony were completely out of sight in the dust the herd kicked up. She pulled the bandana up from her neck to cover her face.

†

The sun broke through the cloud cover by late morning, a trickle of sweat rolled down Coal's back. Several steers had broken away from the herd, and she and Shadow had chased them down and returned them safely after a brief run. She welcomed the respite from the monotonous plodding while the herd moved north, and hoped another would attempt a breakaway soon.

"Heads up, big boy. Maybe another steer will break away," she told Shadow when they'd brought the last steer back to the herd.

†

The herd was slowing down when Gene raced back toward them. Nancy motioned for the rest of the crew to join her at the rear of the herd. When they had all arrived, she looked at Gene for a report.

"We've found a good spot to bring the herd across about a mile ahead. The water isn't very deep and isn't fast-moving like other spots we looked at."

"That's good news. Has everyone had a chance to snack, or do we need to take a break before we move on?"

"I think we can keep moving. Once we get the herd safely across the water, we can take a short break if we need," Coal chimed in. "I don't know about y'all, but I'll rest easier once we're across the river."

"This will be the only difficult part of the drive," Nancy assured. "It's a slow incline from there until we get to the mountain pastures."

"Let's do it, then," Gene eagerly replied.

Nancy grinned at his excitement. "You and Tony can start them across and keep them moving forward. I'm thinking it'll take about twenty minutes or so to get them all across, so keep them moving north for a half hour and the rest of us will catch up with you when we're across."

"Yes, ma'am." He tipped his hat and cantered ahead of the group.

"You heard the man. Let's do it. You okay in the back with me?" Nancy asked Coal.

"Yes, ma'am,"

The crew got the herd moving once more while they took their positions, and Coal remained vigilant for any breakaways.

†

The herd began to stretch out in a narrow line when they approached the river. Gene and Tony drove the head of the herd into the water, keeping them organized to cross in the area they had selected. After they began to cross safely, he and Tony left the frigid water for dry land to keep the cattle moving.

Coal could see Stormy and the rest of the crew when they entered the water as the bulk of the herd crossed over. She and Nancy had the last grouping of twenty head to push across. Nancy was off to the right, and she looked over and smiled at Coal when they were close enough to see the water.

The majority of the herd had crossed by the time they reached the riverbank. The passing of the cattle ahead of them had dredged out a path across the river, and when the first of their grouping hit the water, she and Nancy could see it was deeper than originally reported. The cattle sank into the water up to their bellies as they struggled across.

Coal grimaced as a steer stumbled in the deeper water. This can't be good. Please just let us make it across.

They only had three more animals to push across, when a steer hit a soft spot in the riverbed and sank to his shoulders. He tossed his head and struggled against the current, which only brought the water closer to his nostrils, increasing his risk for drowning. Coal raced toward him and flew out of the saddle and into the river, where she grabbed his head and lifted it above the rushing water. The adrenalin rushing through her veins kept her from feeling the frigid water as it soaked through her clothes.

Nancy pushed the last two across and turned to find Coal struggling with the stranded steer. She left her horse on the riverbank and rushed back into the water to help Coal as she struggled to free the steer.

"Damn, this water is cold," Nancy cried out as the water rushed up to her knees while she waded out to the steer. "How can I help?"

"I'll hold his head out of the water if you'll grab my rope, and Shadow can help us pull him out."

Nancy approached Shadow, took the rope, and secured it around the steer's head.

"Tie it off to my saddle horn and come help him keep his head up out of the water," Coal instructed.

Nancy worked quickly, and when she returned, the panicked animal was struggling to free himself from the muddy bottom.

"Keep his head up," Coal said. When Nancy nodded, she asked, "You ready?"

"Hell yeah, let's get out of this cold-ass water.

"Shadow, back," Coal yelled. "Back, big boy."

Shadow backed up, taking up the slack on the rope while Nancy kept the steer's head above water. Coal wrapped her arms under the steer's front shoulder and lifted, trying to free his front legs as Shadow pulled him forward. As the steer began to move forward, she strained harder to lift his legs free from the sucking mud. Shadow reached solid ground where he could pull with more force, and suddenly the steer broke free and lunged forward, knocking Nancy off her feet. Coal reached forward to steady her, and Nancy's momentum sent them both into the water.

"Damn," Coal cried when she returned to her feet with Nancy in her arms. Their bodies pressed together, and their faces were only inches apart for several long moments. An image of kissing her flickered through Coal's mind. She smiled at Nancy, and lifted her to her feet, fighting off the urge.

Nancy felt the firmness of Coal's body when she held her to keep her from falling below the water's surface. For a brief moment, she thought Coal may lean in and kiss her, and had to admit she was disappointed when she only smiled and helped her to her feet. Her smirk turned to a frown.

They were both soaked as they emerged from the river onto solid ground.

"Good boy," Coal called to Shadow while he kept tension on the rope, preventing the confused steer from moving back toward the dangerous water. She moved them farther away from the water, then removed the rope from around the steer's neck. She looked back to find Nancy standing beside her horse already shivering.

"Shit, that's cold," Nancy groaned, her teeth chattering.

"We need to get to the campsite quickly and get out of these wet clothes."

"Let's catch up with the herd and then ride ahead. I'm ready to be near a blazing fire."

Coal mounted Shadow. "I hear you. I needed a bath, but not that way."

"The faster we go, the sooner we'll be there." Nancy swung up in her saddle.

They quickly caught the steer that was now in a full run, eager to rejoin the herd. Stormy was the first to see them approach while she munched on a strip of jerky.

"What on earth happened to y'all?" She grinned.

"We had a steer get bogged down and we had to pull him out," Nancy told them. "If y'all can bring the herd in, we're going to ride ahead and get out of these wet clothes and get a fire started."

"Yes, go ahead, boss, we've got this," Tony assured her.

Gene turned in his saddle, untied a blanket, and handed it to Coal. "I don't have any extra clothes, but this may help until Georgia arrives with dry ones."

"Thanks, Gene," she said.

They collected two more blankets, then raced ahead of the slowly moving herd.

"Damn that has to feel miserable," Gene said to Stormy.

"That's one way of getting Coal out of her clothes." She grinned back at him.

Gene shook his head. "Girl, you are so not right. Is that all you think about?"

"Most of the time."

They rode out to take up their positions.

†

When Coal and Nancy arrived at the next campsite, they quickly dismounted. Charles, the man Nancy had sent ahead of them had left firewood prepared in the fire pit, just waiting for a flame to bring it to life. They looked at the stack of wood, and Nancy turned to Coal. "Damn, that fire pit is ready, but I have no way to ignite it."

Coal grinned, the dimple on the left side of her face growing as she smiled, and walked over to Shadow. Nancy watched her rummage through her saddlebags. "I've got this. I keep a Zippo and waterproof matches in my saddlebags."

Nancy lifted an eyebrow. "Are you always this well prepared?"

"If I was, we'd have dry clothes on by now."

"Good point. I'll unsaddle the horses if you'll get the fire going."

Coal nodded. "Get out of those wet clothes, then you can wrap up in the blankets."

Nancy picked up the reins and led the horses to two trees with a rope stretched between them. She tied them off and began removing the tack.

Using pinecones and dried grass, Coal got the fire started. The flames licked up the sides of the wood and slowly grew into a blaze. She pulled her boots off and placed them next to the fire pit to dry, then walked over to the horses.

Nancy had stripped down to her underwear and was reaching for a blanket when Coal arrived. Her face grew hot when Coal appraised her nakedness and then with a grin began to undress.

"Wrap up tight in a couple of those blankets and hang out your clothes. I left my boots by the fire, hoping they'll dry out overnight. The fire's lit, so go get warm and I'll finish up here."

"Thanks, Coal. I thought he would drown before we could get him out."

"Not with us around. Go before you catch your death of cold."

Nancy wrapped one of the blankets around her and tucked the end under her arm, then took another blanket to wrap around her shoulders and stepped over to the fire. Taking advantage of Coal's back being turned, she sneaked her own peek at Coal. Her face changed from a smile at the sight of the tattoo, to a frown when her gaze landed on the scars scattered down Coal's back and shoulder.

Coal hung out her wet clothes and wrapped a blanket around her. She draped her socks over her boots, hoping they would dry quickly so she could put them back on. Nancy sat on a log next to the fire and stretched her legs out in front of her.

"Man, this feels good," she remarked when Coal sat down beside her. "I'm not trying to get fresh," she said as she opened the blanket Nancy had around her shoulders and wrapped it around them before moving in close to Nancy. "If we share body heat, we'll both warm up faster."

Nancy chuckled. "I wouldn't even mind if you were getting fresh if it means I can get warm."

Coal picked up a bag of jerky and offered it to Nancy. "Care for some jerky?"

"That sounds good." She took a strip and handed the bag back to Coal, then took a bite and moaned. "This tastes like steak."

"Not quite, but it'll do for now until Georgia arrives. We both could use something hot to drink."

"Some hot chocolate would go down nice right now," Nancy admitted.

"How much longer do you think before she'll arrive?"

"Hard to tell. If she made a good crossing, I'd say no more than two hours."

"That will be about the time the herd arrives, won't it?"

Coal could see her squint as she calculated the time. "Probably so. Maybe we can get into some dry clothes before they get here."

"That would be nice." Coal ran fingers through her own damp hair.

They chewed on the jerky in silence, the popping of the wood the only sound near them other than the rushing water of the river off to their left.

"This would be a nice spot if we weren't freezing our asses off," Nancy replied, breaking the silence between them.

"Yeah, it would. It's a beautiful spot for a campsite."

Nancy shivered when a chill raced through her. Coal briskly ran her hand up and down Nancy's back to generate some heat. "Better?"

"Much, thank you." She looked up at Coal. "You seem to know a lot about survival skills."

Coal nodded. "Uncle Sam trains us well. The time I spent in the desert taught me a great deal about cooling down and staying warm. The temps could soar above a hundred degrees and then drop down near freezing at night."

"That must have been miserable."

"I hope to never see another desert," Coal replied with a far-off look in her eyes.

Nancy imagined Coal was reliving a memory, so she let her contemplate in silence as Coal stared into the campfire.

†

Warmth slowly returned to Coal while they huddled beneath the blankets. Nancy had fallen asleep and rested her head on Coal's shoulder. She jerked awake when the logs collapsed in the pit.

"Sorry, I guess I drifted off."

"No problem. How are you feeling?"

"Toasty except for my feet." She chuckled.

"Let me put more wood on the pile and we can wrap our feet in the blankets," Coal suggested and crept from underneath the top blanket. She placed several large logs on the pile, and when she turned away from the fire, she saw a plume of dust in the distance. "I think Georgia will be here soon. That's too far to the east to be the herd."

"I hope you're right. We can get clean, dry socks and some warm clothes. Do you have an extra pair of boots or shoes?"

"I've got both thankfully," she answered while she snuggled under the blanket.

†

"Well, this certainly looks like it has an interesting story behind it," Georgia said with a grin when she pulled to a halt at the campsite. "What on earth happened to the two of you?"

Nancy smiled at Coal. "She can fill you in while I get some dry clothes on." She climbed into the back of the wagon to retrieve her gear.

Coal chuckled and helped Georgia down from the wagon's seat. "I guess you could say the river crossing didn't go like we expected. We made it down to the last group to go across and one of the steers got bogged down in the mud."

"I reckon the entire herd passing through the same area left it pretty rough."

"That it did. The steer was in jeopardy of drowning after he sank in the soft mud, so I jumped down to lift his head above the rising water." They walked toward the fire pit. "Nancy and I used Shadow's help to pull him free, but we weren't expecting to get him unstuck from the mud so quickly, and she lost her balance."

"Now I see. You rushed to catch her and you both took a dip," Georgia said as if she had been there to witness the event.

Coal grinned. "That's about the size of it. So we both rode ahead of the herd to get out of our wet clothes and get warm by the fire."

Nancy emerged from the wagon fully dressed in dry clothes. "If she hadn't caught me, it would have been much worse. Damn, that water was cold too." Her eyes smiled when she looked at Coal. "Your turn. Thanks for letting me go first."

Coal climbed into the wagon and pulled out fresh underwear, thermals, jeans, a flannel shirt, and her thickest wool socks. *Ah, now this feels much better.* She slipped into her spare boots and emerged from the wagon to find Nancy and Georgia around the fire. "I'd love to have something hot to drink," she said as she walked over to them.

"Of course. I don't know what I was thinking. Coffee or something else?"

"Nancy mentioned hot chocolate."

"That's easy. I'll be back." Georgia climbed into the wagon.

"This is so much better." Coal lifted her hands to warm them as she stood by the fire.

A few minutes later, Georgia returned carrying three mugs of hot chocolate. "Here you go."

Coal placed both hands around the mug. "This feels better already."

They turned their heads at the sound of hooves to see the herd approach.

"I guess I'd better get started on some dinner," Georgia said.

Coal turned to Nancy. "Let's finish our drink and set up camp. Maybe we can get the tents up before the others arrive."

†

Cam was sitting on the top rail of the corral looking at a group of horses delivered to the MC2 for training. They were a fine-looking bunch, and she was lost in thought when Harley walked up to her.

"Hey, Doc, whatcha doing?"

"Just looking over the stock that arrived today. They look like a healthy herd."

"The young'uns will be delighted to hear they have horses to train when they return from Montana."

"I hope they're having a good time on the drive."

"I'm sure they are. How are you doing Doc? Getting settled in okay?"

"You, Melissa, and the others make it feel like home."

"I hope you'll make it home for a long time." He climbed up beside her.

"I'd like that too," she admitted. "Are you excited about the trip to Montana to watch them rodeo?"

Harley grinned at her. "Before our Christmas trip I hadn't been there since I was a young man. I do remember it is beautiful country, though, especially this time of year."

"I'm looking forward to watching them later this year." She turned at the sound of a closing screen door to see Melissa and Bo stepping off the porch to join them.

Harley caught her glance. "He's recovered well from the snakebite, hasn't he?"

"Nothing short of a miracle, but I'm afraid Gene's going to return to find his pup spoiled rotten."

Harley chuckled while he watched them approach. "If that ain't the God's truth, I don't know what is. Hey, boss."

"Hey, are you two about ready for some dinner?"

"I'll never turn down your cooking," Harley answered, then he climbed down from the railing.

"I've got smothered pork chops, rice, corn, and biscuits ready if y'all are."

"I'm all over that." Cam stepped down too.

"Too bad Coal isn't here. That's one of her favorite meals," Harley stated.

"I'll be glad when they get back. It is way too quiet around here," Melissa told them as they walked toward the house.

†

Across the pasture, Mary Leah was making a salad while she talked on the phone with Del. "Yeah, they should just about be halfway through with the drive."

"I hope they're having a great time. I don't know about you, but I miss the hell out of Stormy."

"I know what you mean. It's so quiet in the house, I think I can hear my heartbeat."

Del chuckled. "Do you want to meet me for dinner and a movie tomorrow night?"

"That would be great. Call me tomorrow and we'll decide where to meet," Mary Leah answered and ended the call. She took her salad to the table and looked down at

169

Dolly, Bo's sister. Her warm brown eyes looked sad to her. "I know you miss her too, don't ya, girl?"

The dog's wriggled her rear end in excitement.

"It won't be much longer until she'll be home," she assured the pup.

†

"That was an excellent meal, Georgia," Nancy told her before she stood and stretched.

"I'm glad you enjoyed it. Would you like me to put a pot of coffee on?"

Nancy nodded. "That would be great. I don't think the chill has left me entirely."

"Y'all picked a heck of a time to take a dip," Gene teased.

"That's got to be the coldest water I've ever felt," Coal answered.

"It was wicked cold. I'm glad you were able to get warm by the fire and get some dry clothes," Stormy replied.

"I've never been so happy to see Georgia pull up in the wagon," Nancy told them.

Gene knew Coal was still feeling the effects of the cold water while she sat huddled in her coat by the fire. "Why don't the two of y'all skip a shift tonight and get a good night's sleep in a warm sleeping bag," he suggested.

"I can handle my shift," Coal answered.

"We know you can," Stormy jumped into the conversation, "but there's also a huge chance of you getting a chill that turns into something more."

"They're right Coal," Nancy admitted. "We really haven't recuperated fully yet."

"You can make it up to us later." Gene grinned and shot her a wink.

Coal shook her head. "Okay, you got it."

"Would you like to take the first shift with me?" Gene asked Stormy.

"If y'all can handle the shift until midnight, we can handle the rest of the night," Tony offered.

"That sounds like a good plan to me," Gene agreed. "You ready to saddle up?' he asked Stormy.

"I'll have a thermos of coffee ready for y'all by the time you're ready to ride," Georgia called from the wagon.

"Let me grab my coat and I'll meet you at the horses," Stormy told him, then returned to the tent.

"Thanks," Coal told Gene.

"You'd do the same for us." He smiled.

"Yeah, I would." She grinned back at him.

"See you at breakfast," he replied and went to saddle his horse.

Tony stood and stretched. "We're going to catch a few hours of sleep," he replied, leaving Nancy, Coal, and Georgia alone at the fire.

"Let me get that thermos ready," Georgia stated before returning to the wagon.

Coal added fresh logs to the roaring fire before returning to sit beside Nancy. She picked up her mug of coffee and took a sip. "That still feels good going down."

"It's not going to hurt either of us to have a full night's sleep."

"I know you're right, but I still feel slightly guilty about not carrying my load."

"You've done more than your share on this drive, so don't sweat it."

"Will we still reach the mountain pastures tomorrow?"

"Hopefully by late afternoon so we can all enjoy a good night's rest."

Georgia returned with the pot of coffee and refilled their cups. "If we get there early, I'd like to grill the steaks before our dry ice dies."

"That sounds really good," Nancy agreed.

Darkness fell around them while they chatted around the fire. Georgia took their empty mugs and retired for the night. The rippling of the river and crackling of the fire filled the night, broken occasionally by the lowing of the cattle or the cry of an owl. A blanket of stars filled the sky.

"It's really peaceful out here, isn't it?" Coal asked.

"I was just thinking the same thing. I think I'll fall asleep to the sound of the water tonight."

"I'll build up the fire if you want to call it a night," she told Nancy.

"Thanks again for everything, Coal." Nancy nodded and left the fire pit.

Coal added several thick sections of wood to the fire that she hoped would keep it burning deep into the night. She looked into the darkness but couldn't discern any movement that would indicate Stormy and Gene were near, so she slipped quietly into her tent.

†

Coal listened to the sounds of the night until her eyes grew heavy. The sleeping bag wrapped around her like a warm cocoon. She slept deeply, waking only briefly when a chilled Stormy crawled in with her.

"Sorry to wake you," Stormy whispered.

"No problem, I'll go right back to sleep," Coal snuggled into Stormy's chilly body to share her warmth. "Good night." "Good night." She pulled the sleeping bag over them, a smile playing across her face.

†

Her aching bladder woke Coal just as the sun was coming up. She crept from the tent to relieve herself, slipping her coat over her shoulders. Seeing no other sign of life in the camp, Coal went about bringing the fire back to life. The embers still glowed with heat and welcomed the dried wood she positioned across them to start a blaze. The flames grew and the wood crackled as Coal took a seat on a log, looking across the field, searching for movement.

A bank of fog rolled across the surface of the river, limiting her vision. The herd rested quietly while she enjoyed the peacefulness of the morning. Several minutes later, she heard movement behind her and turned to find Georgia walking toward her.

"Good morning."

"Good morning. Are you ready for some coffee and company?"

"Of course." Coal smiled at her.

†

Georgia sat beside her after handing her a mug of coffee, and Coal smiled. "Thanks." She watched her breath form a fog in front of her.

"Still kinda cool out here, isn't it?" Georgia asked.

"Yeah, it is, but peaceful too."

"Did you sleep well?"

173

"I barely moved all night. How about you?"

Georgia smirked. "Not bad once Nancy quit snoring."

"I think we were both extremely tired after yesterday's excitement."

"The shock of being that cold can really sap your energy. I'm glad you were able to get warmed up when you did."

They turned when they heard a zipper sliding down and saw Gene creeping out of his tent. "Morning," he whispered.

"Help me up and I'll get some coffee for you," Georgia said.

Gene gave her a boyish smile. "Sit tight and I'll get it. Either of you need a refill?"

"You can bring me one." Coal handed him her mug.

When he returned and sat beside Coal, Georgia looked at him "Do you think you could eat some pancakes this morning?"

"Oh yes, ma'am! I love your pancakes."

"They should be enough to hold you until we arrive at the mountain pasture."

"Do you need some help?" Coal asked.

"Nope, I've got this, but thanks for asking."

"I'll go wake Sleeping Beauty, then, and we can start breaking down the camp. Nancy wants to get an early start."

Gene chuckled. "I'll feed the horses and start packing up my stuff too."

†

Tony and John arrived just as Georgia finished the first batch of pancakes, and she handed a plate to Gene.

"I thought I smelled food cooking," John stated.

174

"Tend to your animals, and I'll have another batch ready in just a few minutes."

Coal and Stormy were rolling up their tent when Nancy stepped outside of her tent and stretched.

"Good morning, ladies," she called. "Did I sleep that late or are y'all getting an early jump on breaking down camp?"

"We thought we'd start on camp while Georgia cooked breakfast. Tony and John just rode in, so once we eat breakfast, we can finish breaking down camp and get the herd moving," Coal told her.

"Good idea." Nancy went back inside, presumably to roll up their sleeping bags.

Coal and Stormy helped her break down the tent after placing their gear on the wagon.

"Take a break and come eat," Georgia called out to them.

"We'll be right there," Stormy answered before shooting a grin at Coal.

"I'll meet y'all in a minute. I've got to answer the call of nature," Nancy told them before disappearing into the woods.

†

"Man, I can't wait to get to the cabin," Tony stated while they rode out to start moving the herd.

"What cabin?" Gene asked.

"The cabin we're going to be staying in for the next two nights." Tony grinned. "There's a small cabin at the mountain pastures. So if you want a break from the cold ground, you can sleep on a cot inside."

"That will be a nice break,"

"Let's get a move on then, cowboy."

175

Gene looked at Coal and Stormy. "You heard the man, let's get this party started."

†

The sun was bright while they moved the herd up the steadily increasing incline. Coal couldn't believe what she was experiencing, but the air seemed even fresher the farther north they rode. The breeze had a slight chill as it blew into her face while they pushed the herd toward their destination. She was thinking about how fast the time had passed when she heard a whoop from the front of the herd. She looked up to see what had got the men hollering. In the distance, she could see a cabin tucked into the tree line, smoke rising from the chimney disappearing into the dense forest ahead. She shivered as the temperature seemed to drop with every step forward. Steam puffed from the nostrils of the herd while they plodded forward, eager to feed on the sweet grasses of the mountain meadow ahead.

Something cold and wet landed on her cheek. *This can't really be happening.* But several small flakes of snow were swirling through the air, melting the second they made contact with the ground or anything else solid. She watched with wonder as the flakes landed on the coats of the animals, leaving glistening droplets of water behind. She couldn't help but smile at the beauty of the moment.

Stormy rode back to where Coal was staring up at the sky. "I bet you never thought this would happen, did you?"

"Not in a hundred years. Do you think it will stick?"

"Sadly no, the ground is too warm and the temperature isn't low enough to maintain the flakes."

"It's still beautiful." Coal smiled when she looked at her friend.

"That it is. It probably won't last long." She fell into stride beside Coal. "It will be nice to be under a roof tonight, won't it?"

"Definitely. I'm looking forward to sleeping on a cot tonight."

"Are you still glad we came?"

"Absolutely, I've had a blast on this drive and hope we can do it again."

"Me too, and Gene's excited about the possibility of returning to bring the herd back down in the fall."

†

When the last of the herd arrived in the meadow, Nancy motioned the crew to come to her. "Let's tend to the horses and then join Georgia in the cabin. I hope she's got some hot coffee brewing."

"I hear that, boss." Tony grinned. "It's dropped a good twenty degrees from this morning."

"The snow flurries were a surprise," Nancy told them. "We've only encountered snow once in the last ten years."

Coal unsaddled Shadow and brushed him before placing the thick blanket over his back. She filled his feed bin and water. "I'll see you a bit later," she promised and went inside the cabin.

†

"I've got to run into town for supplies. Is there anything you need?" Cam asked Melissa.

177

She looked up at Cam and forced a weak smile. "Not that I can think of, but thanks for asking."

Cam noticed her lack of energy and frowned with concern. "Are you okay? You don't seem your normal chipper self."

"Is it that obvious? I'm actually missing the kids. I didn't realize how attached to them I've become."

"I know where you're coming from, but I don't see any of them as kids."

"Yeah, I know they're all adults, but in a sense I feel like they are mine. Mitch and I were never blessed with children, so I guess I've kind of adopted each one of them as they've come into my life."

Cam smiled. "They'll be back home soon. I miss them too. It is way too quiet around here without their banter and teasing, and I don't know them like you do, so you must be missing them a lot more. Why don't you ride to town with me and you can tell me about them. I'll even spring for lunch."

"There's not much going on here, so yeah, I'll ride with you. Would you mind stopping by the pharmacy so I can check on Mary Leah? I haven't talked to her in a couple of days."

"I need to get some supplies there too, so that's no problem. Do you want to give her a call and see if she can join us for lunch?"

"Yeah, that's a good idea."

"I'll bring my truck around and pick you up when you're done."

"See you in a few, then." Melissa smiled and left the office.

Cam watched her leave, then picked up her supply list. She found herself smiling when she thought of Melissa. *I need to be careful and not tread too close to the fire with this one.* Cam had decided she would never have another love for her, but her growing feelings for Melissa had her questioning that decision.

She drove her truck to the front of the house to wait for Melissa. Cam was scrolling through radio stations when she looked up to see Melissa bounce across the yard toward her truck. *Damn, damn, damn, she sure looks sexy.*

Chapter Eleven

Coal sat by the window sipping coffee while watching the snowflakes swirl through the air and disappear when they reached the ground. *This is so beautiful. I wish Mary Leah were here to see this.* When footsteps approached, she turned to find Nancy beside her. She leaned down and placed a hand on Coal's shoulder while she looked out the window.

"It's beautiful, isn't it?"

"Yeah, it is. For a moment I found myself hoping it would stick."

"It's not entirely impossible after nightfall, but highly unlikely. Come back in the winter and you'll get all the snow you want." She removed her hand to brush back a lock of hair that had fallen into her face.

Coal smiled up at her. "Yes, it's beautiful up here in the winter."

"I hope the three of you know you'd have a job with us if you ever tired of Texas."

"We appreciate that. But it may be a long time before any of us gets tired of Texas. I do hope, though, you'll allow us to help with future drives."

Nancy chuckled as she gazed out the window. "What are you doing in about five months?"

"Coming back to Montana maybe?"

"We'll need help to bring the herd home."

"You know how to reach us. We'd jump at the chance."

"It will definitely be cooler and your chance of real snow will be much higher then."

"So what's next?"

"We'll spend another day here to make sure the herd is settled in and all accounted for, and then we'll head back home. You've got a date to run with the mustangs in two days."

"I'm so looking forward to that."

Nancy turned back toward the kitchen. "Tanya seemed pretty excited too. I'm going to check on dinner."

Gene and Stormy strode into the room, laughing and wiping snowflakes from their arms. Gene looked over to see Coal sitting by the window. "Man, coffee sounds good."

"Grab some and come join me. We need to talk."

Stormy cocked her head at Coal. "That sounds mysterious. We'll be right back."

Coal watched them shed their coats before entering the kitchen. "Something smells great," Gene stated as they helped themselves to the coffee.

Georgia smiled up at them. "Steaks with veggies, and biscuits. Dinner will be ready in about a half hour."

"Wonderful." Gene grinned. "Do you need our help?"

"No, I've got this, but you can carry more wood in from the porch for the fireplaces."

"Not a problem," he answered. "Let me finish this coffee and I'll get right on it."

"Coal and I'll help too so it'll go faster."

†

Cam and Melissa dropped Mary Leah off at the pharmacy after lunch, and then headed back to the ranch. After they'd pulled into the drive, Cam turned to Melissa. "I'm going to store these supplies and spend some time out in the office."

"I'll check in with Harley and Stan. Do you have any preferences for dinner?"

"I'm so full from lunch I can't think of food right now."

Melissa chuckled. "I'm sure you'll change your mind in a few hours."

"In a few hours, yes. Do you want me to drop you off at the house or the bunkhouse?"

"You can park and I'll walk across the yard. Do you need help with the supplies?"

"Nope, I've got this. I need the exercise so I can eat another huge meal."

"I'll see you later, then."

Cam watched Melissa disappear inside the bunkhouse and then with a smile she carried the first of her bags into the office. After two more trips, she stored the supplies in the cabinets and added several items to her medical bag. Tomorrow she would take inventory of the supplies in her truck storage compartments and restock what she needed. She planned to spend the rest of the day scheduling appointments for the next week. Melissa and Harley would leave for Montana on Thursday with Del and Mary Leah, leaving her alone at the ranch, and she would need something to keep her busy while they were gone. She picked up the phone to begin making calls.

†

"Welcome back," Harley called when Melissa entered the bunkhouse. He and Stan were sitting at the table reviewing some paperwork.

"What are you two up to?"

"Taking a look at this year's rodeo schedule. It came in the mail today," Stan answered.

She walked to the coffeepot, poured a cup, and joined them. "Does it look like we can get the hay season in between events?"

"That shouldn't be a problem." Stan scratched his head. "Maybe even train a few head of yearlings."

"I know four cowhands that will enjoy hearing that information." Harley chuckled.

"That they will. I wonder how the drive is going for them."

"They should be on their way back in a day or so, I'd think," Harley replied. "A couple days' ride back to the ranch and they'll be ready to load up and head to the rodeo grounds."

Melissa took a sip of coffee. "Do you still think we can drive it in two days?"

"Easily," Harley answered. "We won't be pulling a trailer, so it will be much faster for us."

"Del suggested we take her Land Rover. Are you okay riding in that?" she asked Harley.

"As long as I can drive."

"I don't think anyone will argue with you over that. Now how does that schedule look?"

They pored over the schedule until Stan stood up and stretched. "If you don't need me for anything, I'll head out for the night. Is there anything in particular you want me to do while you're gone?"

"Check on Doc Bo to see if she needs anything."

"Okay, I also thought I'd do some maintenance on the equipment to make sure it's ready to begin the hay season in a few weeks."

"That's not a bad idea, and you should be uninterrupted with us gone."

"That's what I was thinking." Stan grinned. "Will I see you before you leave Thursday?"

"That's a possibility. I don't think we'll need to leave at the crack of dawn."

"I'll see you tomorrow, then." He left the bunkhouse.

Harley poured refills of coffee and sat beside Melissa. "Speaking of Doc Bo, what's she doing?"

"She was going to put away her supplies and do some work in the office."

Harley smiled. "She seems to be fitting in well in our little community. I've heard several compliments about her skills already."

"Word travels fast among ranchers. It's nice to have her nearby if we have any emergencies."

"That's an added bonus. I was thinking it's time for some chicken-fried steaks. I'll cook everything else if you'll make the gravy. You know, after all these years I still can't make a decent gravy."

Melissa chuckled. "Some things just aren't meant to be, my friend. Would you mind if I asked Mary Leah to join us?"

"Of course not, the more, the merrier."

"I think I'll head back to the house to give her a call and start some laundry. Is there anything you need?"

"No, ma'am, I'm good here. I think I'll take Doc Bo some coffee and check on her before starting dinner. Is dinner at six okay with you?"

"That sounds fine. I may even whip up something for dessert."

"Now we're talking." Harley stood to pour coffee for Doc Bo.

"See you later."

"Bye, boss." He stirred some sugar into the cup and went to the barn.

†

Cam hung up the phone and penciled in another appointment on her calendar.

Next few days are going to be busy, but that'll help the time pass more quickly. I can't believe how attached I've become to my new family so fast. It's been years since I felt so close to anyone.

She was deep in thought when Harley walked into the office and held out a cup of coffee. "Mind if I join you?"

She smiled at him as she reached for it. "You're welcome anytime, especially if you're bringing coffee."

He looked at her desk calendar. "It seems like you've been busy."

"I thought I'd visit some of the other ranchers while everyone is gone."

He took a seat across from her. "It's not too late for you to join us."

"Thanks, but it's too soon to ask Doc Cone to take calls for me after he's just retired. I'll be more settled and ready to join y'all for some of the Texas rodeos, once the season starts here."

"We haven't had much time to talk since you arrived. Are you comfortable here?"

"Are you kidding? This place feels right to me. It's been the first time since Sheila—died that I actually have a home and family."

"You fit in well with our motley crew."

"I can understand why you love it here. Do you ever miss the rodeo circuit?"

"Like I'd miss a toothache. Going to a few events every year with the crew here is plenty for me, and I don't wake up stiff and sore. Rodeo is for the young ones, and these old bones will not qualify as young anymore."

"Surely there are events you could compete in. Team roping or some of the speed contests, maybe?"

"I'd rather just watch the crew here kick some cowboy butt."

"Some of them quite literally, I take it. Coal seems to have a storm of emotions running through her."

"She's had a hell of a life so far, but there's no one I'd rather have in my corner in the midst of a shit storm. She can kick some ass, but she'd just as gladly give someone the shirt off her back."

"Quite the enigma." She took a sip of coffee.

"That would be a good descriptor for Coal. There's also loyal, passionate, damaged, courageous, to name a few."

"Like a daughter to you?"

"I'd be honored to have a kid half as good as Coal. When she showed up at the MC2, she was pretty shattered, but through hard work and a lot of therapy, she's pulling her life back together."

"I'm sure she's learned a lot from you. You're a good friend, Harley."

"Thanks. She's also a good friend."

"I've enjoyed getting to know her—all of them, actually. They are quite a diverse group."

Harley chuckled and picked up his coffee cup. "You got that right. We're having chicken-fried steak tonight at six."

"Is there anything I can help with?"

"Melissa's making the gravy and a dessert, I think, but you can come keep me company when you're done here."

"That sounds easy enough. I'll finish up here, take a quick shower, and see you soon." She handed him her empty coffee cup. "Will you put on a fresh pot?"

"Absolutely." He left the barn.

Hank strolled into the office and jumped up on the desk, ready to have his chin scratched.

"Aren't you the charmer?" Cam scratched his uplifted chin. Satisfied, the handsome black cat stretched out across the front of the desk, fixing his green eyes on her as she worked. She finished making her notes and slipped the pen into the holder.

He watched as she stood and stretched. "I bet you thought I forgot." She went to a cabinet, opened the door, and pulled out a can of cat food. Hank stood to watch her, and when she pulled the tab, he jumped to the floor. She removed the lid, stepped over to where his food bowl was waiting, and dumped the can into it. Hank rubbed against her legs to show his appreciation and began eating his treat.

Cam turned off the overhead light and left the office, depositing the empty can in the trash on her way out of the barn.

A nice hot shower and a good meal and I'll be out like a light tonight.

†

Melissa called Mary Leah to invite her to dinner, then put a load of laundry in the wash. She was eyeing the contents of her pantry when inspiration hit and she decided to make a bowl of banana pudding.

"Sorry, Gene, I know how you love this, but maybe you're having a great meal tonight too."

She finished preparing the dish and placed it in the refrigerator to chill. Tossing the clothes in the dryer, Melissa decided she'd take a shower before dinner.

†

Cam entered the house and heard the dryer running but saw no sign of Melissa. She assumed she had already gone to the bunkhouse to help Harley. She entered her room, stripped down to her shirt and panties, then grabbed a fresh towel to head to the bathroom.

She opened the bathroom door and froze. Melissa had just stepped out of the shower and was reaching for a towel.

Cam's cheeks burned from the blush that covered them as her gaze traveled down Melissa's body. As hard as she tried, she could not look away.

Melissa smiled and grabbed her towel to begin drying.

"I'm sorry, I didn't realize you were in here," Cam finally stammered as she backed out of the bathroom, her face still ablaze.

"No problem, Cam. I'll be done in just a few, and the shower's all yours."

"Thanks." She pulled the door shut behind her, then hurried to her room and closed the door before leaning back against it. "Holy shit." Her heart hammered.

†

Melissa couldn't suppress her smile as she dried her skin. No one had looked at her in a long time with the appreciation Cam had just shown her. She never thought she could feel an attraction to another person after Mitch, but Cam was making that a very real possibility. Melissa could see Cam's attraction in the way her gaze caressed her. She'd been unable to turn away or at the very least avert her eyes, as any embarrassed person would have. Now she had to decide whether she was ready to admit to a mutual attraction. *What a dilemma.* She wrapped the towel around herself and opened the door. Looking down the hall, she found the door to Cam's bedroom closed. She walked to it and knocked. "All yours," she called out and went to her room to dress.

"Thanks." Cam had slid down the door and was sitting there while her mind raced. She couldn't possibly deny a physical attraction to Melissa. Hell, she couldn't kid herself; the attraction went way beyond physical. "What do I do now?"

She waited until she heard Melissa leave the house and confirmed her departure with a quick glance out the window.

189

Then she went to the bathroom, hoping the pulsing water could clear her head.

†

Melissa was halfway to the bunkhouse when she heard Mary Leah pulling into the yard. She turned toward the car and waited for her sister. "Hey there, sis," she said as Mary Leah approached, then pulled her into a hug.

"Did you have a good afternoon?"

"Yeah, I did. How about you?"

"My afternoon was starting to drag, and then you called to tell me Harley was doing chicken-fried steaks. That was enough to help me make it through the shift."

"That is a great source of motivation. Come on and let's go see how he's doing."

†

Harley whistled when he cooked, and he was whistling away when they entered the bunkhouse.

"You sure have it smelling good in here," Melissa told him.

"Thanks. I'll be done with the steaks in just a few minutes. The potatoes are boiled and ready to mash, and the corn is on simmer."

"Do you want me to mash the potatoes?" Melissa asked.

"That works for me. I have to know, did you make dessert?"

"Crap, I forgot all about that. Mary Leah, will you go over to the house and bring the bowl of banana pudding from the refrigerator?"

"Oh hell yes," Mary Leah answered and left.

"Where's Doc Bo?" he asked.

"She was showering when I left the house," Melissa answered with a smile.

Harley caught a glimmer of something in her eyes as she smiled at him. He cocked his head at her, but refrained from asking what was making her smile so brightly. In the months after Mitch's death, he feared she would never smile again, so he welcomed it now. *But still, I wonder....*

†

Cam sat on the bed and pulled on her boots. The shower had done little to clear her head. She took a deep breath and left the room, hoping her face wouldn't give her away when she walked into the bunkhouse and looked at Melissa. She might be able to fool Melissa, but she was sure Harley would be able to tell what was going on if she didn't get her shit together. She had a great opportunity here and didn't want her attraction to Melissa to screw things up.

She stepped out of her bedroom just as someone entered the kitchen. *Good, I can do this here, just the two of us.* She walked to the kitchen, expecting to find Melissa, but instead she found Mary Leah removing a bowl from the refrigerator.

"Oh, hi, Doc Bo. Melissa sent me for the dessert she made for us. Have you had her banana pudding yet?"

"No, but I bet it's delicious. I haven't eaten anything in a week that wasn't."

Mary Leah chuckled. "Welcome to mealtime at the MC2."

"You want me to take that for you?"

"I think I can handle one bowl."

"I know, but if you're carrying it, I can't accidently get a taste."

"Good Lord, you're as bad as Coal."

"I'll take that as a compliment." Cam held the door open for them.

Thunder rumbled in the distance as they crossed the yard. Mary Leah looked at the darkening sky. "We may get some rain tonight."

Cam turned to look at the thunderheads growing in the distance. "You may be right." She followed her inside to the bunkhouse's kitchen.

†

Melissa used an electric mixer to whip up the potatoes as Harley removed the last of the steaks. Without looking up from her task, she gave them instructions. "Stick that in the fridge and y'all can set the table and pour some drinks."

"Yes, ma'am," Cam answered, glad to turn her back to Melissa for a few more seconds as she pulled plates and glasses from the cupboard. When she turned around, Melissa was looking directly at her and smiling. Cam's heart lodged in her throat, but thankfully, she didn't blush. She averted her eyes as she walked to the table. *Damn, damn, damn. She's going to kill me with those eyes.*

"I think we've got rain moving in," Mary Leah said. "It was thundering in the distance just now."

"A nice slow rain would do us good," Melissa replied. "It would be good for the hayfields."

"That and maybe kill some of this dust for a day or two," Harley added. "I've got to ride some fence line tomorrow, so it'd be nice to not eat dust all day."

"You need some help with that?" Melissa asked.

"Nope, I'm good. Besides, you need to pack for our trip."

"What about your packing, when you going to do that?"

"I've been packed and ready for two days now."

"That figures." Cam chuckled. "You always did travel light."

"That's the deal. So let's eat up so everyone can get home before this rain hits." He brought a platter of steaks and corn on the cob to the table while Melissa finished the gravy.

"Mary Leah, will you grab the potatoes and hand me a bowl for the gravy?"

"You got it, sis."

†

"My word, that was a great meal," Mary Leah groaned after swallowing a bite of steak.

"Don't forget we have dessert," Melissa reminded them.

"I certainly haven't forgotten." Harley stood and walked to the refrigerator and returned with the bowl. Then he retrieved three bowls from the cupboard and carried them to the table.

"Didn't you forget one?" Cam asked.

"Umm, no, so I suggest you get all you want the first time around, because I get what's left." He grinned and picked up his spoon.

"He's not kidding," Melissa said.

"Well, alrighty then." Cam filled up a bowl and passed it to Mary Leah. "One down, two to go."

"You can make mine half that size," Melissa requested.

"You sure? This is your only chance."

Melissa grinned. "Yeah, I have a second smaller bowl for later if you want more."

Cam passed her a bowl, and when their fingers touched briefly, her cheeks warmed. She quickly pulled away and filled her bowl, then pushed the other bowl to Harley.

Melissa took a bite and moaned. "Very tasty if I do say so myself."

The moan vibrated through Cam. *I wonder if she's intentionally trying to kill me.* She fought off a shudder and concentrated on her dessert. "This is great."

A rumble of thunder broke the silence as they enjoyed the pudding. "It's coming in fast," he said. "If you're finished, you need to head home before this storm hits, Mary Leah. Take the bowl with you if you want."

"Nope, I'm good." She put her spoon in her empty bowl. "Thanks for a great meal."

"You're welcome. Call to let me know you made it home," Melissa said as Mary Leah stood to leave.

"Yes, Mama. I'll call you in a few."

Melissa walked her to the door.

"Let me help you get cleaned up," Cam told Harley.

"No, you two need to go too. I can handle this."

"It won't take long if we both work on it."

"I've got all night, so go already."

"Okay, we'll see you tomorrow. You ready?" Melissa asked.

"I'm right behind you."

Harley watched as the two women stepped off the porch. When they'd taken three steps, the clouds opened up. As they dashed for the house, laughing, Harley couldn't help but smile. Melissa skidded to a halt when she reached the porch and waved to him. Harley waved back and returned to the kitchen, shaking his head.

"Whew, that was cold," Melissa cried out when they entered the house, and then broke out laughing again.

They were both sopping wet, but Cam couldn't prevent herself from joining Melissa's infectious laughter. When she could finally stop, she looked at Melissa, who was still bent over laughing. Her wet hair framed her face when she looked up at Cam, whose chest tightened, making it hard to breathe. Cam slid down to the floor, unable to look away from Melissa. "What in the world are we laughing at?"

Melissa sat down in front of her. "I have no clue, but I'm having a hard time stopping."

"I noticed." Her own laughter threatened to erupt again until she turned her eyes away from Melissa.

I have to do this now before I lose my nerve. Melissa leaned forward, taking Cam's face in her hands and turning it toward her. When Melissa looked into Cam's eyes, she saw a longing in them she could not resist. She leaned in farther and softly brushed her lips across Cam's chin, then up to her lips.

Holy shit, she's going to kiss me. Breathe, dammit, breathe. When Cam looked into Melissa's eyes, she saw excitement, and a look of wonderment crossed Cam's face. Is she battling the same demons as me? Are we betraying Sheila and Mitch by being attracted to one another? There, I admitted it. I do want her to kiss me so badly.

Dear God, her lips are softer than I imagined. A faint moan filled the air between them, and Melissa was surprised to learn the sound came from her. She wanted more, but she would not push Cam. *Her eyes tell me she wants me too, but we can't rush.* Melissa sat up straight, her eyes never leaving Cam's once she ended the kiss. She watched the smile on Cam's face grow from her cheeks to her eyes, glistening as they filled with tears.

Tears, oh my God, what have I done? "I never meant to hurt you, but I had to kiss you to know," she whispered to Cam.

"You haven't hurt me by any stretch of the imagination. What is it that you need to know?"

Melissa took a deep breath and let it out slowly. "I needed to know if you wanted the kiss as much as I did."

"I did and I do," Cam answered as a tear slid down her cheek.

Melissa used her thumb to brush away the tear. "Why are you crying?"

Cam shook her head. "Like your laughing, I have no idea why I'm crying."

"Well hell, aren't we a pair?"

"What do we do now?"

"First thing is to get out of these wet clothes."

Cam cocked her head and looked at Melissa curiously.

"To put something dry on, you goof." Melissa punched her arm lightly. She stood and offered Cam her hand. "Then, my friend, we need to talk."

Cam nodded and took Melissa's hand to stand up. "Coffee or something stronger?"

"I think we'd be wise to stick to coffee. I'll start a pot and meet you back here in a few minutes."

†

Cam nodded again and went to her room to change clothes. *Wow, just fucking wow, such a tender, yet powerful kiss.* Her smile grew as she traced her lips with a finger. Just moments ago, Melissa had kissed them. *Should we be doing this?* Cam grabbed a towel and began drying her skin. She opened a drawer and selected a pair of sweatpants and a T-shirt. She slipped the pants up her hips and was about to slide into the T-shirt when her nipples grew hard. She pulled a sports bra over her head. It wouldn't keep them from showing, but they would be a little less obvious. Sliding her feet into warm house shoes, she ran her fingers through her still-damp hair and left her room.

†

Melissa started the coffee brewing and entered her bedroom. She shed her damp clothes and briskly rubbed her skin with a towel to take the chill from her. When she went to the dresser, her gaze landed on the photograph of Mitch and Tessa. She touched the glass and trailed her fingers down the photo. "I miss you so much. Would you forgive me for loving someone else?" His handsome face smiled at the camera, at Coal who had taken the picture.

He understood the love Coal and Tessa shared, but would he approve of me loving Cam? So many questions and I have no answers. Whoa, me loving Cam. Where did that thought come from? She dressed in a pair of Mitch's pajamas. Worn soft from years of use, they felt comforting against her skin. She slipped her feet into thick socks and then took a slow, deep breath that she held for several long moments. She let it out slowly and returned to the kitchen.

†

The pot had just finished brewing as Cam entered the kitchen. She retrieved two cups from the cupboard and poured their coffee, then carried them to the small kitchen table. She smiled to herself as she took a seat.

Why is it that so many important conversations occur around a kitchen table? Her heart raced as footsteps came down the hall.

Cam looked up when Melissa entered. Melissa gave her a tentative smile. She could feel the warmth in Melissa's eyes as they locked on her. She sat down beside Cam.

"I went ahead and poured your coffee."

"Thanks, you make it taste so good." Melissa lifted the cup to her lips and took a sip, then returned it to the table and looked at Cam, who waited to see who would bring up the subject first.

Melissa traced the rim of the cup with her fingertips. "I can't say I'm sorry for kissing you, because it would be a lie."

Cam watched Melissa's fingers and her imagination went into overdrive. She imagined how they would feel circling her nipples, making them grow painfully hard and pressing against her bra.

I need to stop allowing my imagination to run wild and concentrate on what she's saying.

Melissa hesitated, as if searching for the words she wanted to say.

"I can't deny I enjoyed the kiss. I've been wanting that with you all evening," Cam said.

"Since the shower?"

Cam nodded.

"The way you looked at me made it hard to breathe. I don't know if I can explain that, but your eyes told me how much you wanted me. Does that make sense?" Melissa finally said.

"Probably more so than any explanation I can offer. I have no words to accurately describe how you make me feel when you look at me."

"Do you feel a twinge of guilt? Like you're cheating on your partner?"

"For a brief second, it did cross my mind, but I know she would want me to be happy, and if being your friend would make me happy, I have no guilt."

"I think Mitch would want the same. But I want more than to be your friend. I never dreamed I would fall in love again after he died, and I haven't been interested in anyone until you arrived." She paused for a second. "I'm not saying I'm in love with you yet, but I do want to give us a chance."

Cam sat speechless as she listened to Melissa. Her throat felt parched, and she attempted to swallow while forming a response. She ended up clearing her throat and wiggling in her seat. She was sure she and Melissa could grow to be great friends, but did she want to risk losing that friendship if a relationship didn't work? It was a lot for them to take into consideration. The kiss could change her world forever if she let it. Was she ready to open her heart and risk letting it get broken?

"Cam, are you all right?"

"Yes, no, hell, I don't know," she answered as honestly as she could.

Chapter Twelve

"I'm pretty sure I know what your answers will be, but Nancy has invited us back to bring the herd down in the late fall. It'll be a lot colder with a better chance of snow, but we can do this if you want," Coal said.

"Oh hell yes," Gene cried. "I'm surprised you even asked."

Stormy grinned. "I'm in, and by that time Lucas may want to join us too."

"He'll probably need a break from changing diapers by then," Gene agreed.

"I'll let Nancy know we're in after dinner."

"Saaaweet," Gene answered.

"We have another day here, and then we start back to the ranch. We'll be running with the mustangs in two days," Coal reminded them.

Stormy stood to return to the kitchen. "This trip just gets better and better. Drink up, and let's get this firewood hauled before it gets dark."

They gathered their coats and gloves, then spent the next half hour stocking split wood and logs by each of the three fireplaces in the cabin. They were storing their coats when Georgia called them to dinner.

†

After a filling meal, Coal went outside to the small corral to check on Shadow. The snow had stopped falling, and had mostly melted from the ground and trees leaving little evidence to prove it had snowed earlier. "So much for our snow, big boy." She stroked down his neck. "I have to admit, my friend, you look rather handsome in your thick blanket." Athena, Nancy's mare, walked over to them. "Hello, beautiful." She stroked down the mare's face.

Footsteps crunched behind her, and Coal turned to see Nancy approaching. "Hey, boss."

"I thought you might be out here."

"Just checking on the horses," Coal answered as Athena nudged her with her muzzle.

"I think you have another admirer," she replied, nodding toward her mare. "She's usually selective with who she likes, but then again, animals sense good people."

"Yeah, they do."

"They're getting ready to play some poker if you're interested."

"Thanks, but I'll pass. I think I'll enjoy this beautiful evening and then turn in early."

"The campfire's burning well if you'd like some company."

"That would be nice." She stroked Shadow's head and then Athena's. "Good night, you two," she said and turned to follow Nancy out of the corral.

They took seats in canvas camp chairs near the roaring fire.

"This is nice." Nancy stretched her long legs out toward the fire.

"Careful you don't melt the soles of your boots," Coal warned.

She pulled her feet back a bit. "It's been really great having the three of you on this drive."

"It's been a great experience, and we'd like to come back to bring the herd home at the end of fall. Lucas, another of our crew, may want to come too. He and his wife just had their first, so he couldn't make this trip, but I know he'd love to come."

"The more, the merrier. Will you be busy once you return?"

"Oh yeah, we'll have two cutting seasons for hay, yearlings to train, and at least two rodeos, three if we score high enough to make the finals."

"You really love this life, don't you?"

"What's not to love about it? I get to be outside, not cooped up between four walls all day. I get to work with animals and great people. Rodeo is our reward for having a good hay season. We work for a great woman. Melissa springs for all the expenses, so it's like a paid vacation."

"She's a lucky woman."

"We're lucky to work for her. She treats us like family."

"Your partner is her sister, right?"

"Yes, Mary Leah and I have been together a few years now." She knew a sparkle filled her eyes as she spoke Mary Leah's name.

"She's a lucky woman too. If anything ever changes, you'll have a home with us if you ever need one."

"Thanks, and no offense, but I hope I'll never have to leave the MC2."

"I hope you won't either, but remember you have options if you ever need them."

Coal gave her a bashful smile. "That means a lot."

They listened to the crackling and popping of the wood in the fire for a while in a comfortable silence. Coal heard a soft sizzle and then felt a chill on her cheek. She looked up and saw flakes spiraling to the ground.

"Well I'll be damned." Nancy chuckled. "Twice in one day and this late in the spring is just strange for us."

"Beautiful," Coal whispered as the flakes floated to the ground and disappeared.

†

"What should we do now?" Cam stammered, but before Melissa could answer, a bolt of lightning struck close and thunder filled the night. The storm raged outside, stirring the air with electricity, while a different type of current built between the two women.

Melissa had opened her mouth to answer when the telephone rang, making them both jump in their seats. She walked over and picked up the phone. "Hello. Oh, hey, Mary Leah. Glad you made it home. Okay, call me tomorrow. Love you too, sister."

Cam looked at her with wide eyes as she hung up and turned back toward the table.

"Mary Leah made it home safely," Melissa said.

"That's good." Cam took a sip of coffee.

Melissa walked back and covered Cam's hand with hers. "I don't know where we go from here."

'Cam reveled in the warmth of Melissa's hand as she brushed her thumb across her knuckles. "I think we both need to spend some time thinking about our futures. We need to ask ourselves if we're ready to move on from Mitch and Sheila. You also need to determine if you're ready to deal with the stigma of being labeled a lesbian."

"The last part will probably be the easiest. I don't care what others think about my love life. Frankly, labels don't really mean anything to me. Gender doesn't matter to me as long as we're happy and treat each other with love and respect."

"That's easy to say in theory, but society still doesn't accept that two women can love one another. It may be difficult, especially when those who you've known for years turn their backs on you because of your choices."

"I think maybe it's a good thing we'll be apart for a few days. That will allow us time to think. I don't imagine I would be able to do that as clearly with you a few rooms away. I have to be honest, Cam. I find myself growing more attracted to you every day."

"I can't deny it either, but that doesn't make it right for us." The pain in Melissa's eyes made Cam's stomach churn with anxiety. "Maybe a few days apart will bring some clarity to our situation." She brought Melissa's hand to her lips and kissed her knuckles.

Lightning streaked to earth close by and the electricity flickered twice, and then the lights went out.

"Well, there goes our power," Melissa said.

"You're not scared of the dark, are you?"

"No, ma'am." Melissa stood, taking Cam's hand. "We might as well get comfortable while the power is out. No television, no radio, so maybe it's a good time for us to learn more about one another." She led Cam to the sofa.

†

"This is a great night." Nancy nodded toward the tree line. "Snow and Northern Lights in the same night."

Coal looked to the north above the trees and could see a faint green and yellow glow. "That is beautiful."

"When you come back in the fall, you will see the whole show. They'll be in full force then. These are just the last flares of the season."

"I'll look forward to that."

Nancy stood and stretched. "I think I'll call it a night."

"I won't be far behind you. Good night, boss."

"Good night."

Coal watched the brilliant colors dance across the sky for several minutes. Then with a sigh of complete contentment, she returned inside. Most of the crew sat around the table playing cards as she made her way to the bunks. She kicked off her boots and stretched out on a cot.

†

After talking for several hours, Cam and Melissa decided to call it a night. Melissa leaned over to blow out the candle she had lit earlier.

"Thank you for sharing things about you with me tonight," Melissa said as they walked down the hall.

"It was my pleasure, and it was fun to get to know you better."

When they reached Melissa's bedroom door, they stood facing one another like two awkward teens. Melissa stepped forward and pulled Cam's face down for a kiss. When their lips made contact, Cam's parted to welcome Melissa inside.

Cam's strong arms wrapped around her as their bodies melted together and their tongues danced sensually, bringing a moan from deep within Melissa. She knew trying to restrain the moan was useless, and instead let it vibrate in their mouths as her muscles began to quiver with need. Sensing the time wasn't right, she broke the kiss. "Sleep well, and I'll see you for breakfast."

"Sweet dreams," Cam replied, then spun on her heel to continue to her room.

Melissa understood the quivering of Cam's body as they pressed together, and she knew neither of them would sleep without sweet dreams.

Melissa walked to the window to glance into the darkness. A river of rain streaked down the window as a single tear flowed from her eye. She reached up to brush it away. Cam made her feel excited and alive again, so it was a happy tear.

Just two kisses and you've got my heart racing. You feel so right for me.

She undressed and slipped between her sheets, trying to keep her thoughts from dwelling on the woman sleeping so close down the hall.

†

Cam groaned as the phone rang beside the bed. She opened an eye to discover it was barely 5:00 a.m. and reached for the phone.

"Hello. I understand. Yes, I'll be there as quick as I can."

She dressed quickly and scribbled a note to Melissa that she had an emergency call and then rushed to the office to grab her bag and suturing supplies.

Harley was leaning against the side of her truck holding a thermos she prayed he filled with coffee.

"Harley Boone, you're a godsend if that's some strong coffee."

"I guarantee it will wake you up. What's the emergency?"

"Luther Bronson's got a mare who got tangled up in some barbed wire during last night's storm. He's managed to free her, but she's cut up and losing blood."

"You need some help?"

"Thanks, my friend, but I'll be doing a lot of suturing, so there's nothing you can help with. Please let Melissa know I'll see her later today if you would."

"Will do, Doc. Drive safe, and you know where I am if you need me."

She took the thermos and climbed into her truck. As she started down the drive, she twisted the lid off and took a sip.

"Phew, you weren't kidding." She chuckled and took another sip of the strong coffee.

The Bronson place was a twenty-minute drive, and when she arrived, a teenaged girl with tearstains on her cheeks met Cam outside the barn.

"Are you Doc Bo?"

"Yes, I am. Can you take me to the mare?"

"Follow me. Is Misty going to be okay?" she asked as they started walking.

"I'm going to do my best to make her as good as new."

A man rushed toward her as they entered the barn. "I'm Luther Bronson." He held out his hand. "And this is my daughter Ginny."

"Doc Bo," she said as she took it. "Where's Misty?"

He looked at the young girl and put a hand on her shoulder before leading them to a stall.

She went to work assessing the damage, then drew a vial of sedative. "I need some blankets and a portable shop light if you have one."

"I'll get some blankets while you set up the light," Ginny told her dad and rushed from the barn.

"Easy, girl," Cam soothed as she approached to take a closer look at the mare's injuries. Misty was standing, but her appearance was agitated and her eyes were wide with fright and pain. Somehow Misty had gotten one of her back legs tangled, and in struggling to free herself had made a mess of the flesh on the inside of her leg. The outer portion of her leg covered by a thicker coat hadn't received the same intense damage as the sensitive inner leg; none of the cuts there required suturing.

Cam placed the filled syringe between her teeth and pulled out a jar of salve that she spread over the mare's back leg.

Ginny rushed into the barn carrying three large blankets.

"Help me spread them out beside her, Ginny," she instructed. "Luther, set the light up there." She pointed to an area far enough away that the bulb wouldn't increase the temperature in the air around her, but close enough to give her more light.

"Okay, here's the plan. I'm going to give Misty this sedative, which will take effect quickly, and I need you to turn her head back toward me to help me guide her to the ground. Then I'll start an IV to give her fluids and keep her sedated. I'll be stitching for several hours here."

"What can I do?" Luther asked.

"Ask your wife to keep me in coffee. You can do something else, but probably not today. You can get rid of that danged barbed wire and install horse panels."

"I know I should have done it sooner."

"Just get it done when you can."

"I'll get the panels delivered Monday."

"Go tell your wife about the coffee and come back here quickly." She looked at Ginny. "Once she's down, I want you to put her head in your lap and talk to her and let her know she's going to be all right. Can you do that?"

Ginny sniffled, struggling to hold back the tears and put on a brave face. "Yes, ma'am, I can."

"Good, here we go." Cam found a vein in the horse's leg and gave her the injection, then moved around to her other side. "Ginny, take her halter and pull her head back down and toward her tail. I'll help guide her down onto the blankets."

The maneuver went better than Cam expected as the horse's front legs buckled and Cam pulled her down onto her side. Misty's eyes glazed over from the medications. "Okay, get to it." She nodded to Ginny.

Ginny took the mare's head in her lap and soothed her as she stroked it while Cam started an IV and hung the bag of fluids and medication on the stall railing.

Luther returned. "The coffee will be here in a few minutes. What can I do?"

"Do you have a lead or soft rope? Use that to secure her left leg while I stitch. It doesn't have to be tight, but secure enough to keep the leg out of my way."

"I got it."

Cam placed her bag near the horse and kneeled to begin suturing the torn flesh. She looked over at Ginny. "You okay watching this?"

Ginny nodded. "I'm okay."

†

Four hours and two pots of coffee later, Cam finished suturing. She straightened up on her knees stretching her back muscles. She felt every minute that had passed between her shoulders as she sat in that uncomfortable position. She reached into her bag for the salve and handed it to Ginny.

"You need to put this on her cuts twice a day. Not heavy, but just enough to cover each tear. Got it?"

"Yes, ma'am."

She looked over at Luther. "Release her leg and I'll start bringing her around." She injected another medication into the horse's vein and removed the IV. "It's time for you to move, Ginny. She'll start trying to stand in a few minutes."

Cam moved her bag and supplies away from the stall, then returned to the horse's side. Several minutes passed, then the horse stirred, pulled her legs underneath her, and climbed to her feet.

"That's a good girl," Cam soothed as she stroked down the mare's neck. "Keep her in the stall until the sutures come out in ten days." She reached back into her bag and pulled out a box of wrapped treats. "Pain medicine." She handed the box to Ginny. "Give her one later tonight and then twice a day when you put the salve on for the next five days."

"Is there anything else?" Luther asked.

"A bathroom would be nice."

"Of course, Doc. Come with me."

"Call me if you have any questions." She handed Ginny her card.

Ginny looked relieved that Misty would be okay. "Thank you." Ginny hugged her tight.

"You're welcome."

†

Melissa thought she heard a car door close but assumed she'd been dreaming and fell back asleep. When she woke an hour later, she dressed and walked into the kitchen. The house seemed eerily quiet until her eyes came to rest on the note Cam had left her on the counter by the coffeepot. *Emergency call, see you later*, the note read. She was all alone in the house, which explained the silence.

Harley may know what's going on.

She entered the bunkhouse as Harley was sliding an omelet onto a plate. "What perfect timing you have. Grab a cup of coffee and I'll pour you some juice," he said.

"I don't want to eat your breakfast. Come eat and I'll fix my own."

"Sorry, boss, but my omelets are better, so sit and eat."

"You've got me there. Do you know where Cam is this morning?"

"She had an emergency call at the Bronson place. One of his mares got spooked during the storm last night and got tangled in some barbed wire."

"That's got to be ugly." She poured a cup of coffee, then took it and the omelet to the table.

"Do you want toast?"

"No thanks, I'm good. This omelet is huge."

He whipped up another omelet and poured it into the frying pan, then took two glasses of orange juice to the table.

"What time did the power come back on?"

"About two, I think," he answered.

"We sure needed that rain."

"Yeah, we did. It'll be great for the hayfields."

"Are you still planning to ride the fence line today?"

He flipped the omelet before answering. "Yes, I need to make sure none of our herd spooked in the storm last night."

"I've got my last load of laundry in the dryer, if you wouldn't mind some company." She didn't want to be alone this morning, and she suspected Harley could tell.

"That would be great. After breakfast, I'll load supplies onto the gator while you finish your laundry."

"Thanks," she replied between bites. "You're right, your omelets are so much better."

"Lots of practice." He chuckled.

†

"Change of plans," Nancy announced over breakfast. "The herd is in good shape, so we're starting back for home today."

"That doesn't break my heart," Georgia groaned. "I'm ready for a long, hot shower and a nice soft bed."

"Let's pack up and ride as soon as we can. I'd like to make it back to the site where we meet with Tanya and Thomas by nightfall. Do you think you can make that, Georgia?"

"That won't be a problem as long I get across the river easily. Would you mind sending a couple of the boys along with me in case I run into trouble?"

"Nope, Tony and Roy can ride along with you. We'll take the tents and get camp set up and a fire going while we wait for you."

"That works for me."

"Gene, since you never chew your food, you can be in charge of gathering the tents and strapping them on Roy's horse. Can you handle that?"

He chuckled at her comment. "I'm all over it, boss." Gene left the cabin.

"Thanks for a great breakfast," Coal said as she handed over her dishes.

"You're welcome. I'll see you tonight," Georgia said.

"Yes, ma'am, I'm going to start saddling the horses."

"Hang on, I'm coming with ya," Stormy called.

"I'll see y'all in a few minutes," Nancy told them.

†

Cam climbed wearily into her truck. She wanted a hot shower, some food, and a nap, not necessarily in that order. Even after consuming all that coffee, she knew she'd have no problem falling asleep. Remaining in that cramped position for so long had exhausted her.

She parked the truck and carried her bag to the office to restock it before returning to the house for her much-deserved shower. She didn't see Harley or Melissa and the gator was gone, so she assumed they were riding the fence line together. Thinking of Melissa brought a smile to her tired face as she entered the back door and went to her room for clean clothes. She started the water in the shower, and after undressing stepped under the strong flow of water.

Dear Lord, this feels heavenly. She reached up to change the setting on the showerhead to a pulsating flow and let the water pelt against her tight shoulders as she leaned against the front wall of the shower. After several delicious minutes, she reached for the shampoo and washed her hair, then her body before emerging from the shower.

She slipped into shorts and a T-shirt, then left the bathroom. She was hungry but too tired to fix anything, so she opted to walk to the kitchen for a drink. She'd fix something to eat after a nap. Cam downed half the bottle of water as she went back to her bedroom and placed it on her nightstand before collapsing onto the bed.

†

Harley and Melissa rode miles of fence line without finding any damage.

"I think it's safe to say we don't have any issues. Are you ready to go home, boss?"

"Yes. I don't know about you, but I'm getting hungry."

"You're beginning to sound like Gene," Harley teased.

"I can't believe how much I've missed them."

"It has been awfully quiet around here, hasn't it?" he asked.

"I'll be glad to see them in a few days."

"Me too."

"So what are we having for lunch?"

"Persistent, aren't you? How about some sandwiches, and I'll cook spaghetti later for supper?"

"Wonderful. Do you want me to make a salad and some garlic bread?"

"Okay, now you're making me hungry."

Melissa chuckled as they bounced across pastures until they reached the cattle pens. A smile filled her face when she saw Cam's truck. "Ah, the good doc's home."

Harley liked the smile on Melissa's face when she talked about Doc Bo. "Yes, she is. Will you see if she'd like to join us for lunch while I return the gator to the barn?"

"Sure," she answered, and when he pulled the gator to a halt, Melissa started toward the house.

†

Melissa stopped at the door to Cam's room. Cam was stretched out on the bed facedown, softly snoring. Melissa leaned against the doorframe, admiring the view. The shorts and T-shirt fit Cam's lean form, exposing her strong arms and legs.

Do I wake her to see if she's hungry or let her sleep?

Cam made the decision for her when she rolled over and opened her eyes. "I thought I felt someone enter."

"I was trying to decide if I should wake you or not. Harley and I are about to make some sandwiches for lunch. Have you eaten?"

"Not yet. I was too tired to make anything when I got back."

Melissa stepped inside the room. "Do you want to join us, or I could bring you a sandwich over if you prefer."

"Let me slip on some clothes and I'll be over in a minute."

"Okay, see you in a few." Melissa left to join Harley in the bunkhouse.

†

Coal enjoyed the scenery on the return trip from the mountain pastures. Without the stress of watching the herd, she noticed much more of the environment. A pair of nesting eagles took turns flying overhead, hunting small prey to feed their eaglet, she assumed, while the other stood guard over the large nest. She pulled out her camera hoping the batteries had enough charge left to take a few pictures.

"Maybe, just maybe," she said as she lifted the camera to her face and snapped off several shots of both birds.

Stormy smiled at Coal as she lowered the camera and turned toward her. "You really love it out here, don't you?"

Coal took a shot of Stormy with mountains in the background. "I love being outdoors, period, but you have to admit, it's gorgeous up here."

"Yeah, it makes me miss home, but life in Texas is too good to give up."

"That is so true. It's beautiful and I really enjoy visiting, but it's not home for me."

"I know a tall, blonde cowgirl who would love to change your mind," Stormy teased as she nodded toward Nancy.

"It's nice to have options should I ever need them."

Stormy cocked an eyebrow at her in surprise. "Would you ever consider that option?"

"Only if things changed significantly in Texas." She lifted the camera to her face, took several more shots, then stowed it.

"Hey, Coal," Gene hollered. "You gonna take a swim this time?"

They had reached the river and were looking for a safe spot to cross.

"Only if I have to jump in to save your ass," Coal hollered back.

"Too cold for me, so I'll be careful," he promised, then guided his horse into the water.

Nancy shook her head at their banter. When she looked up at Coal coming up beside her, her eyes sparkled. "Care for a dip?" Coal asked.

"Hell no, once was definitely enough for me. The next water I want to dip into will be a nice hot bath."

"I hear that," Coal answered with a chuckle. "I'm beginning to offend myself."

"Just one more day," Nancy reminded her. "There are only showers in the bunkhouse, but you're more than welcome to use one of the garden tubs in the main house."

"Maybe after I'm a bit less funky and hairy," Coal answered.

"You know I'm going to miss you guys. It's been a real pleasure having you on this trip."

"I think it's safe to say you can count us in on future drives now that we know what to expect. It's been a great experience for us as well. We'll have some nice cool memories to relive when we're scorching in the heat this summer baling hay."

"I bet it can get brutal down there."

"Yeah, it can."

Gene's horse plunged through the river, kicking up the water. "Damn, that's cold," he hollered.

"Suck it up, buttercup," Stormy yelled back to him.

Nancy chuckled at the exchange. "Do they always work this well together?"

"We make a great team, and the competition between us keeps us all on our toes."

"Speaking of competition, are you excited to rodeo up here?"

"Absolutely, that was the icing on the cake for all of us in deciding to come up."

"Well, it won't be long now."

†

217

They rode for another two hours before reaching the campsite. Working quickly, they set up camp and prepared a meal. The group had just finished eating when the sound of thundering hooves filled the air and a plume of dust appeared beyond the tree line.

"I do believe the mustangs have arrived. I think I'll walk over and see if Tanya and Thomas want to come over for a hot meal. I know Georgia cooked extra for them," Nancy said.

"Would you mind some company?" Coal asked.

"Not at all, you need to stretch those long legs?"

"Yes, sitting in the saddle all day makes them ache."

"Let's go track some mustangs, then." Nancy offered her a hand up from the log they'd been sitting on.

†

They started across a field of lush, green grass that just days before had fed the herd they had driven north. The fresh smell of the evergreens filled the air, and Coal breathed it in deeply as they strode toward the tree line. They were nearing the trees when a wolf bounded out of a densely wooded area and slid to a stop a hundred yards ahead of them. Coal instinctively reached for the pistol holstered on her shoulder.

Nancy reached for Coal's arm. "You can relax, it's just Gimp following Tanya and the herd."

Coal remembered the conversation about Gimp and she recognized the unique gait Tanya had described. The wolf fixed them with his yellow eyes for several long seconds and then trotted into the woods.

"See, he's no threat to Tanya or the mustangs."

Coal relaxed and they resumed their trek. The sound of the herd settling in led them through the forest to another open pasture, where the herd grazed on the lush grass as Thomas and Tanya set up camp. Thomas was gathering wood to start their fire while Tanya pitched her tent. She looked up to see them as they stepped into the open.

"Well hello, strangers. I didn't expect to see you for another day or so."

"We were getting antsy and the herd was settled in well, so we started back earlier than planned," Nancy said.

"That's great timing. We're running close to the border of the rez tomorrow, so it will be right on your way for a few hours before you split off back east."

"That does sound like perfect timing. Georgia made extra food if you two would like a hot meal tonight."

"That sounds wonderful. We'd never pass on her cooking." Thomas grinned. "Give us a few minutes to set up camp and we'll be over."

"We can help with that. I'll help you gather some wood and Nancy can help with the tent."

"Awesome," Thomas said.

†

Half an hour later, with the sun sinking below the mountains, they returned to camp. Georgia fixed them all plates and they joined the rest of the crew around the campfire.

"Damn, that was so good, would you mind if I have seconds?" Gene asked Georgia.

"Go right ahead, there's still plenty," she answered with a grin. "I still can't figure out where you put all that food."

"In his wooden leg," Coal answered.

"I'm a growing boy," Gene shot back at them.

Coal watched him disappear back into the wagon and then turned her attention to the growing night. Dots of yellow-green light flickered to life in the meadow as the fireflies began their courting dance. A cool breeze had picked up after the sun set, bringing the smell of the forest and the grazing herd on its currents. For a moment, Coal's memory drifted back to the desert, where she'd gazed up at the Milky Way with Tessa, until the laughter around the fire brought her back to the Montana night.

"We should make it back home after a hard day's ride tomorrow," Nancy told the crew.

"I'm so ready for a shave and a hot shower," Gene said between bites.

"I'm so ready for you to get a shower in too." Coal smiled as she waved a hand in front of her face.

"Well, not all of us decided to take a mud bath in the river," he was quick to remind her.

"Oh, trust me, I'm ready for a shower and shave too." She grinned back at him.

"We'll wait for you to break camp in the morning before we start moving the mustangs so anyone that wants to run with us can do so," Tanya reported. She stood and handed her plate back to Georgia. "Fantastic meal as always. Thank you."

"I think our Texas crew will join you and the rest of us will proceed at a slower pace to stay with Georgia," Nancy replied. "We'll meet back up at the ranch tomorrow late."

"Just save us some hot water," Tom said and punched Gene in the shoulder.

"I'll try my best," Gene answered with a grin.

†

"We're going to be leaving for Montana day after tomorrow. Are you sure you won't change your mind and come with us?" Melissa asked Cam.

"I'd love to, but I've got way too many rounds to make. I will definitely be going to the rodeos this summer, though."

A look of disappointment flickered across Melissa's face. Harley was pleased his two best friends were becoming acquainted, but he sensed something deeper was happening between them. As bad as he wanted to ask, he bit his tongue. When and if the time was right, one or both of them would confide in him.

"What do you have planned for tonight?"

Melissa looked at Cam and shrugged. "Nothing that I know of. What did you have in mind, Harley?"

"I'd be proud as punch if you two lovely ladies would join me in town for a steak dinner and a movie."

"I haven't been to the movies in ages," Cam said.

"No time like the present, then, Doc Bo."

She looked at Melissa, who was smiling at her. "Let's do this. I need to go check on the mare I spent the morning stitching up, but after that I'm free."

"That sounds like a plan to me. I'll call for reservations for dinner at five if you'll check out the movie listings, boss."

"I'll gladly do that."

"Let me go get showered and complete my visit so I'll be back in plenty of time for dinner," Cam said. "Thanks for lunch."

"My pleasure, Doc. See you later," he added as she headed toward the bunkhouse door.

†

Tanya and Thomas stayed to share coffee with the crew as they enjoyed their last night on the drive together. Coal watched the faces around the fire and smiled at the excitement in their voices as they talked about the drive.

"This has been great for us," she said to the group. "We'd never have an experience like this in Texas, and the scenery and company has been terrific."

"Consider yourselves welcome to join us any time," Nancy told them. "It's been great having you three here and sharing some of your experiences in Texas. I bet Dad is about to burst his britches waiting for us to return so we can get our rodeo on."

"Yeah, now we're talking," Gene hollered.

"Y'all are staying for the rodeo this weekend?" Tanya asked.

"We've been asked to ride for the Circle T," Stormy answered. "We're really looking forward to it."

"I guess we'll have to ask for the weekend off so we can come. We'd love to watch the competition."

"The more, the merrier." Gene grinned.

Tanya stood and stretched. "We'll see you guys in the morning. Ride over once you break down camp and we'll get the mustangs moving."

"Why don't you two join us for a hot breakfast?" Georgia offered.

Nancy grinned. "That's a great idea. How about it, guys?"

"How can we pass up a chance for Georgia's cooking?" Thomas asked.

"We can't," Tanya answered. "We'll see you in the morning."

"Good night," Nancy called after them.

"I think I'm going to call it a night too," Coal told them.

"See you in the morning." Gene grinned at her.

Coal doubted he would sleep much tonight from his excitement at running with the mustangs. She was excited too, but the nights of broken sleep had caught up with her.

Just one more night on the ground and I'll be back in a comfy bed. She entered the tent and pulled off her boots, then climbed into her sleeping bag.

†

Harley opened the truck doors for Doc Bo and Melissa. "I can't remember when I've had so much fun, especially with two beautiful ladies. I was the envy of several men tonight," he crowed as he got them settled safely in the truck.

"You are such a charmer, Harley Boone," Cam said. "It was fun tonight. We should do it more often."

"I'd like that too," Melissa said.

"I'd be honored to take you ladies out anytime."

They had driven halfway back to the MC2 when Cam's phone rang. "Doc Bo," she answered. "No, it's not a problem to call. Oh, that's great news, honey. Yes, keep a close eye on her tonight and call me if you need me. That second dose should keep her temperature down now that she's broken the fever. Yes, thanks for notifying me. I'll see you in a couple of days. Good night." She ended the call and saw that Melissa had turned in her seat to watch her.

"Is everything okay?"

"Yes, the mare I spent half the night stitching up was running a low-grade fever. Her young owner was calling to give me an update. The fever has broken, so she should be on her way to a full recovery."

"No permanent muscle damage?" Harley asked.

"I don't think so. None of the tissue damage was very deep, so I think she'll be fine."

"That's great news. Maybe you can get a full night's sleep."

"Maybe so," she answered.

Harley cleared his throat after a few minutes of silence. "Are we loading up for the trip tomorrow, boss?"

"Yeah, I'd like to be ready to leave early Thursday so we can make it at least halfway to Montana before we roll into a hotel."

"That shouldn't be a problem if Harley's driving. He's got one heck of a lead foot," Cam teased.

"What can I say? The older I get, the harder it is to hold it off the gas pedal."

Chapter Thirteen

Coal stretched as she stepped out of the tent, and her gaze fixed on the horizon where the last waves of Northern Lights were fading to make way for the morning sun. The drive had gone too quickly, and by the end of the day, they would be back at the Tucker ranch. While the thought of a hot shower and soft bed was enticing, she feared she would miss the smell of the aspens in the fresh morning air and the glimpses of snowcapped mountains.

Yeah, I could live here if I ever wanted to leave Texas.

The sound of hooves alerted her to Thomas and Tanya's arrival. Georgia heard them as well and emerged from the cook wagon with the coffeepot. Coal breathed in the aroma of frying bacon as she approached Georgia.

"Is there anything I can help you with?" she asked.

"You can get our guests set up with coffee. I'll have the early birds' breakfast ready in five."

"Morning, guys." Coal took the pot from Georgia, who went back into the wagon. "Grab a cup and I'll pour."

"Good morning, Georgia," Thomas said as he peeked inside the wagon. "Can I offer you any help?"

"Nope, but thanks for asking. Breakfast will be ready in just a few."

Coal filled three mugs, and Tanya took two, then handed one to her brother.

"It looks like we'll have a great morning for a run. The fog is low but will burn off with the sunrise," Tanya said.

"Sounds perfect." Coal smiled. "I'm surprised Gene isn't up yet."

"He just went to sleep a few hours ago." Georgia chuckled. "He was up well into the early morning swapping stories with the boys. I heard your name come up more than once."

"We've had some great times together."

"He worships you just a bit."

"I reckon so, but I'm nothing special, just a hard-working cowgirl."

"You're one hell of a fighter too, if Gene's stories are accurate."

"I've been in a few scraps since arriving at the MC2; I won't stand by to allow friends to be bullied. I was trained to protect others, and instinct has a way of kicking in."

"Is it true you kicked a guy's teeth out?" Georgia asked.

Coal hung her head. "Like I said, instinct kicked in and he did something very stupid to endanger my horse and myself. I'm not proud of my behavior, but it did teach him a lesson about stupidity."

Gene walked up behind them. "You must be talking about Bubba."

"Yep, one and the same. I heard you were up swapping stories last night."

"I was too wired to sleep."

"I knew that was going to happen." Coal smirked.

†

Coal finished eating and packed a clean outfit into one of her saddlebags before tossing the rest of her belongings into the back of the wagon. She placed a blanket on Shadow and tied her saddlebags onto the back of her saddle.

"Are you ready for a long run, big boy?" She slipped the bridle over his head and mounted.

Gene and Stormy had just arrived to saddle their horses. "I'm going to ride over to meet Thomas and Tanya. See y'all in a few," Coal told them.

"We're all loaded up too, so we won't be far behind you," Gene replied with a smile.

She eased Shadow out of camp and cantered across the open space to the tree line. As predicted, the fog was burning off, and Shadow's breath puffed out in front of him in the crisp morning air. Coal breathed in the fresh smell of the aspens. In just a few more days, she'd be back in the Texas heat, and within weeks, the crew would be in full-bore haying mode. The bright side to summer was training young horses, and of course, the rodeos.

She slowed Shadow to a walk, and they picked their way through the small copse of trees. When they stepped into a clearing, Coal's smile widened. The field rippled with the beautiful movements of mustangs of all colors and sizes. Shadow's muscles quivered with excitement beneath her.

"It won't be long now," she promised and ran her hand down his neck.

When the crew assembled, Tanya explained how they would ride out. "Thomas and Gene can take the head of the herd, you and Stormy can flank them, and I'll push any stragglers from the rear. We'll start slow and it'll take about three hours to get to the pasture at the rez."

"Hey, y'all have room for one more?" Nancy called out as she emerged from the clearing. "I just realized our Texas buddies wouldn't know the path back to the Circle T."

"We were so excited we didn't think of that," Coal admitted.

Nancy smiled. "It actually gave me a good excuse to come run with the ponies too."

"You know you're welcome at any time. You can bring up the rear with me," Tanya told her. "If everyone's ready, Thomas, you and Gene can get us moving."

The boys nodded.

"I'll take the right flank," Coal volunteered, and they trotted through the milling herd.

The group started out at a slow trot, but within minutes, the speed increased until they were in a full run. Shadow's black mane blew in the breeze as he ran at a comfortable speed, easily keeping pace with the herd. Time flew by, and their pace slowed as they approached the river they would cross, marking the halfway point. Coal grinned as the herd began to descend into the water. She doubted she'd ever make a river crossing again without thinking of her muddy swim with Nancy.

Nancy must have been having similar thoughts. "Last chance for a swim," she called as she rode up to Coal.

"Thanks, boss, but I think I'll pass."

"Me too," Nancy replied as Athena entered the water.

The herd slowed long enough for a drink and emerged on the far bank to make the run for home.

†

When small houses began cropping up, Coal knew they were on reservation land. She didn't need to see the black-haired, dark-skinned children running out to see the ponies to know they'd arrived. More than one set of shining, dark eyes smiled at them as their owners waved while the herd cantered by home after home.

Once the herd settled, Thomas and Tanya took the group to their home and introduced Coal, Stormy, and Gene to their parents, who were delighted when the Texans and Nancy agreed to stay for lunch. When they finished and Tanya walked them out to their horses, Nancy asked if she and Thomas would be going into town to watch the rodeo.

"Normally, we would pass, but we have friends competing, so count us in."

"That sounds great." Coal tightened Shadow's girth strap and swung up into the saddle. "See you again soon, then."

"I'll be looking forward to it."

"Thanks for inviting us to run with you this morning," Coal said.

"You're welcome anytime, and if you come back in the fall, I hope to see you then."

"It's sounding pretty good for a return visit."

†

Cam had gotten last minute instructions for caring for Bo and Dolly from Mary Leah before seeing the group off on their adventure to Montana. She hated to see them go without her, but she had a business to run and new clients to meet. Without the distraction of the beautiful woman down the hall, she hoped to get some work done. The pups followed her to the office, and she made a pot of coffee, hoping to catch up on paperwork she had been neglecting, before the sun rose.

Her concentration wandered back to Melissa and the kisses they'd shared. She had never been with a "straight" woman before and found herself smiling at the old joke about winning a toaster oven for converting a woman to "the dark side."

A toaster oven could come in handy in the office. She laughed at herself and poured another cup of coffee. She'd be loaded with caffeine by her first appointment. Stan, Melissa's foreman, would watch the pups while she made rounds.

Focused on her computer, she barely heard Stan pull up and enter the barn. Dolly was the first to sense his approach and trotted to the door of the office just as he entered.

"Good morning, Doc. Did the crew make it off okay?"

"Hey, Stan. Yes, right on schedule too. Harley was joking this was the first time ever that he traveled with three women and left at the scheduled time."

"I sure hope he knows what he's bitten off with the three of them."

"Harley's right in his element. He'll be just fine."

"Are you still planning on making rounds this morning?"

"Yes, sir. Now that you're here I'll hit the road. You've got my number if you need me."

"I do indeed. Come on, pups, let's ride."

Bo and Dolly trotted happily after him.

Cam watched through the window as he climbed into a gator and the pups piled in beside him. When they drove off, the silence draped around her. Even the birds were barely awake as she walked back into the office and packed her bag.

Already missing Harley's cooking, she decided to stop and grab a biscuit for breakfast before beginning her rounds.

†

There was no rush to get back, so they took a leisurely ride to the Circle T. Coal scanned the scenery as she rode, and she chimed into the conversation when necessary.

Stormy saw the look of contentment on her face as she rode beside her. "You really like this place, don't you?"

"I guess I never realized how beautiful it is here. When we came up for Christmas, all I saw was a blanket of white, but there's so much more beauty here than the snow."

"Do you think you could live here?"

Coal thought for several long seconds. "If I ever chose to leave Texas, I'd sure have to give Montana a second thought. Colorado too, but I'm happy in Texas."

They plodded along the trail, Gene bringing up the rear. Coal turned in her saddle when he cried out and saw him fly off his horse to land with a thud on the hard ground. "What the hell?"

His horse ran past them with a look of terror in his eyes.

"I'll get him, you go check Gene," Coal told Stormy and then urged Shadow into a run after Gene's spooked horse.

"What on earth is going on back there?" Nancy asked as she turned around to look at them.

Gene was just climbing to his feet, knocking the dust off his pants when they arrived. He looked to his left and pointed to the tree line. "That's what happened," he growled.

Gimp stood at the edge of the trees, and his expression looked to Stormy as if he were smiling.

"Gimp just arrived to say good-bye." Nancy chuckled.

"Are you okay?" Stormy asked.

"Nothing bruised but my pride." Gene picked up his hat.

"You okay?" Coal asked as she and Shadow arrived with Gene's horse in tow.

"Yeah," he grumbled. "Gimp spooked my horse and caught me off guard."

"I'm glad you're okay. Are you ready to ride?" Coal asked.

Gene took the reins and swung onto the horse's back. "Yeah, I'm good to go."

"Hold on tight, cowboy," Stormy taunted him.

An hour later, Nancy leaned down and opened a gate to an immense pasture. "Here we are, home, sweet home."

"I can't believe the drive went so fast," Gene groaned.

"I hope y'all will come back in the fall," Nancy said. "It's been great to have you here."

Coal grinned at Gene and then Stormy. "I think that's highly likely."

"The temperatures are usually starting to drop when we bring the herd back down from the mountain pastures."

"Is there any chance of snow?" Gene asked.

"This is Montana. There's always a chance, so it never hurts to be prepared."

The sound of a motor reached them and they turned to see Nancy's father approaching on a gator.

"Hey there, Dad."

He coasted to a stop. "Welcome back. I was hoping y'all would be back today."

"Why's that?" Nancy asked.

"I've got steaks getting ready for grilling."

"I feel like I could eat half a steer," Gene said.

"Did we not feed you well enough?"

"Oh no, sir. Georgia was fantastic, but I'll never pass on a great steak."

"He's still a growing boy," Coal reminded them with a grin.

"Nuttin' wrong with that. I love to see a healthy appetite," Nancy's father said.

"Well I am definitely your man, then."

"Let's go get y'all cleaned up, and you can tell me all about your drive while I get supper started. Will Georgia and the rest make it back today?"

"I'd say they were an hour or so behind us," Nancy replied.

"Perfect, let's go home."

†

Coal dismounted and led Shadow into the stables to unsaddle him and give him fresh water and feed.

"You've been a great pony on this drive. I hope you enjoyed it as much as I have." She brushed her hand down his back. "Tomorrow I promise you a bath and some rest before we head out to the rodeo."

Gene grinned at her and then at Stormy. "I'll finish up here if you two want to go ahead and hit the showers."

"I'm going to give Mary Leah a call, so why don't you get started, Stormy?"

"Sounds good. See you in a bit."

They watched Stormy leave the stables. "You sure you got this?" Coal tossed her saddlebags over her shoulder.

"It's just a matter of taking care of the tack and brushing the horses down. I think I can do that. Besides, it takes me about a third of the time it takes you two to get cleaned up."

"Are you going to shave?"

"I don't know. I may keep the beard for a bit. What do you think?"

Coal had never seen Gene with a full beard, and she had to admit, a close-cropped beard looked good on him and made him look more his age. "You'll probably want to cut it once we get back in the Texas heat, but keep it until then."

"Yeah, it'll be hot as heck once we get back. I wonder what Susan will think?"

"You'll find out tomorrow, right?"

"Yes, she'll be at the hotel to meet me for dinner."

"I bet you're excited."

"That I am."

"Okay, let me go see if I have any juice left in my phone."

†

"Hey, I'm glad you called. Have you made it back in already?" Mary Leah asked, sounding excited.

"Yes, we just got back to the Circle T about a half hour ago. Where are you?"

"Somewhere in or near Colorado is all I know. Melissa had Del come out to stay at our place last night so we could leave at the butt crack of dawn this morning. We loaded our bags last night so we were all set."

"Sounds like y'all have made great progress today. Harley must be driving."

"Yes, he's been our chauffeur all day. The longer the day grew, the heavier his foot became."

"You all aren't excited or anything," Coal teased.

"I think we're all having withdrawals, even Harley."

"We've missed you all as well, but this has been a great experience. Today we got to run with a herd of wild mustangs."

"Oh wow. I bet you loved that."

"You know I did. It's also beautiful here in the late spring. The mountaintops still have snow, but everything is so fresh and green."

"Are you planning on coming home?"

"Of course, why do you ask?"

"You've got that dreamy quality to your voice that tells me you're in love."

"That's because I'm talking to you."

"Nice try, cowgirl, but thank you. How is Stormy?"

"She's in the shower. We just literally got back to the Circle T."

"I bet you're looking forward to one as well."

"I'm definitely in need of a shower and shave."

"I haven't seen any reports about Big Foot sightings in the area."

"Very funny. Besides, it would probably be Sasquatch in this area," Coal teased back. Her phone beeped. "My battery is low and I've no idea where my charger is. I'll find it and call you back later."

"That sounds great, Coal. Love you."

"Love you too."

Gene walked into the bunkhouse as she ended the call. "Aw, I love you too, Coal. Are you done talking already?"

"My battery is low, and I've got to find my charger."

"You want to use mine? I left it here in the bunkhouse."

"Yeah, that'd be great. I think mine's on Georgia's wagon with the rest of my stuff."

Gene went to his room and tossed her the charger when he returned. "I'm off to the shower."

235

"You're not going to call Susan yet?"

"Nope, I'm gonna clean up first and give her time to get home from work."

"Save me some hot water," she teased. Coal plugged in her phone, pulled out clean clothes from her saddlebag, and slipped out of her boots before heading to a shower.

†

The bunkhouse was quiet and empty when Coal emerged from the shower room. She dropped off her dirty clothes and stepped into her newer pair of ropers, then sat on her bunk and relaxed for several minutes. Mary Leah had quickly picked up on her love of the area, and Coal smiled thinking about seeing her lover and friends again. *It is beautiful, but it's not home.*

†

Coal was surprised to find the sun rapidly descending when she emerged from the bunkhouse. Metal rattled, and she looked up to see Georgia's wagon crossing the field to the ranch. She detoured into the stable to check Shadow's food and water and then met Georgia as she pulled the team to a halt just outside of the stable.

Gene and Stormy emerged from the house followed by the Tuckers.

"Welcome home." Roger helped Georgia down from the driver's bench.

"Thanks, it's good to be home."

"Why don't you go get cleaned up and we'll get the wagon unloaded and the animals tended," he suggested.

"You won't get any argument from me. I'm bushed."

"I'm cooking supper tonight too, so take your time and relax a bit."

"That sounds even better." Georgia grinned and trudged toward the house.

"Let's get this wagon unloaded," Nancy instructed.

Coal and Nancy climbed into the back of the wagon and handed items out to the rest of the crew while Roger directed them where to put the items. Within ten minutes, the wagon was empty and Tom was leading the team to the stable for food and water. The Texas crew grabbed their belongings and carried them to the bunkhouse.

"You boys staying for dinner or heading for home?" Nancy asked her local crew.

"Going home, ma'am," each answered.

"Thanks again. We'll see you Saturday at the rodeo."

†

"Mr. Tucker said to come up to the house when we're ready. He said he's got a cooler of cold ones on ice," Gene reported.

"That does sound good," Stormy said.

Coal's arms were full of muddy clothes. "Y'all go ahead. I'm going to put these in the washer. I'll join y'all in just a few."

"Getting the jump on us, huh?" Stormy asked.

"Yeah, I want to knock it out tonight so I'll be ready for the rodeo."

"That's a good idea. I'll wash when you get done," Stormy said.

"There are two washers if you want to start a load."

"If you can finish in two loads, go ahead and I'll start later."

"No problem."

"I'll save you a beer or two." Gene grinned and slapped Stormy on the back. "Let's go."

†

Nancy was sitting on the patio with her dad when Gene and Stormy walked around the house. She frowned when she didn't see Coal. "Where's Coal?"

"She decided to get some laundry started. She'll join us later," Gene reported.

"Well, grab yourself a beer and have a seat," her father instructed. "Nancy was just telling me about the swim she and Coal took."

"It was more like a mud-wrestling match, I think," Stormy laughed. "I don't know who won, though; they were both covered."

Nancy chuckled. "I think Coal got the worst of it when the steer finally broke free. Damn, that was some cold water too."

"You're lucky both of you didn't come down with pneumonia," her dad said.

"We rode like the wind into camp and got dried out and warmed up by the fire as fast as we could."

He looked at Gene with excitement sparkling in his bright eyes. "Did you two enjoy yourselves?"

"Oh yes, sir, it was a great experience. Thank you for the opportunity."

Her father let out a soft laugh. "Thank y'all for helping us out. It would have been more difficult for us if I had to put my old butt in the saddle."

"You're not old, Dad."

"Too old to be sleeping on the ground."

"I'm sure you've been on your share of drives," Stormy said.

"More than I can remember."

"What was you're most memorable drive?" Gene asked.

"That's easy. During the spring drive in 2000, we woke up one morning to a foot of snow. Needless to say, it was totally unexpected, but we managed to slog through it and made it to the next camp just a few hours later than usual."

"I remember that one. The temperature dropped so quickly, and the snow fell like crazy that night."

"Yep, you and I lucked out and got first draw for night watch. We were tucked into our sleeping bags before it got nasty."

"The next day was still miserable. That was the last time I forgot to pack thermal underwear."

"Hard lesson learned." Her father smiled at Nancy.

"That it was." Nancy walked to the beer cooler and grabbed two bottles. "I'll be back in a few."

Three heads turned to watch her walk toward the bunkhouse.

†

Coal was transferring clothes into the dryer when someone tapped behind her.

"You mind some company?" Nancy asked.

Coal turned to see her leaning against the doorframe, holding two bottles of beer. "Let me put another load in and I'll be right with you."

Nancy nodded and walked into a small den area and sat on the couch. Coal enjoyed the view as she turned to leave.

She sure can fill a pair of Wranglers nicely. She shook her head at the thought and placed a load of Stormy's clothes in the wash. When she entered the room, Nancy had stretched out with her boots propped on a small table. She looked up as Coal approached and smiled warmly at her.

"I thought I'd bring you a beer." She held it up for her.

"Thanks, nice and cold too." Coal took it, twisted off the top, and took a long drink, then sat beside Nancy.

"I wanted to thank you again for helping us out on this drive. I do hope you will consider joining us again in the future."

"I'm pretty certain we'll be back. This has been a great experience for all of us. The weather has been a welcome relief too. When we get back, it'll be time to start the hay season and the heat will be brutal."

"Dad made an excellent decision a few years ago to hire a contractor to come in and roll our hay for us. With our difficulties finding reliable help, it reduces the stress of providing hay for the winter months."

"That does make good sense. We still do it the old-fashioned way with bales. Melissa sells a few thousand bales to local ranchers every year."

"That's hot, miserable work."

"Don't I know it, but it's something we need to do every summer. It keeps us in good shape and looking forward to the rodeo season."

"We are so excited to have y'all ride for the Circle T. Dad says we're going to put some of the local ranchers on their butts with your help."

"I hope he's right. We need the practice for our season too, so it's a win-win situation."

"Do you still plan to drive into town tomorrow before the rodeo starts?"

"Yes, our friends will be coming to town late afternoon, and I'd like to get the horses settled and the humans settled into the hotel to wait for them."

"Is your Mary Leah coming?"

"Yes, she is. Melissa, our boss; Del, Stormy's partner; and Harley, our mentor, will be here. Gene's girlfriend is also in Montana and will join us for the weekend."

"Mary Leah's a lucky woman."

"Thanks, but I think I'm the lucky one. She and her sister, Melissa, have given me a real family."

"I bet they say the same thing about you, and Gene and Stormy worship the ground you walk on."

Coal was in full blush and heat rose from her neck to her ears. The buzzer on the dryer sounded, giving her an excuse to exit the room. "I'll be right back."

"I'll let you finish your chores. Don't be too long. Dad is chomping at the bit to cook for y'all."

"Tell him to fire up the grill and I'll be there shortly."

"I will." Nancy reached for Coal's empty bottle before leaving the bunkhouse.

Coal folded her laundry and transferred Stormy's into the dryers.

†

"Here she is," Roger said when he looked up to see Coal walking toward them. "I'm glad you made it."

"Thanks. I wanted to get my laundry done." She looked at Stormy. "Yours is in the dryer." She turned to Gene. "You didn't leave yours out, so you're going to have to put it in. The washers are free if you want to get it started."

"I'll be right back."

"Thanks for getting mine washed," Stormy said as Gene walked off.

"No problem. I was waiting on mine to dry."

Nancy walked over and handed her a cold beer. "I hope you're hungry. I think Dad got confused between steaks and roasts."

"With Gene around, nothing goes to waste," Coal said.

"Hey, I heard that," Gene yelled on his way to the bunkhouse.

"You know you can't deny it," Coal hollered back at him.

"Nope, I can't."

†

"I can't eat another bite," Gene groaned as he pushed his plate away.

"Those are words we don't hear very often." Coal chuckled.

"That was one fantastic meal, Mr. Tucker."

"Gene, will you please call me Roger before you go?" He laughed.

"Yes, sir, Roger."

"That was great, Dad."

"I should let you cook more often," Georgia replied.

Roger softly laughed. "Do you really want me in your kitchen, Georgia?"

"Oh right. What the hell was I thinking?"

He looked at Coal. "What's the plan for tomorrow?"

"We thought we would leave here around lunchtime to get the horses settled at the rodeo grounds and get checked into the hotel. The rest of our group should arrive late afternoon. We'll be good to go for the opening ceremonies Saturday morning."

"Was there something you needed, sir?" Gene asked.

"Yes, but give me a second."

Roger left the room, and Nancy shrugged when they looked at her. "I have no clue either."

When he returned moments later, he was carrying envelopes. He handed one to each of them. When Coal opened hers, she saw the amount of the check and looked up at Roger. "This is much more than we agreed on."

"Consider it a bonus for staying for the rodeo, or a bribe to get you to come back." He grinned. "By the way, I've also paid all the entry fees for the rodeo, so don't let them double-charge us."

"Thank you for that. No bribe is necessary. We've already discussed coming back in the fall, granted we can get Melissa's approval."

"That is fantastic news. You'll love being here then."

"I have no doubt of that." Coal glanced toward Nancy.

Gene stood. "I'm going to finish my laundry. Can I help with the dishes before I go?"

"No, go ahead, we can handle this," Nancy assured him.

"Stormy and I'll help," Coal offered.

"Seriously, I think y'all have done plenty for our family. Get a good night's rest and we'll see you tomorrow," Roger stated.

"Would you mind if I let Shadow spend the night in the arena?"

"He's welcome anywhere you want him." Nancy grinned.

"Thanks. I think he'd like to stretch his legs tonight, and he loves being out under the stars."

"A romantic horse?" Nancy asked.

"Maybe." Coal chuckled.

Roger and Georgia started to clear the table.

"Are you sure there's nothing we can do to help?" Coal asked.

"Just stay out of her way," Roger warned. "She's a hurricane in the kitchen."

"Will you be ready for breakfast by eight?" Georgia asked.

"I'll be ready anytime you're ready to cook," Coal answered. "Thanks again for such a great dinner."

"You're welcome. Good night, ladies," Roger said. "I'll see y'all in the morning."

Nancy walked with them to the door. "I hope you both sleep well tonight."

"I doubt either of us will have any problem," Stormy answered.

"I'll see you in a bit. I'm going to get Shadow settled and make sure he has fresh water."

†

The motion-activated lights triggered when Coal stepped inside the stables, and several pairs of chocolate-brown eyes followed her. She opened the gate to Shadow's stall and stepped inside. "Would you like to spend the night in the corral?"

He nuzzled her shoulder and she placed her hand on his halter to guide him out. "Let's go, then, big boy."

They left the stables, and when she opened the corral gate, he bolted through and raced across the open space, kicking his hind legs high in the air. Coal grinned as he demonstrated his appreciation of freedom. She closed the gate and leaned against the railing to watch her beloved friend. Fresh water bubbled in the trough, so he could have a cool drink after his display. Darker than the night, he was easy to see in the pale light of the nearly full moon.

"He is a beautiful animal," a deep voice spoke from behind her, and she turned to see Roger watching Shadow. "I know it's pointless to offer to buy him. Any fool can see the love you two share."

"He's the best cow pony I've ever had, and a great friend."

"It really shows in how well the two of you work together. I can't wait to see you in action this weekend."

"It'll be nice to knock some rust off before our rodeo season begins."

"I hope you know that if you ever tire of Texas, you'll have a home here."

Coal looked into Roger's sparkling eyes, the same eyes Nancy had. "I appreciate that. It's always great to have options, and you never know what the future may bring."

"That is all too true. I believe that even more now I'm growing older. I'd like to know that when I'm gone, Nancy has someone here to rely on to help her run the Circle."

"Nancy is a very competent woman and will fall right into your footsteps."

"Yes, she is, but I haven't seen her smile like she does when you're in the room, and I know she gets lonely being out here."

"Roger, if I didn't know better, I'd say you were trying to play match maker."

"Very poorly too, might I add. I know my daughter's heart almost as well as she does, and I can tell she holds a special place in her heart for you."

"I've enjoyed getting to know her, but my heart is in Texas right now. But I do appreciate the offer, and I will keep it in mind for the future."

"That's all an old man could ask for. Good night, Coal, sleep well."

"Good night, Roger." She watched him walk to the house.

Shadow ambled over to her and placed his head over the railing. "That was a great offer. Do you think you'd like living here?" She stroked down his neck and hugged him. "A day of rest tomorrow, and then we get to have some fun." She stroked down his face. "Get ready to kick some Montana cowboy ass, my friend."

Shadow tossed his head in agreement, and Coal softly laughed. "Good night."

"Goodnight, Coal," Nancy whispered into the darkness of her room as she watched Coal move to the bunkhouse.

†

"Here she is now. Yes, I'll tell her to call. Love you too." Stormy ended the call with Del and smiled up at Coal. "They're settled into their hotel if you want to give Mary

246

Leah a call. Del told me she tried to call earlier but got no answer."

"My phone was still charging. I'll give her a call in just a minute. How's Gene coming with his laundry?"

"Almost done, and thanks for getting mine started too."

"You're welcome." She reached down to unplug her phone and walked over to the couch as she dialed. "Hey, I got your message," she said when Mary Leah picked up. "Yeah, I was tending to Shadow. No, it was a long day, but a good one. Where are y'all?" Coal smiled over at Stormy as she stretched out on a bunk. Mary Leah must have been talking ninety to nothing, Stormy thought. "Wow, y'all made good time. Harley must have done most of the driving. Yeah, that's what I thought. We'll be heading into town after lunch, so we should be checked in when you get here tomorrow, or at least close by." Coal chuckled as she listened to Mary Leah speak. "It sounds like Melissa is eager to be here too. It's gorgeous up here. I can't wait for you to see the photographs I've taken. Yes, I'll be sure to charge the battery so you can take some rodeo pictures. Okay, honey, yes, I love you too. See you tomorrow."

"It sounds like she was as wound up as Del. Makes me wonder how much caffeine they've had today," Stormy said as Coal hung up.

"Probably way more than either of them is used to. That usually happens when you're traveling."

"I hope they save some of that energy for when they get here tomorrow night." Stormy wiggled her eyebrows for effect.

"I'm sure your doc will have plenty for some loving."

"I hope so." Stormy climbed into her bunk. "Damn, this is heavenly."

"What, you don't miss snuggling with me on the cold ground?"

"The snuggling part yes, the cold ground, not so much."

"Good night, Stormy. I'll see you in the morning."

Coal walked to her room, changed into a nightshirt, and climbed into her bunk just as Gene entered.

"You ready for lights-out?"

"Yeah, I'm all settled," she answered. "Try to get some sleep tonight. Hey, did you talk to Susan?"

"Yeah, I called her from the laundry room. She'll meet me at the hotel at three." He grinned.

"This is going to be a great weekend," Stormy called from the next room.

"Good night, you two," Coal said and rolled onto her side.

†

Cam took a sip of her coffee as she watched the fireflies dance across the front lawn. Bo and Dolly were stretched out on the porch, lulled to sleep by the chorus of crickets. She smiled at the pups and the tranquility of the evening. The crickets were the only sound except for the occasional whisper of a breeze though the oaks in the yard.

Her thoughts drifted to Melissa. Were her hormones leading her astray, or did Cam have a genuine attraction to her? Melissa was beautiful, holding her sure felt good, and the kisses were familiar, yet exciting. It was too early to declare that she was in love with Melissa, but she felt her attraction was the real deal. She hoped their time apart would help Melissa sort out her feelings and they could have a long conversation when she returned. Cam felt it was time for her to move on from grieving for Sheila, but her heart worried Melissa wasn't prepared to make such a life-changing decision.

"I guess only time will tell," she said and both pups looked up at the sound of her voice. "Are you kids ready for bed?"

Bo and Dolly bolted to their feet and raced to the door.

"I guess that's my answer." Cam walked into the house just as the sky lit up with streaks of heat lightning.

†

Melissa knocked on Del's hotel room door.

"Is everything okay?" Del asked when she opened it.

"I'm not sure. Do you have a few minutes to chat?"

"Absolutely, come on in. I was about to fix a drink. Would you like one?"

"Yes, that would be great." *Maybe it'll help calm my nerves a bit.* Even though she and Del had had many personal conversations before, Melissa was anxious about this one.

"Here you go. You're going to have to pretend this is a real cocktail glass instead of Styrofoam," Del said as she handed the cup over.

Melissa laughed, calming herself. "Thanks."

"So what's on your mind?" she asked, settling beside Melissa on the small couch.

"I've got a bit of a dilemma I'd like to talk through with you, if you have time."

"I'll always have time for you, my friend."

"Thanks." She took a sip of the strong drink and a deep breath. "Do you think it's too soon for me to move on after Mitch?"

"I think you've mourned him long enough, but that call is ultimately yours. Do you feel it's time for you to move on?"

"I think I do, but this is something very different for me."

"Different? How so?" Del raised an eyebrow in interest.

"I've always felt I was strictly heterosexual, but now I have to question that."

"Do you think you're only attracted because you're curious?"

Melissa puffed out her breath, blowing a lock of hair off her forehead. "I don't think so. I mean it feels like real attraction. I just don't know what to do."

"What does your heart tell you to do?"

"Relax and enjoy, but my head tells me to run like hell."

Del chuckled. "Why do you think that?"

Melissa blushed, the heat rising up her neck. "I know it's not easy for you and the others to be labeled as lesbians."

"Are you attracted to this person because she's a woman or because she appeals to your heart?"

"Of course she appeals to my heart."

"I've got something I must ask. I've never known you to be concerned with labels, so why now?"

Tears pooled in Melissa's eyes. "I don't want anything to tarnish my memories with Mitch or my reputation as his wife."

"I never met Mitch, but I bet he'd want you to be happy and fall in love again, regardless of who brought you happiness."

Melissa took a few seconds to digest Del's comment. "Yes, you're probably right."

Del gave her a reassuring smile. "Is it Cam?"

Melissa's cheeks heated more and she nodded. "Yes, I find myself very attracted to her."

"Um, this is a bit personal, but have y'all done anything?"

"We've shared a few very nice, intense kisses. We've talked about our feelings and want to take things slowly."

"Cam is a handsome, well-grounded woman, and I think she would complement you well. Have you talked with Mary Leah about this?"

"No, not at all, and I can't really explain why."

"That's okay, I was just curious. I believe that as long as you're both comfortable with each other, you should explore your feelings. You may be surprised by how well you complete one another."

"I found kissing her very exciting, and I don't think it was because she is a woman. I felt like I was compelled to kiss her if that makes any sense."

"I think it makes perfect sense. Just be prepared to have some apprehension moving forward. Being a lesbian isn't always champagne and roses. There will be hard times, and some of your friends may treat you differently. You'll have to determine if your feelings for Cam are worth fighting for and potentially losing friends over."

"If they can't accept who I love, then they aren't really friends."

"No, they're not," Del agreed.

Melissa smiled. "I feel so much better just talking about her."

"How about talking to her?"

"Huh?"

"Have you talked to her today?"

"Not since we left."

"Well, what are you waiting on? Go call her, woman."

"I think I just might." Melissa finished her drink in one long gulp.

"You want another for the road?"

"No, I think I'm sufficiently giddy. Thanks for being a great sounding board."

"It's always my pleasure. You just needed to confirm the feelings you're experiencing, and I hope you've done that tonight."

"Yes, I do believe I have. See you for breakfast."

"Good night."

†

Cam's phone rang in her pocket as she freshened the water bowl for the dogs. She was tired after a long day and hoped it wasn't an emergency call. She took it out and grinned as she saw Melissa's name on the screen. "Hello, how are you?"

"I'm great, and you? Did you have a good day?"

"Yes, it was busy, but I accomplished a great deal today."

Silence filled the air for several long moments. Finally, Cam continued, "I was just thinking about you."

"I was thinking of you too and thought I'd call to say good night."

"The pups and I just had a relaxing time on the porch, and I found myself wishing you were here."

"I was thinking that today as we were driving into Colorado, of how beautiful it was and how nice it would be to share the scenery with you."

"I would like that. Colorado is a gorgeous state, no matter the season, there's always tons of things to do."

"I miss you."

"I miss you too. I want you to have a great time, but I can't wait for you to come home." "Home," that sounds good rolling off my lips. It seems like forever since I've had a home.

"I'm sure the weekend will be so busy, it'll pass quickly, and I'll be home before you know it."

"Just have fun and be safe."

"What are your plans for the weekend?"

"To finish catching up on some paperwork and do some relaxing if possible. Hopefully no major emergencies will arise."

"I hope you can relax. You've been pretty busy since you hit town."

"That's the life of a vet." Cam let out a husky laugh. "You think you can handle that?"

"I'm sure willing to try."

"I really like the sound of that."

"Okay, I won't keep you, because I know you've been up long hours and didn't have the luxury of a nap like I did."

"Will you call again tomorrow so I know you've arrived?"

"You bet I will. Good night and sleep well."

"You too." Cam ended the call with a huge sigh of contentment.

†

Melissa entered the room she shared with Mary Leah just as she was ending a call with Coal.

"Are you okay?" she asked as her sister frowned.

"Yes, I've got a nagging headache. I wonder if it must do with the change in altitude. I remember having headaches like this at Christmas when we were in Montana."

"Have you taken anything?"

"Yes, I have. You're rooming with a drug dealer, remember."

"That's right, the roving pharmacy. Can I get anything for you?"

"A Coke. Maybe some caffeine will help."

"It certainly can't hurt. I'll be right back."

"Where did you go earlier?" Mary Leah asked when Melissa returned.

"I talked with Del for a little while and then called Cam to check on everything at the ranch. As I was coming back inside, Harley caught me, so we talked for a few minutes too." She handed the coke to Mary Leah who opened it and took a sip.

"Sounds like you've made the rounds."

"Are you excited to see Coal?"

"Gosh, it seems like she's been gone a month."

"You don't miss her much, huh?"

"I didn't think it would be this bad, but I feel like I've got a hole in my heart."

Melissa sat on the bed across from Mary Leah's. "That's very sweet."

She cocked her head at Melissa. "What's up with you? You've had a shit-eating grin plastered on your face all day."

"Cam and I have become good friends, and I think there may be more than that between us." She held her breath as she waited for Mary Leah to respond.

"Shut the door! What are you telling me?"

Releasing a breath, Melissa grinned at her. "That I may be falling in love with Cam." *There, I've spoken it aloud and didn't get struck by lightning or turn to stone.*

"That's fantastic. When did you realize this?"

"Just in the last few days, but we've agreed to move slowly and not rush into anything."

"Wow, just wow. I'm very happy for you. Cam is a real sweetheart, and you deserve someone special in your life."

"I never thought that special person would have turned out to be a woman, though," Melissa admitted.

"Are you ready for that? It's not the easiest life."

"Yes, I'm pretty sure I am. If people refuse to understand my feelings for Cam, then I don't need them in my life."

"That's the spirit." Mary Leah offered her a high five. "So have you...you know?"

Melissa felt her face burning. "No, not yet. Is that all lesbians think about? Del asked the same thing."

"So you haven't been thinking about it?"

"No, I can't deny that I've been thinking about it a lot."

"Touché, then, sister."

Melissa rolled her eyes at her sister's comment, then changed into her sleep clothes and climbed into the bed. "How's your head?"

"Easing up a bit, I think. Are you ready for lights-out?"

"Yes, if you are. Tomorrow's going to be an exciting day."

"Yes, it is. Good night."

"Good night." Melissa reached over to turn out the light.

Chapter Fourteen

Coal was the first to wake the following morning. Her attempt at sleeping in ended at six, when a dream woke her, so she crept as quietly as she could into the bathroom to take a shower, dressed, and walked over to the house. She was almost positive Georgia would be awake and in the kitchen, drinking coffee while she dreamed up a wonderful breakfast to serve them before they packed and left for the rodeo grounds.

She stopped at the stable to fill a bucket with food for Shadow and walked to the corral. He raced to meet her at the gate and nuzzled her briefly before turning his attention to the bucket.

"Enjoy your breakfast, my friend." She placed it on the ground and turned toward the house.

Roger met her at the front door. "Good morning. I thought you were going to sleep in today."

Coal ran a hand through her damp hair. "So did I, but that didn't seem to work out."

"Come join us old folks for some coffee, then."

"Who are you calling old?" Georgia called from the kitchen.

"I beg your pardon, Miss Spring Chicken."

"Here you go, Coal." Georgia offered her a steaming mug of coffee as they walked into the kitchen. "You can get your own refill." She grinned at Roger.

"Yes, ma'am," he answered and sauntered over to the coffeepot on the counter.

"I thought I heard stirring in the kitchen." Nancy rubbed her eyes as she entered. She smiled at Coal and then removed a mug from the cabinet. "How'd you sleep?"

"Very well, thanks. It was much warmer and softer than the ground."

"You never get used to that on a drive," Roger stated as he poured coffee for himself and Nancy. He grinned at Coal. "I've got the three of you ladies signed up for all three of the speed events, and you with Gene on the team roping. Gene is also registered in saddle bronc, steer wrestling, and the roping competition."

"You need to add one more event to Stormy's schedule."

"What's that?"

"She also competes in the saddle bronc competition."

Roger nearly choked on his coffee. "Are you serious?"

"Why, does that surprise you?"

"She's the first woman I've ever heard of competing in saddle bronc." He smiled at Coal. "I guess nothing about you two should surprise me."

"Stormy loves to see the look on the men's faces when she outscores them."

"I can see that," Georgia said just as the door to the house opened and Gene and Stormy asked to enter.

"Come on in. We were just talking about you. Coal informed me that I have another event to enter you in."

Stormy's face lit up, "The saddle bronc competition?"

"Yes, I hear you're quite good."

"I try my best."

"Are you guys up for some SOS for breakfast?" Georgia asked.

Gene looked confused. "For what?"

"Shit on a shingle." Coal chuckled.

"Excuse me?"

"Also known as dried beef on toast. Trust me, you'll love it," Coal answered. "You want me on toast duty, Georgia?"

"Nope, that's Roger's chore for calling me old."

"I earned that." Roger started for the toaster.

"So we should be all set for the rodeo," Nancy said.

"Are you coming into town tonight?" Coal asked her.

"No, Dad, Georgia, and I will be there in the morning in time for the opening ceremony."

"It's going to be a great weekend." Gene grinned. "I hope you've got room on that mantel for the top cowboy trophy."

"I'll clear a spot later today," Georgia called from the kitchen.

†

"Oh my goodness that was fantastic," Gene said after finishing his tenth slice of SOS. He looked at Coal. "You've known how to make this all this time?"

"Trust me. Uncle Sam fed me a barrel full of this stuff when I was in the service. I'll teach you how to make it when we get back home."

"Awesome." He looked over at Stormy. "You ready to get our stuff loaded?"

"You aren't excited, are you?" Roger asked.

"Are you kidding? This crew lives to rodeo." He grinned. "No pressure, but I'll add a $250 bonus for each of you if you bring home top cowboy."

"Bring your checkbook," Stormy said.

"I'll be out once the kitchen is cleaned," Coal told her friends as they stood to leave.

"Go ahead, we've got this," Nancy said. "Just check in before y'all take off."

"We will. Thanks for all the great food, Georgia."

"I don't know if you'll see me, but you'll definitely hear me in the stands. I wouldn't miss it for the world."

"Sounds great, see you in a bit." She followed Gene and Stormy.

"I'm going to miss those kids," she heard Georgia say as she reached the door.

†

After saying their good-byes, the crew piled into the truck and drove to the rodeo grounds. Coal had programmed the address into the GPS, but they didn't need directions. All Gene needed to do was follow the flow of horse trailers as they entered town.

Gene pulled the truck into a lot adjacent to the stables, and they walked over to find the manager.

"We're looking for Ron Simpson," Gene told an official-looking man standing just inside the stables.

"I'm Ron, what can I help you with?"

"Roger Tucker said he had arrangements for our stock."

"Yes, welcome. You've got stalls four through six," he replied, pointing to the right. "Let me know if there's anything you need. Roger said to treat you like family."

"Thank you, sir." Gene offered his hand.

"You're welcome and good luck."

Gene nodded and walked back to the trailer as Stormy and Coal unloaded the horses. The sun gleamed off Shadow's coat as Coal handed Gene the rope lead for his horse. "We've got stalls four through six, so let's get 'em settled in," he said.

"This place is much bigger than I imagined it would be," Stormy said as she walked between her friends.

"Everything looks clean and modern too," Coal noted as they stepped inside the stables. "You might get spoiled here," she told Shadow as she led him into the center stall. "Fresh running water and clean sawdust, this is very nice."

"Do you folks need feed and hay?" a tall man asked.

"No, sir, I think we're good to go," Gene answered.

"I've got some fresh-cut alfalfa if you change your mind. Just let Ron know, and I'll deliver."

Gene looked at Coal, who nodded. "Why not? These guys have worked hard lately."

Gene grinned at the man. "You heard the lady. Three bales it is, please, sir."

"I'll be right back." The man limped out of the stables.

Coal smiled as Gene raced to catch up with him. She knew he'd noticed the man's limp, and with his heart of gold, Gene would never let him carry the bales by himself. She turned to look at Stormy, who was also smiling. "We're so lucky to have him on our crew."

"Yes, we are. They don't make many like him."

Once they got the horses bathed and settled, they checked back in with Ron and gave him their contact numbers.

"Don't worry about a thing, we've got security all night long, and a vet on standby," he said.

"That's comforting to know." Gene held out his hand. "Thanks."

"You're welcome, son. Where you all from? You're much too polite for locals."

"Up from Texas. Mr. Tucker hired us to work a cattle drive and promised us some rodeo fun when we were done," Gene replied.

Ron chuckled. "That sounds like Roger. He's a good man, and that daughter of his is a looker with a great business head on her shoulders. I expect they'll roll in early."

Gene grinned. "Yes, sir, well in time for the opening ceremonies."

"Well then, good luck to you and have some fun. If you've been on a drive, you've earned it."

"That we have." Stormy smiled and slapped Gene on the back. "You're probably ready for lunch, and then we can go check in at the hotel."

†

After a filling meal, they arrived at the hotel. Coal called the MC2 group, and they were still three hours away.

"I think I'm going to unpack and take a nap," she announced as they entered the elevator.

"I'm too wired to sleep," Gene said.

"Me too," Stormy agreed.

"Fine, you two can scope out the restaurants and make us reservations for tonight."

"Yeah, we can do that. Can you meet me in my room when you're unpacked?" Stormy asked Gene.

"See you in a few, then." He slid the key into his door and stepped inside the room.

Coal's room was next. "I can't wait until they get here. Seems like weeks since we've seen them."

"I hope they'll be just as eager to see us," Stormy said. "I don't know about you, but I could use some loving."

"Why do you think I'm napping?" Coal winked and stepped into her room.

†

Miraculously, the group from the MC2 arrived at the hotel at the same time as Susan. Gene was pacing the lobby waiting on them, and when Susan entered with Melissa, he rushed to her side and gave her a sweet kiss.

"I'm so glad you made it." He released her from the hug and stepped back.

Susan stroked the closely cropped beard on his chin. "This looks nice, but it tickles."

"Wow, where did our Gene go?" Melissa teased.

Gene tore his gaze off Susan and looked at Melissa. "Hi, boss, glad y'all made it too." He blushed.

"I know it's only been a bit over a week, but I swear you've grown, and that beard does make you look older."

"I'm not sure about keeping it on a permanent basis, but it was easier than shaving on the drive."

"Looks good on you, so don't let their teasing get to ya," Mary Leah warned. "Are you all checked in?"

"Yup, Coal's napping, and I left Stormy watching a movie." He turned back to Susan. "I've got your room right next to mine. Here, let me take your bag." He reached for it.

"Harley, I guess that leaves you and me to check in," Melissa said.

262

Gene nodded and looked at Del and Mary Leah. "Would you like me to show you to your rooms?"

"That would be great." Del smiled.

"Do we have a dinner reservation already?" Melissa asked.

"Yes, ma'am, for seven at a local steakhouse."

"That sounds wonderful," Harley groaned. "I'm starved."

"Have they not been feeding you?" Gene chuckled.

"I've never eaten so much salad as I have the last two days."

"You've got to watch your girly figure." He grinned.

"I've got your girly figure, smart-ass." Harley pulled him into a hug.

"How's Bo doing?"

"He was doing great when we left, but I don't know how he'll survive the weekend," Melissa answered.

"What?" he cried.

"Cam has both the pups and they are already getting so spoiled." She grinned.

"Damn, boss, don't scare me like that."

"Doc Bo's made him as good as new," Harley said.

"What happened to Bo?" Susan asked.

"He was bitten by a rattlesnake and I thought I'd lost him," Gene answered, his voice cracking with emotion. "Thankfully Doc Bo, our new vet, was arriving at the time we needed her most."

"That was good fortune."

"Yeah, it was." He smiled. "Let's go get y'all settled."

"Meet us back here at six thirty," Melissa told the group.

They rode the elevator to their floor, and Gene pointed out everyone's rooms and led Susan to her room.

†

Mary Leah knocked softly on the door and looked over at Del. Del grinned back at her. Both were excited to see their lovers.

Coal opened the door and Mary Leah flew into her arms.

"Hey, did ya miss me a bit?" She stepped out to grab Mary Leah's bag and grinned at Del. "Hiya, Doc."

"Hey, Coal," she answered, then Stormy opened the door and Del's attention was lost.

"You are never going anywhere without me again," Mary Leah said as Coal rolled her bag into the room.

"I missed you too." Coal took her lover into her arms for a deep kiss.

"Wow, I've missed those." Mary Leah was nearly breathless when Coal ended the kiss. "So did you have a great time on the drive?"

Coal led her to the small couch. "You wouldn't believe how much fun we had. I've got so many beautiful pictures to share with you, but they can wait until later. How are you?"

"I'm good, but I've got a bit of a lingering headache. Do you have a soda? I could use the caffeine and some pain relievers."

Coal frowned at her answer. "I'll hit the vending machine while you find your meds."

"Thanks, it's probably the increase in elevation and the different pollens in the air." She stood and walked to her bag as Coal headed to the door.

Coal left the room to get a soda. She vaguely remembered Mary Leah having some problems with the elevation when they were here for Christmas. She hoped either that or the pollens was the only thing wrong with Mary

Leah. She returned to the room with two Cokes, and placed one in the mini fridge and handed Mary Leah the other.

"Do you want to take the meds and stretch out for a little while? I can go check on Melissa and Harley while you rest."

"No, I want you here with me. Will you come cuddle with me until the meds kick in? If I fall asleep, you can go check on everyone."

"With pleasure." Coal kicked off her boots and got into bed.

Mary Leah climbed up beside her and snuggled into her warmth, laying her head on Coal's shoulder.

Coal softly stroked her hair as Mary Leah relaxed. "Is it easing up at all?"

"Yes, a bit," Mary Leah's voice was sleepy.

"Just relax, and I'll make sure you're up in plenty of time to prepare for dinner." Coal kissed the top of her head, and resumed stroking her hair.

†

Cam filled the pups' bowls with kibble and placed them on the floor, then took her plate to the kitchen table. She had eaten her salad and was cutting her baked chicken breast, when she felt eyes watching her. She looked to the right and found both pups staring at her with interest.

"You two didn't take long to eat." Bo was wiggling his nub of a tail so hard, Cam was afraid he'd fall over. She took a bite and let out a soft moan. Both pups licked their chops as they begged for a bite with their eyes. "Okay, I get the hint." She returned to the counter, sliced up the breast she had cooked for tomorrow's lunch, and divided it between their bowls. "Chew this time and let me eat."

The pups devoured the chicken, took a drink from the water bowl, and left the kitchen. She heard them push the screen door open and looked up to see Dolly following her brother across the yard. She watched them play for several minutes while she finished her meal.

It had been a long, productive day, but her attention had drifted to thoughts of Melissa often. They would be in Montana, settled into the hotel and probably on their way to dinner by now. She would pick up the kitchen and relax on the porch for a while.

Hopefully Melissa will call when she settles in for the night.

She took her cup of coffee to the front porch and sat in one of the rockers as Bo and Dolly romped in the yard. Bo's recuperation had been miraculous. To look at him now, she would never have guessed he'd just been at death's door. She smiled as they played.

A slight breeze brought relief from the heat of the day, and she began to nod off. The yipping of the pups and the tapping of raindrops on the roof snapped her awake. Bo and Dolly shook the rain from their coats after they reached the cover of the porch.

"Hey, I've already had a shower," she cried out to them. They danced in front of the screen door as a flash of lightning filled the sky and the boom of thunder followed. "Okay, chickens, I'll let you back inside." Another close strike made her jump, and she grabbed her coffee cup and rushed inside, laughing as she watched the pups disappear down the hall. As she rinsed her cup, she had a good feeling she was going to have company in her bed tonight. The lights were flickering and she wondered if the power would go out altogether. Just in case, she grabbed a flashlight before walking to her room.

†

"That was a fantastic meal," Melissa said as they emerged from their vehicles into the hotel parking lot. "What time do we need to meet for breakfast?"

"The opening ceremonies begin at eight," Gene answered.

"Do you guys plan to ride in them?"

"Naw, why break with tradition?" Gene grinned. "We'll get the horses warmed up for the beginning of the speed events."

"Good night, then. Get plenty of rest. Meet up at six?"

"That should give us plenty of time to grab some breakfast, boss," Harley answered.

†

Melissa rushed to her room and dialed Cam's cell phone. It rang with an odd crackling sound and no one answered. Frustrated, she ended the call and dialed the house number.

"Come on Cam, pick up."

"I'm sorry, but all circuits are busy. Please try your call again later," an automated female voice said.

She paced the room, trying both numbers again to no avail. "Damn." She slumped onto the couch and turned on the television. Horror filled her as the Weather Channel showed footage of an outbreak of tornados in Texas. "Oh no, Cam, please be safe."

267

Someone was pounding on her door. She walked over and opened it to find Harley outside. "Did you see the weather news?" he asked.

"Yes, it looks horrible. I haven't been able to reach Cam on the phone." Melissa settled back on the couch, and Harley sat beside her.

"I couldn't reach her either. Cam's been through all kinds of bad weather. I'm sure she's okay. The phone lines are probably down, due to the storm."

She knew he was trying to calm and reassure her, but she'd known him long enough to recognize the worry in his voice. "I'm sure you're right," she replied, unsure if her voice was any more convincing than his had been.

†

The lights flickered then went out as Cam entered the bedroom. She turned on the flashlight just as a pelting sound began. She rushed to the window to find hail striking the panes.

"Okay, kids, I think we need to take some shelter."

She rushed into Melissa's bathroom and placed Dolly inside the deep garden tub, and Bo jumped in beside her.

"Make room for me," she told them as she crawled inside and pulled the two young dogs under her arms.

The hail continued to pelt the house as the rain poured from the skies. The wind howled around the house, and when the howl changed to the roar of a freight train, she ducked her head and began to pray. A loud crack followed by a crash made her jump.

She felt the air suck out of the house, then reenter in a sigh as the storm cell passed over the house. Cam waited a

268

few more minutes, and when the winds remained calm, she climbed from the tub. The pups jumped out and danced around her, unaware of the danger they had just escaped.

The power was still off, so Cam plucked the flashlight from her back pocket. After illuminating the room, she crept toward the back door. The rain was still falling, but gently now instead of the heavy downpour that had passed through moments before. A quick glance toward the barn revealed no damage. She guided her light up to the roof of the house. Some shingles were missing, but everything else seemed sound. When she reached the front yard, she saw that the large oak there had split, and a large section had landed only a foot from the front porch.

"Damn, that was close."

Cam looked south toward the town and saw the flash of lightning and power transformers exploding as the storm moved through. Sirens filled the air, warning the residents of the approaching storm cell. Rain trickled down her face as she walked back to the porch and entered the house. She stripped out of the wet clothes and dried her body with a towel before slipping into dry clothes. She located her phone, but as she feared, there was no service.

"We might as well get some sleep," she told the pups before climbing into bed.

†

Stormy took Del in her arms when they returned to the room. "I've missed you."

"Was your trip everything you hoped it would be?"

"That and then some, but I'm happy to be back in your arms."

269

"I've missed you too," Del admitted as she slipped her hands beneath Stormy's shirt and pulled open the closure of her bra. She ran her hands up Stormy's sides. "You've lost some weight."

"It was hard work and long days. We ate well, but we burned through the calories working and staying warm."

"I bet it felt good to get a hot shower and to sleep in a bed again."

"It was like heaven, but tonight will be even better." Stormy shrugged out of her shirt, then lifted the sweater above Del's head and pulled her close. "Umm, your skin's so warm," she sighed as their bodies joined and she bent down to kiss Del. "I want to kiss you all over." Her warm breath caressed Del's neck.

Del's moans filled the room as she worked Stormy's belt free of her jeans and unfastened them. She then pulled the zipper down and slid her hand into the back of Stormy's jeans to cup her muscular ass.

"I'm so glad you didn't lose this." Del gave it a good squeeze.

Stormy guided Del backward onto the bed, then knelt to pull Del's boots off and slide her jeans down her legs. She sighed when her gaze landed on Del's black lace bra and panty set.

"Are these new?" She toyed with the waistband of the panties.

"I bought them for tonight. I know how much you like them."

Stormy brushed her lips down Del's neck, across her collarbone, and down between her breasts as she reached behind Del's back to release the bra. She lowered the straps from Del's shoulders to help her slip out of it. Del's nipples were erect from the excitement of Stormy's tender caresses. Stormy slowly lifted her gaze, devouring each inch of Del's body until she reached her lover's passion-filled eyes.

"You are so beautiful," she whispered as she pushed her jeans off and joined Del on the bed, where she pressed Del onto her back while she lay beside her. She traced a finger down Del's forehead and across her nose to her lips. "So soft." She smiled as she trailed it lower, down her neck to circle her swollen nipple as their lips met in a soft kiss. Fingers joined in a light pinch, eliciting a moan from Del, swallowed by Stormy's kiss.

Her hand moved lower to find the lace panties soaked with excitement. A slow undulation of Del's hips invited her inside, and Stormy moved her hand into the panties, parted Del's lips, and buried her knuckles deep in the velvety warmth of Del's core.

"Someone's ready for some loving." Stormy's voice was husky and filled with passion.

"Yes, please," Del moaned.

Stormy slowly withdrew her fingers, Del's muscles convulsing around them, and entered her again, her movements matching the rhythm of her hips as they rose to meet Stormy's fingers. Del pushed the panties down her raised hips, and Stormy removed them and tossed across the room. Her mouth captured Del's and their tongues swirled together as Stormy thrust her fingers deeply into her. She moved to straddle Del and felt Del's hand slide inside her boxers, easing between her soaked lips. She rocked into Del's hand as their fingers plunged deep, orgasms rising until they came together in a rush of passion, their moans echoing through the room.

Stormy broke off the kiss. "Now it's time for a taste." She moved down Del's body.

†

Two doors down, Coal took Mary Leah into her arms. "How are you feeling?"

"Better." But Coal could see the pain in her eyes.

She stepped back to look at her. "I want you to see a doctor if you don't feel better tomorrow."

"I'll schedule an appointment when we go home. I promise."

"Come on, let's get some rest. Maybe that will help." Coal pulled the covers back on the bed.

Mary Leah frowned. "I know that's not what you expected tonight. I don't want to disappoint you."

"I'm not disappointed. I'm worried about you."

"I'll be fine. Maybe a night snuggled up to you will help."

Coal pulled a T-shirt over her head and climbed into the bed. Mary Leah followed her, and Coal wrapped her arms protectively around her lover. She held her until Mary Leah's breath slowed, indicating she'd fallen asleep. A tear ran down Coal's cheek as she held her close and drifted off to sleep.

†

After Harley returned to his room, Melissa tried to calm her nerves by watching television, but she couldn't help but return to the Weather Channel to follow the reports coming out of Texas. At midnight, she decided to try calling Cam one last time before climbing into bed. She was hopeful when the phone rang and she didn't receive the recorded message, and her heart skipped a beat when Cam picked up on the fourth ring.

"Thank you for answering. The phones have been out for hours. Are you okay?"

"Yes, we're fine here. We had a tornado move through, but the house and barn are safe. I can't say the same for the oak in the front yard, though. It split and barely missed the front porch."

"I'm not worried about anything but you."

She could almost hear Cam smiling. "I'm good. The dogs and I tried out your garden tub."

"I'm so relieved you're safe. The television has been showing horrible shots of devastation in the area."

"We were lucky the storm moved through quickly. I could see the lightning strikes and transformers exploding on its path into town."

Melissa sighed in relief.

"I hope you've made it to Montana safely."

"Yes, we got here late this afternoon. It was great to see the kids. Gene looks all grown up all of a sudden. He's grown a beard."

"Oh my goodness, he's lost his baby face."

"Yes, but it looks really good on him." Melissa fell silent for several long moments. "I really miss you."

"I've been thinking about you all day," Cam said. "I should have made arrangements to go with you."

"That would have been nice, but hopefully we'll have other opportunities to travel together."

"Yes, I think we will. Is the crew all set for tomorrow?"

"Set and ready to go. I'm not sure how much sleep anyone will be getting tonight, though."

"Too excited?"

"Yes, that, and reuniting with partners." She let out a soft laugh. "The look Stormy was giving Del at dinner could have caused an inferno."

Cam laughed. "She does appear to be pretty hot-blooded. How's Coal? Was the trip all she hoped for?"

"Yes, I think she had a great time. She seems very relaxed and at home here."

"That's great to hear. I know she's had a rough life for one so young."

"Yeah, she has. She's got a heart of gold, and I wouldn't trade her for anything in this world. She's come a long way since she rolled up in my front yard when I was expecting a cowboy."

"Yeah, I bet the name has confused a lot of people. She fits well at the MC2."

"She's become the heart of the crew. They all love her like a sister, or daughter in Harley's case."

"Yes, he's very fond of her."

"Gene worships the ground she walks on, and I don't think Stormy is too far behind him."

"Definitely not far. Are you excited about the rodeo?"

"I love to watch them rodeo. I feel like an excited mama."

"Well, excited mama, it's almost one, so I'd suggest you get some sleep. Call me anytime you want tomorrow."

"I'll call Stan to get someone out to remove the tree."

"Do you want me to give him a call?"

"Sure, if you wouldn't mind."

"No. I don't mind at all. Sleep well and I look forward to hearing from you tomorrow."

"Good night. I'm glad you're safe."

"Me too, and I'm glad y'all arrived safely. Good luck to everyone tomorrow."

"Thanks."

"Good night, Melissa."

Chapter Fifteen

When they met for breakfast, Melissa shared what Cam had told her about the tornado. They were all relieved the ranch hadn't sustained any major damage and were glad Cam and the pups had sheltered safely.

"I can't wait to see Bo." Gene grinned as they cleared the tables in preparation for leaving.

The crisp morning air felt good against her skin as Del emerged from the hotel after breakfast. They loaded into the trucks and drove to the rodeo grounds to prepare for the opening ceremonies.

When they pulled into the lot, Coal pointed out the Tuckers' horse trailer as it pulled in after them. "There's Nancy and her dad. Pull in next to them if you can, Gene."

"Not a problem." He did as she asked.

Harley followed Gene's lead and parked in the spot beside Gene's truck. They all climbed out and regrouped at the rear of Roger's trailer. He emerged from the truck and smiled when he saw Coal and the crew from the MC2.

"Well, good morning," he said as he walked toward them.

Del watched as a tall blonde walked around the end of the trailer and her face lit up when she saw Coal. She also noticed the brilliant smile on Coal's face and a slight blush when Coal caught Del watching her closely. *This could be trouble.*

"Mr. Tucker and Nancy, I'd like you to meet the rest of the crew from the MC2 and our friends." Coal introduced the two groups.

"What's this 'Mr. Tucker' stuff?" he asked her. "Hi, I'm Roger."

"We've heard a lot about y'all," Melissa stated. "The crew really appreciated being a part of your drive."

"They saved the day for us," Roger said. "I'd take this group on a drive anytime. I do hope you'll allow them to return in the fall to bring the herd in."

"Oh, they've already started planning a return trip," she answered.

Roger grinned. "That's what I love to hear."

Coal smiled at Nancy again. "You want help unloading Athena?"

"Sure, I never pass on good help."

"May I have the privilege of escorting you ladies into the stadium so we can pick out good seats?" Roger asked and held out his arm for Melissa.

"Oh, what a charmer." Gene snickered.

"I'll join you in a few," Harley told Melissa. "Let's get your tack out and into the barn," he said to Gene and Stormy.

†

"She's a real looker," Mary Leah whispered to Del as they followed Roger and Melissa toward the stadium.

"Definitely a tall drink of water, and she looks so much like her dad," Del agreed. She hoped Mary Leah hadn't caught the quick exchange between Coal and Nancy. "How are you feeling this morning?"

"Much better. A good night's sleep and the cooler weather seem to help."

"You really should get checked out."

"I promised Coal I would make an appointment when we get home."

"Good, we all hate to see you in pain."

"Trust me I don't like it any more than y'all."

Roger and Melissa were chatting away as they climbed the concrete steps into the stadium and located seats under the awning, away from the glaring sun. They found seats near the center of the arena and several rows from ground level.

"Will this spot do for you ladies?" he asked.

"This looks perfect," Melissa answered.

"May I get anyone coffee?" Roger asked, then turned as two women and a man approached them. He introduced the three as Georgia, Tanya, and Thomas, and then left with an order for five coffees and Del in tow to help.

"Gene just raves about your cooking," Melissa told Georgia.

"He should, that boy ate enough of it over the last week. He's got quite an appetite."

"Yes, he does. I almost didn't recognize him with that beard when we arrived yesterday, and I think he's filled out a bit more on this trip."

"He's a fine young man, and all three are some of the hardest workers I've ever met. Not one complaint out of them the whole trip, and it was a hard trip. We never could quite guess what the weather would be like from one minute to the next."

"Gene was ecstatic about seeing snow again. Being a Texas native, he hasn't seen it often."

"It was beautiful, and we had several nights of a show from the Northern Lights."

"Coal gets all dreamy-eyed when she talks about how gorgeous it was out there," Mary Leah added.

"With good reason. We covered some of the prettiest landscape in Montana."

"I'm starting to get jealous," Melissa replied.

"You should come join us for a drive, then," Georgia offered.

"No way I'm giving up hot showers and soft, warm, beds for the cold ground, but thanks anyway. I'll just live vicariously through the kids."

"I understand. I don't know how many more drives these old bones can take."

Roger and Del returned. "What old bones? You're still a spring chicken," he reminded her with a wink.

"I wish you'd make up your mind. Yesterday I was an old woman."

He cringed at her words. "Damn, I hoped you'd forgotten that blunder."

"I may be old, but I've still got a good memory. It may be weeks before you live this one down."

Roger chuckled and passed cups of coffee around. "I reckon I'll never learn my lesson."

The announcer saved Roger from any more embarrassment as he welcomed the guests to the first rodeo of the year. Roger sat between Georgia and Melissa and quietly sipped his coffee.

As the ring cleared and the rodeo clowns set up for the barrel racing competition, he clapped and cheered, "Here we go."

You aren't excited much, huh, Mr. Tucker?" Tanya teased.

"I've waited all week for this day."

†

They had drawn earlier for run positions, and Nancy was the first of the three to make her run. Stormy was next, and Coal was the second-to-last competitor.

Harley smiled. "Good luck, ladies." He followed Gene and Susan to the grandstand to join the others.

"Thanks Harley," Stormy called after him as they left the warm-up ring and rode toward the arena.

The first two riders put in mediocre times, and Nancy set the bar for the rest of the competition. She and Athena put in a near-perfect run. Coal looked at the time flashing on the scoreboard. *That's a good time, but we can beat that.*

Stormy whistled. "Damn, that was fast."

"Yeah, it was. It's going to be hard to beat that."

Nancy and Athena trotted back to them. She was smiling, clearly knowing they had put in a good run.

"Great run," Coal said.

"Thanks, it felt good." She looked up to see her name at the top of the scoreboard.

Stormy grinned. "Let's see if we can get close." She turned away to take up her waiting position.

Athena leaned over and nuzzled Shadow. Coal chuckled and looked at Nancy. "Did you teach her to do that?"

"Do what? I have no idea what you're talking about, Coal Bryan. You know Athena is crushing on Shadow."

"Uh-huh, I think we better go run to get back in focus."

"At least wait for Stormy's run."

Coal settled back in the saddle as Stormy moved into position. After flying out of the starting gate, Stormy put in a solid run but tipped the final barrel as she turned for home. Coal held her breath as the barrel teetered but did not fall. It was just enough of an error to throw her horse off stride, costing her precious ticks of the clock, but Stormy finished the run strong, a little over a second behind Nancy.

Coal watched Nancy squirm in her saddle. "Another good run."

"Yeah, that puts us in great shape for points already."

"It would be nice to take all three-point slots."

"Dad would be on cloud nine with that start."

"Let's see what we can do about it, then." She turned Shadow and gave Stormy a high five as they passed her. "Great run."

"Cowgirls do it in the dirt." She grinned.

"Hell yes, we do," Coal finished their mantra.

"Thanks. The sand's a little soft around the last barrel."

"Thanks for the heads-up."

"Take us on home. I know y'all can beat that time."

"We're going to give it our best."

Coal rode to the warm-up ring. Shadow broke into an easy canter, and Coal could tell he wanted more speed. "Very soon, big boy, you can go all-out."

†

With one rider ahead of her, Coal positioned Shadow near the starting gate. A glimpse at the scoreboard still showed Nancy and Stormy on top. She could feel Shadow quivering with excitement, ready to run, and her heart began to pound. The rider ahead of her finished her run, and Coal moved to the starting position. Her name was called, and when she got the nod from the gate judge, she gave Shadow a nudge and they exploded through the starting gate. Each stride thundered in her ears as they raced for the first barrel, then across the arena to the second for another tight turn. They managed to skirt the soft sand around the final barrel, and then Coal leaned forward and gave Shadow permission to run. Her hair flew out behind her in the wind as they raced for home. She didn't have to look at the clock to know they had a near-perfect run. She pulled him to a stop outside the runway and looked up to see her name flashing on top of the leaderboard.

"Good boy." She leaned down and patted his neck as Gene hollered from the grandstand.

"Nice run," Stormy said as Coal joined them.

"Congratulations. I don't think anyone will best that time." Nancy smiled.

As predicted, the final rider failed to come near their times and they took the top three spots in the event.

†

"Now that's what I'm talking about," Roger crowed. He looked at Melissa. "Are you sure I can't keep these three?"

A resounding no came from Melissa, Del, and Mary Leah.

"Well that's settled." Georgia chuckled.

"Okay, so loan them to me from time to time?"

"That's a possibility."

"We got all the points for that event." He grinned. "What a way to start the day."

"The girls should build us a nice lead in the speed events," Gene said.

"Maybe they should rename it to Top Cowgirl," Del suggested.

"I'd gladly take that honor too." Roger smiled.

†

Coal, Nancy, and Stormy watched as the clowns shifted the barrels to prepare for the flag race, the easiest of the three speed-and-agility events.

"Did you pull our numbers?" Coal asked Nancy.

"Your turn to go first; you got the second slot. Stormy is fourth and I'm seventh. I went ahead and pulled numbers for the pole bending too."

"You're on the ball, boss," Stormy teased.

"Would you look at that smile?" Nancy nodded toward the grandstand. "Dad's about to bust he's so happy."

Stormy and Coal looked into the stands until they found the group. Roger and Melissa were engaged in an animated conversation.

Coal returned her smile. "Your dad and Melissa seem to be hitting it off well."

"He's turning on the Tucker charm."

Coal blurted out without thinking, "So you get it honestly."

Nancy blushed. "Yeah, I guess I do."

"I think they're getting ready to start," Stormy said. "Get us a good time." She winked at Coal.

"You got it." Coal and Shadow trotted over to the starting gate.

†

By the end of the morning, the Circle T was well ahead of the competition in the race for the top cowboy award. The ladies had done their job to build a lead by winning all three-point slots in the speed events. After the pole bending, Harley, Gene, and Roger met them at the stables.

"Congratulations on a great morning." Roger beamed.

"Good job, ladies," Harley added.

"That's the way to kick some ass," Gene said.

Nancy smiled brightly. "That was a lot of fun. It was great having teammates."

"It was fun," Coal agreed.

"And look at you taking first in pole bending," Gene praised Stormy.

"I was just lucky Coal missed the last pole and had a time penalty." She grinned at Coal.

"I'll gladly take two firsts and a second any day." Coal glowed.

"I bet you're stoked over the points race, huh, Dad?"

"It's a nice lead, but we still have to get through several other events. Still, it looks good to see the Circle T at the top again."

"We'll do our best to keep it up there," Gene promised.

"You and I and the boys have a busy afternoon." Stormy patted his back. "Let's go get some grub so it can settle before the steer wrestling."

Roger's grin grew. "My treat, so I hope y'all have worked up an appetite."

"You should know by now this group never has a problem with appetite." Harley chuckled.

"Well, let's go get them fed."

"I'll join you in a minute. Shadow's done for the day, so I want to unsaddle him and get him settled."

"Do you want your usual?" Stormy asked.

"Pulled pork sandwich, onion rings, and sweet tea," Coal answered. "If they have it," she added.

"Oh, they have that and more, you can bet on it," Nancy said.

"Awesome, I'm starving. See you in a few."

†

Coal watched the happy group leave the stables, then unsaddled Shadow. "You did really good today, big boy." She bunked her saddle and tack and then picked up his halter and brush. "It felt good to run with you." She wiped the sweat off his back and brushed him until his coat gleamed in the sunlight. She checked his hooves for stones and packed dirt and then gave him fresh water and feed.

†

"I wonder what's taking Coal so long," Mary Leah said when she hadn't arrived by the time the group started eating.

"I'll go check on her," Roger volunteered and stood.

Gene moved to get up too, but Nancy placed her hand on his arm and leaned over and whispered, "Let him go."

Gene nodded and stayed seated.

"Hurry back, Dad. Gene's eyeing your sandwich," Nancy called to him.

"Go get some more if he'll eat them," he called back and tossed his hand up in a wave.

Nancy pulled out a fifty-dollar bill and gave it to Gene. "You heard the man, go get a few more sandwiches."

†

Roger was on cloud nine and he didn't think anything could wipe the smile off his face as he entered the stables. He spotted Coal right away, talking with two cowboys from the Silver Crescent. He knew Randy Booker to be an ornery cuss prone to picking fights, but hopefully he wouldn't be stupid enough to take on Coal. Then again, it was Randy and he didn't have a clue about her background. As he approached, he heard the venom in Randy's voice.

"So old man Tucker brought in some dyke friends of Nancy's to try to topple us from top cowboy," Randy told his partner. "Where you bitches from?"

Roger saw the flash of anger in her eyes.

"First, we're not anyone's bitches. We're from Texas, came up to help Mr. Tucker out since he couldn't find any decent cowboys in the area to help with a cattle drive."

Well done, Coal. He picked up his pace as the stable manager, Ron, approached the group.

"Texas? No wonder. I hear it's full of steers and queers," Randy joked. He and his buddy laughed.

"So you're from Texas too. Does that make you a steer or queer?" Coal replied.

They stopped laughing. "I'm neither, bitch," Randy sneered, and drew back his fist.

"Hold up, Randy," Roger hollered at him.

Randy dropped his fist and turned to glare at Roger, "What do you want, old man?"

Roger landed a right fist to Randy's left jaw, dropping him to the sawdust floor.

Randy looked as shocked as the small crowd that had gathered around them did as he shook his head and wiped blood from the corner of his mouth. The rage of the devil was in his eyes as he climbed to his feet and lunged at Roger. So focused on Roger, Randy didn't see Coal's boot as it slammed into the right side of his jaw. He went down with a thud as the air rushed out of his body. He turned his head to glare at Coal and then slumped back down into the sawdust.

Coal looked at Randy's buddy. "You want to be next?"

"Uh, no," he stammered.

"Okay, that's enough, the shows over," Ron announced as he pushed his way through the crowd. "Jeff, get Randy up and y'all get out of here. Silver Crescent's rodeo is over for this weekend."

Randy shook his head as if trying to clear the cobwebs. "What? You can't do that?"

"Yes, I can, and I just did. Load your stock and gear and get the hell out of here. We don't treat guests, especially women, that way around here." He shot a wink to Coal. "I apologize for his brutish behavior, ma'am," he said as Jeff helped Randy up and the two left.

"Thanks." She turned to look at Roger. "Nice shot, but you're going to need some ice for those knuckles."

"I thought it was a good idea at the time, but dang that hurt."

"He has a very hard head."

"That was one helluva kick. I'm glad you spared his teeth, though."

"Yeah, he doesn't look all that great with them." She placed her arm over his shoulder.

"You better watch your back while you're in town. Ron banished him from the rodeo grounds, but that doesn't mean he won't try something stupid in town," Roger warned.

"I can handle myself away from here."

"That you can." He grinned.

"Should I stay out here tonight so he doesn't mess with Shadow or our other stock?"

"No, Ron will ensure the stock is safe."

The crowd parted like Moses parting the waters to make way for their exit. Roger saw smiles on many of the faces he passed. Several of the older men patted him on the shoulder with an "atta boy" and huge grins.

"Do I need to be worried about being in trouble with Nancy for getting you into a fight?"

"You didn't start it, but you certainly ended it. Besides, I threw the first punch."

"Yes, you did."

†

"Gene, can you go get an ice pack from the concession stand?" Roger asked when they approached the table.

Gene turned to see Roger holding his hand and dropped the sandwich he'd been eating. "I'll be right back."

Roger took a seat beside Nancy, who was eyeing his hand. "What on earth happened?" she asked.

"My fist came in contact with Randy Booker's hard head. He was being rude and obnoxious to Coal and me."

"So you hit him?"

"Yeah, I did. Put him on the ground too."

Nancy looked Coal over. "You look fine."

"Coal was smart. She used her foot to take him the rest of the way down and out," Roger praised. "Didn't even scuff her boot. Too bad it didn't have some manure on it, though."

Coal dared a glance at Melissa. "No teeth involved this time."

"That's a relief." She relaxed back in her chair.

Gene returned with the ice pack and handed it to Roger. He placed it on his scraped knuckles and winced.

"Are you sure nothing's broken?" Nancy asked.

"They're just skinned up. I'll be fine."

"I can take you to the first aid station."

"Hell no, not for skinned knuckles."

"All right, then, come eat your lunch."

"I got you fresh onion rings, since I ate yours," Gene sheepishly told Coal.

She smiled at him. "Thanks, this looks and smells delicious."

"It is good. Gene's already had three sandwiches." Harley chuckled.

"Just don't forget you've got steer wrestling and saddle bronc this afternoon," Stormy warned. "I'd hate for you to cover your boots."

"Well that visual just ruined my appetite," Del groaned.

"Not mine." Coal took a bite from her sandwich. "This is great."

†

By the end of day one, they held a comfortable lead over their closest competitor. After showering, the crew met the Tuckers, Georgia, and the Bearclaws at the same steak house they had eaten at the night before.

"That was just as wonderful as last night," Melissa moaned as she pushed her plate away.

"No dessert for you, then, boss?" Gene asked.

"Heavens no, but I'll enjoy it vicariously through you."

The entire group was amazed with the voracity Gene displayed attacking two slices of apple pie dripping with cheese.

"I swear that kid must have a hollow leg," Harley declared.

Susan tapped his legs with her fist. "Nope, just a hearty appetite."

"I still can't get over how different you look with a beard," Melissa told him with a smile.

"It's been nice to try, but I think it'll get shaved quickly once we start the hay season. It gets hot."

"Maybe it will be your new winter look." Coal elbowed him gently.

Melissa turned to Roger. "Are y'all staying in town tonight?"

"No, we'll head back home but be here bright and early before the roping starts." He flagged the server down for the check. "Tonight is my treat for such a great first day."

Gene's head popped up from his dessert plate. "Where will we go to celebrate winning top cowboy tomorrow?"

"Home," Georgia answered. "Roger's already got a keg of beer on ice and a dozen of the biggest T-bones you've ever seen marinating."

"We've got to double down, then, and be sure to win," Stormy said.

"Even if you don't win, which I think is doubtful, dinner is still out at the Circle T," Roger told them. "It's truly been a pleasure having you all here."

"You'll have to let us return the favor and come to Texas one day soon," Melissa offered.

Nancy looked at her dad. "Maybe we will take a drive south later this year."

"We won't be able to make the finals tomorrow, so this is good-bye for us," Tanya told the group. "I hope y'all do come back in the fall. I may be back in school, but I'll see you on the weekend, so keep an eye out for the herd."

"I can't tell you again how much we enjoyed riding with you two," Gene said. "That was definitely another dream come true for us."

"Good luck and we'll see you in the fall, then." After hugs, she and Thomas left.

†

Later, after everyone had turned in for the evening, Del and Stormy had made love. Afterward, Del turned in Stormy's arms. "Tell me something, darling."

"Anything you wish, my love." Stormy chuckled.

"Did something happen between Coal and Nancy while y'all were on the drive?"

"You feel it too, don't you? The chemistry building between them."

"Yes, it's like electricity fills the air every time Nancy looks at Coal, and Nancy watches her often."

"If it were up to Nancy, she'd be all over Coal, but she was quick to tell her that she was committed to Mary Leah. Tanya was also crushing on Coal."

"I guess our friend's just a chick magnet."

"That she is. She's got women swooning in her wake. She's so deeply in love with Mary Leah, though, no one else matters."

"Come here, lover, and leave me swooning again," Del purred and pulled Stormy on top of her.

†

Mary Leah climbed into bed naked beside Coal and turned out the light. "I'm so proud of you for defending Roger today without getting into an all-out brawl."

Coal stiffened at Mary Leah's comment. She didn't go looking for trouble, but it had a way of finding her. "He landed a good first blow, but I was afraid for him once I saw the look in Randy's eyes."

Mary Leah rested her head on Coal's shoulder. "I know you always do what's right." She slid her fingers beneath Coal's nightshirt.

"You must be feeling better today," Coal chuckled as Mary Leah's fingers teased her nipples.

"Much better, and I need to get naked with you. You up for it, cowgirl? Wanna give me a ride?"

"I think I can manage more than eight seconds." Coal raised up in the bed to remove her shirt.

"That's much better." Mary Leah wrapped her lips around Coals perked nipple and ran her hand down Coal's front.

Coal grew damp as her lover caressed her body. "Damn, that feels nice," she whispered as Mary Leah suckled her breast.

"I want you to feel nice all over," she answered as she parted Coal's damp lips and gently slid into Coal's wetness.

Coal's muscles quivered as her lover teased her, her excitement building with each loving stroke of fingers and tongue. She rolled her hips to match the movement of Mary

Leah's fingers as they reached deeper inside, caressing the places that made Coal's mind explode with pleasure. Coal clenched her teeth, holding back her orgasm as she guided Mary's Leah's mouth down to cover her aching clit.

"Right here?" Mary Leah asked right before she lapped across the swollen flesh.

"God yes, suck it, please," Coal groaned.

Mary Leah pressed it against the roof of her mouth with her tongue, and Coal flooded her hand as she came hard against her fingers.

"Mmm, yes, that's nice, baby," she moaned as she curled her fingers inside Coal.

Coal's skin broke out in a light sweat as she released. *Damn, I didn't realize how badly I needed that.* She reached down, took Mary Leah's hands, and pulled her up beside her. "That felt so good," she whispered as she brought her lips to Mary Leah's neck.

Mary Leah placed her hands on either side of Coal's head. "I'm okay for tonight. I know you must be tired, and truthfully, I am too. I just wanted to make sure you slept well tonight. I don't think you got much rest last night."

"I think I was still adjusting to being in a real bed again." She kissed Mary Leah lightly on the lips. "I'm not too tired if you need some loving."

"Really, it's okay. I can wait until we get home. I know tomorrow will be another long day, and then we'll celebrate."

"Are you sure?"

"Yes, I promise I'm fine. I love you, Coal, and will be happy to have your arms wrapped around me tonight."

"Okay, then."

When Mary Leah turned away from her, Coal scooted up next to her and wrapped an arm around her waist to hold her close.

†

After breakfast, Melissa asked, "Are we doing okay for time?"

"Yes, the first round of bull riding starts off the morning, and then the roping will begin," Gene answered.

"Is it team or individual first?"

Gene grinned. "Team first and then individual."

"The final round of bull riding is the last event. Is that right?"

"Yes, ma'am, it is. Then they'll announce top cowboy, we pick up our winnings and the trophy for Roger, and let the party begin."

"You're pretty certain you'll win?" Susan asked.

"Yeah, even though I don't do bull riding, Coal, and I would have to really bomb in the roping events to drop big points, and that ain't gonna happen."

"I love your lack of confidence," Susan teased him and then kissed his bearded cheek.

†

The cool morning turned into a warm afternoon. As Gene had predicted, he and Coal placed second in team roping and he placed second in individual calf roping. The top cowboy trophy was a sure lock for the Circle T.

Finished with the competition, the crew unsaddled and tended the horses, then loaded tack and other supplies in the trailer. The plan was to take Shadow and the other horses out to the Circle T for the night and they would start for home after picking them up on their way out of town in the morning.

"Do we want to go ahead and load the horses?" Gene asked.

Coal shook her head. "Naw, let's leave them in the stable until after the awards ceremony. It won't take long to load them after."

The overhead announced the beginning of the bull riding finals as Gene and Coal rushed from the stables to their seats. Harley handed them cold drinks as the gate flew open and the first bull lunged out of the chute, all four feet off the ground, before crashing back to earth in a powerful spin, sending the cowboy flying from his back. The crowd moaned at the painful ejection and the clowns distracted the bull from the rider to allow him to safely escape the arena.

"I know that's good money if you win, but it's not worth the risk," Coal groaned as the next rider hit the ground and barely rolled away in time to prevent being stomped on by the bull.

"I agree," Gene said. "I prefer my body to stay in one piece as long as possible."

The crowd cringed every time a rider crashed to earth. Of the ten finalists, only four were able to complete the eight seconds mandatory to score on the ride.

The announcer recapped the top three winners of each event. "Now for the moment we've all been waiting for, the announcement of the top cowboy award. I'm very pleased to announce the return of a crowd favorite from years past. Without further delay, the top cowboy trophy goes to Roger Tucker of the Circle T."

The crowd burst into applause as Roger made his way to the center of the arena to accept the trophy and check for winning the title. The smile he wore was worth every sore muscle or bruise the team encountered during the competition. He called the crew down for pictures, and after picking up their winnings, they all headed to the Circle T.

"We'll see you shortly," Coal told Roger as they reached the stables. "Melissa, Del, and Mary Leah will follow you out and help you get dinner rolling if that's okay."

"Perfect," Roger answered. "Ladies, if you'll follow me."

Susan looked at Gene. "Go ahead. We won't be far behind," he said.

She smiled at him and rushed after the group.

†

As they led the horses out to the trailer, Coal went to see the stable manager.

"Congrats on a great rodeo," he said.

"Thanks, I wanted to stop by to say thank you for everything and to apologize for the drama."

"You don't have anything to apologize for, Coal. Randy just gets stupid sometimes, and yesterday was his day. I apologize that as a guest of our town and our rodeo you were treated that way."

"I've seen it before and it's all a part of being female in a man's world. I can hold my own."

"I'm man enough to admit I was impressed by your ability to put him on his face. I haven't seen that kind of fire in Roger in thirty years either. The only thing better was watching him collect the top cowboy trophy."

"That was pretty awesome."

"I hope you and your friends will consider coming back to rodeo with us. You lit a spark in this old man's heart."

Coal offered him her hand. "I'd like that. Don't be surprised if we're back in the fall to defend our trophy."

"I'll look forward to seeing you then. Safe travels."

Coal tipped her hat and led Shadow to the trailer.

†

The feast they shared that evening was beyond belief. Gene was able to quench his normally insatiable appetite with all the delicious food. Roger never stopped smiling, and while they ate, the trophy sat in the middle of the table for all to admire.

"I'd like to offer up my thanks for Gene, Stormy, and Coal, whose assistance, and skills, brought this trophy back to our ranch after many years' absence." He lifted his glass of beer. "Cheers to the top cowboys and cowgirls of the Circle T, MC2, and my heart."

"Cheers," everyone echoed and took a long sip of the icy beer.

Coal cleared her throat after the cheers died down. "On behalf of myself, Gene, and Stormy, I'd like to thank you and Nancy for giving us the opportunity to fulfill several of our dreams this trip. The experience of the cattle drive and running with the mustangs will live with us forever. We were all born to rodeo, and we're thankful our participation helped to bring the trophy back to where it truly belongs. Also, most importantly, thanks to Melissa for allowing the three of us time to enjoy these experiences and create some beautiful memories."

"Amen," Gene cheered.

Del didn't think she'd ever seen Coal this happy and excited about life. She couldn't help but notice how Coal's gaze drifted to Nancy when she talked of making beautiful memories. Whatever had transpired between the two had definitely had a positive effect on Coal, and for that, she was thankful. Del continued to smile as Melissa's phone rang and she excused herself from the table.

†

"Hey, hang on a second." Melissa walked toward the corral. "I'm sorry, the crew is having such a wonderful time I couldn't hear you. I wish you were here." She propped a leg on the rail of the corral. "Yes, Roger threw a celebration for the crew. He cooked steaks the size of roasts and tapped a keg of cold beer. It was a wonderful weekend." She let out a deep sigh as she surveyed the skies. "It really is beautiful up here, especially at night. The sky is so clear it makes me feel like I can reach up and touch the stars." She chuckled. "I'm glad you think my smile lights up your world. I can't wait to see you in two days. Yes, we plan to leave early in the morning and drive as far as we can. It'll be slower going pulling a horse trailer, but we'll definitely be back Tuesday." Her smile grew as she listened to Cam. "I can't wait to see you either. I'll call tomorrow. Sweet dreams. Good night."

Melissa turned to find Coal walking up. "Everything okay?" Coal asked.

"Yes, it was Cam checking in, and it was so loud I couldn't hear."

Coal instinctively rubbed Shadow's head as he reached out for her. "I love that smile on your face, boss."

"I'm having a terrific time, and it's so beautiful up here."

"Uh-huh," Coal answered. "Your phone call didn't have anything to do with it?"

Melissa smiled. "Maybe, but let's get back to the party." She grabbed Coal's hand and pulled her back to the house before she could ask any more questions.

Coal laughed but allowed Melissa to lead her.

†

At the end of the night, Nancy walked them out to the trucks. She placed an arm around Coal and Stormy. "I'm really going to miss you two. It's been great having you both here, and I want you to know the door is always open for you."

"We will definitely be back," Stormy promised.

"If all goes as planned, you'll see us back for the fall drive. Just keep us posted and give us as much notice as you can so we can make arrangements with Melissa."

Nancy smiled at Coal. "I've got your email and phone number, so I'll keep you posted. See you in the morning."

"Good night, and thanks again for everything." Coal hugged her new friend.

"My pleasure, rest well."

Chapter Sixteen

The road home glistened with sunlight as they headed south. Coal wasn't imagining the tears she saw in Nancy's eyes as they hugged good-bye. A glance in the side mirror reflected the image of Nancy wiping them from her eyes.

It was a fantastic trip, and maybe at a different time in our lives….

"On the road again," Gene broke out in song, pulling Coal's attention back into the truck.

"Dear Lord, Gene, you still can't sing." Coal laughed and sang along with him. Del and Stormy broke into chorus from the back seat as they bumped down the driveway.

†

Two long days of driving brought them to the entrance to the MC2.

"Welcome home, ladies," Gene announced.

"Finally," Coal groaned. "I don't think my ass was this sore from being in the saddle."

"I heard that," Stormy agreed as she stepped out and stretched.

"Dear Lord, what is that smell?" Gene asked as he emerged from the truck.

Coal grinned. "I'm not sure, but I'd bet on fried chicken."

Melissa smiled. "You win the prize, Coal Bryan. Cam has cooked dinner for us."

"That's why you didn't want to stop to eat," Harley said. "It would ruin her surprise."

"We'll take care of the stock if you can help the ladies with the luggage," Gene told Harley. "Do you want to take Shadow home first?"

"No, we'll just put him out in the front pasture and he'll follow us when we go home later."

Gene let out a whistle. "Damn, would you look at that pile of wood? We won't need to chop wood for the fire pit this year."

"No, we won't. It'll be nice to have seasoned oak for the smoker too," Harley agreed.

Cam walked out to greet them. "Y'all have near-perfect timing. Ten minutes and supper will be on the table."

The pups were hot on her tail, and when Bo saw Gene, he rushed to his master. He licked his face and sneezed, the hairs from Gene's beard tickling his nose.

"I know I need to shave it," Gene told him.

Cam smiled at him. "It looks good on you."

"Thanks, but it's going to be too hot for the summer."

"Let's get to work, I'm hungry," Melissa said.

"We're all over it." Gene pulled open the trailer door. "Stormy, will you get our tack while Coal and I get the horses?"

The crew went to work, and within minutes, they unloaded and tended to the stock and took the bags to the bunkhouse and Melissa's house. Mary Leah and Del pitched in to set the table in the bunkhouse and helped Cam carry the food to the table.

†

The crew settled back into their routines, and as she promised, Mary Leah made a doctor's appointment. Coal attended the appointment with her, and they were both relieved to hear that she checked out fine. The X-rays revealed the source of her headaches to be a wisdom tooth that had impacted in her sinus cavity.

"I can't believe you still have your wisdom teeth," Coal said with relief after they left the doctor's office.

"As you can see from the X-rays, they never erupted, but I'll be making a dentist appointment to get that taken care of soon."

"I'm relieved it wasn't something more serious. I was worried about you."

"That's very sweet, but you're going to have to put up with me for years yet to come." Mary Leah pulled her face down for a kiss.

"I look forward to that, my love." Coal took her hand to walk out into a beautiful afternoon.

†

The crew went to work training the herd of yearlings while the fields grew for another week. Melissa and Cam spent many hours talking, taking their time getting to know one another while they watched Coal and the others work their magic with the young horses.

"That method of training is just amazing," Cam said, watching Coal work with a young stallion.

"It's proven so much easier for both horse and rider," Melissa replied. The day had grown long and she leaned into Cam as they looked out into the corral. "You know what I think, Harley?"

"What's that, boss?"

"I think it's time we have a cookout."

"Great idea. How about we barbecue some chicken tomorrow while the young'uns continue the training?"

"Sounds wonderful. Will you go grocery shopping with me tonight?"

"I'd love to," Cam answered, smiling.

Harley smiled at them. He was pleased to see the two women he loved so much falling in love. "I'll head in and make a list while you two enjoy the show."

Returning his smile, Melissa said, "Thanks, Harley."

†

After she finished dressing, Coal paced through the house while Mary Leah dressed.

"Are you nervous about something? You can't stand still."

"No, I'm just eager to get to the cookout."

"Are you starving?"

"I think Gene's rubbed off on me. I'm always hungry."

"I'll be ready in five minutes, but if you can't wait, go and I'll join you."

"I think I'll live another five minutes."

†

303

Del and Stormy arrived at the same time. Coal smiled nervously at Del as she emerged from Stormy's truck. "Hey, Doc, you got a few minutes?"

"Sure, Coal. We'll meet you ladies inside in a bit," she told Stormy and Mary Leah.

They walked over to the corral. "I would ask if you're nervous, but you look almost panicked. Are you sure this is a good time?" Del asked.

"I know we talked through this during my session this week, but this is a huge step for me."

"Yes, it is, but there's no rush."

"I've waited long enough. I need to do this, Doc."

"Then take a few deep breaths and relax. Did you bring it with you?"

"Damn," Coal growled as she patted her pocket. "I'll be right back."

"Come on, I'll drive you. No telling what you might run into today."

"Thanks, Doc."

†

"Where are those two going?" Melissa asked when she looked out the window to see Del and Coal driving off.

"No telling with them. Coal's as anxious as a cat on a hot tin roof today for some reason," Mary Leah replied.

"Come help me set the table," Melissa told Mary Leah. "We can start serving when they return."

Gene and Harley were taking the barbequed chicken off the grill when Del and Coal got back.

"I'm glad y'all are back. The smell of this chicken is driving me insane," Harley said as they approached.

"We can go eat now," Coal answered.

†

Deep breaths and relax.

Coal waited until her family filled seats around the table and finished the blessing before she cleared her throat. "I know this food is going to be fantastic and we're all hungry, but I hope you'll give me just a few more minutes."

I can do this. She looked at Del for a boost of confidence, and received her warm smile and a nod. She stood at the head of the table and looked at Melissa. "Since the day I arrived, I've felt like a part of a family even though I wasn't who you were expecting me to be." She chuckled. "Each of you in your own way made me feel loved at a time in my life when I needed it most." Melissa and Del had tears in their eyes, so she plunged ahead. She reached into her pocket and pulled out a small box.

She smiled at Mary Leah and dropped to a knee in front of her. "Just when I thought my heart would never love again, you came into my life and made me feel whole. Will you do me the honor of becoming my wife?" she asked as she opened the box to offer Mary Leah the engagement ring Del had helped her select.

Mary Leah's gaze moved between the ring and Coal's face, but she remained speechless. Coal's heart pounded as she waited for Mary Leah's answer.

Melissa finally spoke. "Mary Leah, if you don't answer soon, I'm going to accept Coal's proposal."

Her voice was apparently just what Mary Leah needed to bring her out of the shock she'd experienced. With tears flowing down her cheeks, she nodded. "Yes, Coal, I'd love to be your wife."

"Finally," Gene hollered and got a stern look from Melissa. "Congratulations, you two." He slapped Coal on the back.

Coal removed the ring from the velvet box and slipped it onto Mary Leah's finger. "Thank God it fits," she sighed with relief.

Mary Leah took Coal's face in her hands. "It wouldn't have mattered if it didn't." She leaned forward for a kiss.

Melissa wiped away her tears. "I reckon we have a wedding to plan, ladies and gentlemen."

"No eloping or sneaking off to the justice of the peace?" Coal asked.

"Don't even think of depriving me of the pleasure of planning my sister's wedding, Coal Bryan."

Coal threw up her hands in mock surrender. "Yes, boss."

†

As they shared the meal, they chattered excitedly about planning the wedding.

"What time frame are we looking at?" Melissa asked.

Coal looked at Mary Leah. "Will a date sometime around Christmas be okay with you?"

"That would be perfect, especially if we have an outside ceremony," Mary Leah answered.

Coal listened to the conversation as they continued to eat, thankful Melissa would be instrumental in helping to plan the ceremony. She was overwhelmed just thinking about the time and resources it would take and was relieved when Melissa looked up to see her anxiety rising.

"Damn, I forgot the dessert at the house," Melissa said.

"I'll go get it," Coal replied. She needed a breath of fresh air.

"Come on, I'll help," Harley told her. "I have a feeling it's a bowl of banana pudding and I'd hate for you to get lost," he joked.

They walked outside together. Coal let out a deep breath.

"Congratulations. I'm so happy for both of you and proud to call you family."

Coal turned and embraced Harley. "You don't know how much that means to me."

"Yes, I do. I kind of like to think of you as a daughter of sorts."

"Well enough to walk me down the aisle?"

"I'd be honored," he answered, wiping away a tear.

"Goodness, let's go. I can't handle you crying," Coal placed an arm around his shoulder as they walked across the yard.

†

Once the crew went their separate ways, Melissa smiled shyly at Cam. "That was great, and very exciting, but I'm glad we're finally alone."

Cam opened her arms, pulled her close, and kissed her softly. "Me too. It's been a great day, and I'm happy for Coal and Mary Leah." She carried their coffee mugs to the kitchen. "Do you want another cup?"

"No, I want to take a nice hot shower and snuggle with you if that's okay?"

"That is more than okay," Cam beamed.

"Would you care to join me? I've got a spot on my back I just can't seem to reach." Melissa grinned.

"I thought you'd never ask." Cam took her hand and they walked down the hall.

†

Cam's heart raced as she stepped into the shower behind Melissa. It had been so long since she'd shared an intimate shower with a lover. Melissa's firm body was only inches away, yet she hesitated to reach for her.

Is it time for us to take this to the next level?

Melissa turned to face her, and the look in her eyes answered Cam's unspoken question. It was definitely time. She stepped closer to Melissa and kissed her softly as she slid her hands beneath Melissa's hair.

I don't want our first time rushed by the threat of cold water.

Once more, Melissa came to her rescue. "Let's rinse off and head to bed. I want to be with you tonight, Cam."

Shocked speechless by Melissa's remark, Cam could only nod. *Damn, I want this to go so perfectly.*

Melissa turned off the water and they dried their bodies. Amazed by how excited she was at the possibility of being intimate with Melissa, every fiber in her seemed to vibrate. Cam took her hand and led her to the bed.

"You realize I have no idea of what to do, so you'll have to be patient and teach me," Melissa said.

"Light a candle, and we'll learn together."

As they lay side by side, verses from a poem she had read years ago, popped into her head. Staring into Melissa's eyes, Cam rolled her onto her back and spoke. "'Imagine the most perfect kiss, and give it to her,'" she whispered as she leaned down to brush her lips against Melissa's cheek, then down to her lips. She gently parted them with her tongue, and their excitement soared as they took their time to slowly explore each other's mouths. Melissa shivered with excitement with each kiss.

"Imagine the softest touch, and give it to her," she whispered as she ran her fingertips down Melissa's neck and across her chest. Even in the dim candlelight, Cam could see the chill bumps rising on the surface of Melissa's skin in the wake of her touch. She circled the soft mound of her left breast and watched Melissa's nipple harden with desire as her chest rose and fell with each breath.

Melissa quivered as Cam ran her tongue over her lips and leaned down to brush it across her nipple. She moaned as her hand found the back of Cam's head to pull her more firmly onto her breast. Cam eagerly opened her mouth to engulf the offering and rolled Melissa's other nipple gently.

"Oh God, yes," Melissa moaned. "That feels wonderful, Cam."

"Wait, it only gets better," she promised.

Cam brought her right hand to Melissa's center and eased the soft folds open, then slid her fingertips into Melissa's wetness as her lover moaned.

Please give me patience to go slow. I want this moment between us to last a lifetime. Cam felt Melissa's hips rock up toward her hand as her fingers glided smoothly in the wetness, and she knew Melissa's climax was building. She slowed her movements and lifted her mouth from Melissa's breast.

"Imagine the perfect taste. You taste like that," she whispered as she moved down Melissa's body to rest between her opened thighs. She removed her fingers and softly licked the glistening drops of excitement from them with the tip of her tongue.

"Please, Cam," Melissa whispered as she clutched the sheets. "I need you now."

Cam slid her tongue between Melissa's lips, and her sweet taste filled Cam's senses with absolute joy as she lapped the juices flowing from her lover. She brushed her thumb across Melissa's clit and Melissa called her name as she released. Cam slid her fingers deeply inside Melissa again as Melissa's muscles pulsed around them, intensifying her orgasm. She continued to caress Melissa with her tongue until Melissa fell back, calm and exhausted. Cam looked into her lover's eyes to find tears flowing down her cheeks and quickly took Melissa into her arms.

When Melissa spoke, her voice cracked with emotion. "That was beyond perfect."

Cam smiled with relief.

For hours that night, they explored together and learned how to love one another. When they fell back onto the bed totally spent, the candlelight was flickering against the wall, the flame soon to be a distant memory.

Cam's gaze fell to the print of Coal and Stormy that they had given to Melissa as a gift after the first rodeo they'd competed in as a group. "That's a wonderful shot of those two. 'Cowgirls do it in the dirt.'" She read the caption aloud.

"Yes, we do," Melissa answered with a grin.

Bubba's SOS Recipe

Growing up less than prosperous, our mother had to stretch a tight food budget as far as it could go back in the sixties and early seventies. We ate most of what we grew, raised, or hunted for with some grocery store 'fixins' in between. Mom constantly looked for dishes that could go a long way in feeding a family of six, while providing a hot, hearty meal. One dish we ate often, usually for breakfast, was a dish we called SOS or more lovingly known as Shit on a Shingle. Proper speaking folks might also refer to this as dried beef on toast. My younger brother Bubba got the gravy-making gene from my folks, so I'm including this in his honor. To this day, he makes the best SOS in the family. A loaf of bread, a little milk, and gravy, and a couple small packs of meat sure stretched a long way.

1. Combine flour, milk and water in a frying pan to prepare a white milk gravy – For those of you like me, that can't make a gravy without lumps, local grocery stores sell a Pioneer gravy mix that is miraculous. Season with salt and pepper to taste.
2. Pull, slice, or dice, your choice of meats. Dried beef is the usual. You can also substitute pastrami, ham, or other type of thin-sliced meats. My personal favorite is pastrami.
3. When the gravy is thick, but not lumpy, add in the meat torn into small bits and stir until thoroughly mixed and heated.

4. Make buttered or plain white toast in the toaster and spread across a plate. For little mouths, you might want to cut the toast into smaller squares.
5. Cover the toast with the gravy and enjoy!!

About the Author

Ali Spooner

Ali Spooner, a native of Florida, now calls Pensacola her forever home. Ali has been writing for many years as a hobby, and with the assistance of the Affinity Rainbow Publishing team, has taken her love of storytelling to a new level.

Ali's characters range from cowgirls and psychics, to a healthy dose of supernatural beings. She has written stand-alone titles and series. Ali is an avid reader and her other hobbies include photography, outdoor activities and watching college sports.

Other Books from Affinity eBook Press

<u>Faith in Rayne</u> by Dannie Marsden
Welcome back Rayne and Lisbet from *Rayne Comes to Town* and *Rayne's New Beginnings*. Their life has flourished since meeting. Rayne ventures to Telluride, Colorado, where both adventure and trouble land at her feet. Lisbet heads to Telluride to reunite with Rayne, her head filled with dreams of their future only to have her dreams come crashing down. Can she find the strength to fight for Rayne, allowing her faith to guide them back to their love?

<u>Fortunes</u> by Alane Hotchkin
Despite the curves life has thrown Remmy Garrick, her life is going along pretty good except mysterious things keep happening at her job sites. State Investigator Kira Kirpatrick is assigned the case, and everything about Remmy draws Kira to her. Circumstances beyond their control throw their lives into a frenzy. Does Kira have the courage to step up and accept the love Remmy is offering, or will she continue to hide behind her secrets and let them control her?

<u>Captivated</u> by Annette Mori
Juliet Lewis has one too many quirks for her own well-being. Snooping was bound to get her in trouble. Sexy police officer Tanner Sullivan gets Juliet's attention and she wants to know

more. Will Tanner turn out to be her jailor or savior? Sparks fly when the obsessive-compulsive Juliet and the paranoid Tanner cross paths in this quirky thriller with a new twist around every corner.

Pausing by Renee MacKenzie
Jordy Chapman is the Emergency Service Coordinator at Cypress Haven mental health facility in Naples, FL. Keira Yeager's family owns an upscale furniture store in Naples and orchestrates a generous donation of furniture to Cypress Haven. When the two meet, they hit it off immediately. Will a Yeager family's anguish and misunderstanding threaten their new relationship?

Breaking the Silence by JM Dragon
Still grieving five years after the death of her father, Dilana Sterling is a shadow of the woman she once was...a successful author with a string of best sellers, and a longer string of women. Rachael Alderman, a teacher at the local orphanage, lives a quiet, yet satisfying life. When Dilana and Rachael meet, they develop a friendship that leads them on personal journeys of self-discovery. Will their memories of the past prevent them from moving toward each other, or will they find a path that leads to each other so they can experience life together?

The Termination by Annette Mori
Codee is having a bad day and it's only going to get worse. Sawyer, a compassionate young woman, is resigned to her fate. Her only question is what fate is that? After slipping on ice, Codee wonders if she is hallucinating and fallen into an Alice type rabbit hole. The only thing she knows is that she

needs to save Sawyer. Enjoy this satirical romance, with all of its twists and turns, that just might make you go hmm...

The Next Time by Erin O'Reilly
What if you had the chance to make history stop repeating itself? Would you sacrifice today for a chance at a better tomorrow. There is a moment in everyone's life that defines their future. For Jac and Carol, that time is now. Jump ahead twenty-five years and meet Carol's granddaughter Livvy. She is ready for a challenge and is fleeing the nest and getting on with her life. Read this wonderful love story that spans several lifetimes.

Open Your Heart a Sensual Collection by Ali Spooner
Excite your senses, rejuvenate your memories and best of all flirt with the edge of eroticism. Allow us to help you relive that first kiss, flirting with young love, your dream come true, surprise encounters, and your wildest desires... Enjoy these stories of love, sweet seduction, and steamy encounters. Open Your Heart...a sensual collection.

Secret of Stone Creek by Natalie London
Jennifer Cameron arrives in Stone Creek, Wisconsin to sell her grandparents' large Victorian home. While there she is intrigued by a twenty-four-year-old never solved murder. Her attraction to the lovely and mysterious librarian, Diana vies for her attention. Follow this suspenseful whodunit to its conclusion.

The Promise by JM Dragon
An accidental meeting with Melissa Grant, leads to an unexpected offer for Kris Lake—refurbishing a beach

cottage, with the help of Melissa's granddaughter Claire. Do outer imperfections prevent them from reaching the beauty that lives inside and the chance of a happy new life? Find out in this lovely romance that will fill you with heart-warming sensations throughout the story.

Christmas at Winterbourne by Jen Silver
The Christmas festivities for the guests booked into Winterbourne House has all the goings-on of a traditional holiday. The only difference is that this guesthouse is run by lesbians, for lesbians. Join the guests and staff at Winterbourne for a Christmas you'll not soon forget.

The Review by Annette Mori
Silver Lining, a successful lesbian romance writer, has the crazy idea to sponsor a contest where the first reader who posts a review wins a home-cooked meal with an offer to fly the winner to Washington State. Jasmine, the winner, has engaged in subtle flirtations with Silver. Bizarre messages from the unknown fan has Silver questioning the wisdom of a relationship with Jasmine.

South of Heaven by Ali Spooner
Kendra Drake has taken over as Captain of her father's shrimp boat. As a favor to her father, Kendra has agreed to give fellow shrimper, Lindsey Bowen, a chance to work on the boat but first must prove herself to Kendra and her crew. Lindsey finds a way into Kendra's heart. Will it only last for the summer?

Catch to Release by Lacey Schmidt
On the verge of success, lesbian folk-rock star, Shay Greenaura, finds herself caught up in more than just her

music. Threats have her manager hiring a security firm for protection. Addison Weller, a former Diplomatic Security Services agent is called in to assess the threats against Shay. Their undeniable attraction, brewing silently between them, could prove to be a fatal distraction. Follow this fast-paced adventure to its surprising romantic conclusion.

Ready for Love by Erin O'Reilly
Kylie Wilcox's life dramatically changed with the death of her husband. Dr. LJ Evans, a renowned archaeologist, needed and wanted nothing but her work for her happiness. Their worlds are about to collide and lives will be altered forever.

Neptune's Ring by Ali Spooner
In the sequel to *Venus Rising*, Nat and Liz, owners of Venus Rising, invite Levi and Vanessa to join them in a venture for a new club on another island. They find the perfect place in an unfinished resort, Neptune's Ring. While on the island, Levi is drawn into a mystery involving secret compartments and a murder. Join the characters in this page-turning adventure, filled with steamy romance, intrigue, and an unsolved murder.

The Ultimate Betrayal by Annette Mori
Lara is a successful, beautiful, charming, financier. She is also a total control freak, so whatever Lara wants, Lara makes sure she gets. Rachel is Lara's fun-loving, charming, irresistible wife. Sophia's surprise visit to see Lara sets in motion a number of life changing events for them all. Hell has no fury as a woman scorned.

Affinity
Rainbow Publications

eBooks, Print, Free eBooks

Visit our website for more publications available online.

www.affinityrainbowpublications.com

Published by Affinity Rainbow Publications
A Division of Affinity eBook Press NZ LTD
Canterbury, New Zealand

Registered Company 2517228